SERGIO MISSANA

The Transentients

A Novel

*Translated from the Spanish
by Jessica Powell*

McPHERSON & COMPANY
KINGSTON, NEW YORK
2021

McPherson & Company
P.O. Box 1126 Kingston, NY 12402
WWW.MCPHERSONCO.COM
FIRST EDITION
1 3 5 7 9 10 8 6 4 2   2021 2022 2023
Typeset in Stemple Schneider.
Design by Bruce McPherson.
PRINTED IN U.S.A.

Library of Congress Control Number: 2021945309

ISBN: 978-1-62054-043-5

Originally published in Spanish under the title *Las muertes paralelas*
by Era (México) in 2010 and by Seix Barral (Chile) in 2011.

THE TRANSENTIENTS

The Child is father of the Man...

for Ramsay

THE TRANSENTIENTS

ONE

T HE second half of my life got off to an auspicious start. Or that's how it seemed on my fortieth birthday. I couldn't help seeing that day as a template, a microcosm of what my life would be like from then on: reduced to its most minimal components, free of ties and expectations, unpredictable. The lucid sense of euphoria I felt throughout that day was not disturbed even by the rupture during my bath — when time folded in on itself — or by what would prove to be the first episode within an episode. In that dream or hallucination (the neurologist would later insist that it was impossible to dream during an episode of amnesia), I found myself transformed into an elderly woman who was shuffling across an open area, a plaza. That brief "absence" was nothing more than a minor flaw, a tiny defect that only brought the day's sense of possibility into sharper relief.

In an extravagant gesture — that deepened the concern of my closest friends — I decided to spend my birthday completely alone. They had arranged a dinner in a Japanese restaurant the night before. On the morning of my birthday I woke up early, in Manuel's apartment, where I'd spent the last week. I rolled the sheets into a ball and put them in the washing machine. I folded up the sofa bed. I took a shower. I scribbled a brief note to Manuel and his new girlfriend, thanking them for their hospitality and dinner. I picked up my suitcase and duffle and left without making a sound. I went down to the street and hailed a taxi. Just before nine a.m., I officially moved into my new apartment on Rosal Street. Everything was spotless. The housekeeper had come, as planned, the previous afternoon. It took me less than half an hour to unpack and the relocation was complete.

Although I had signed the lease a month earlier and had been paying rent for two and a half weeks, I had waited until that day, staying at friends' houses and even spending a few nights in a hotel, before moving in. In truth, I'd been moving in gradually, buying things and making small repairs, assembling a new bookcase, unpacking my books and movies, making sure the Wi-Fi and the cable TV were working, striking up brief conversations with the super and a handful of neighbors, visiting the local cafés and bookstores, getting acquainted with the neighborhood. I'd just avoided sleeping there. Until then. New chapter, new life. In what was certainly the most alarming decision among a host of alarming decisions for my friends, a month earlier, I had quit my job as creative director at the ad agency where I was also a junior partner, announcing that my last day of work would correspond to my last day as a thirty-nine-year-old. The other partners tried, in a series of meetings and lunches that consumed nearly a week of their valuable time, to convince me to change my mind, employing a succession of powerful arguments: a raise and an increased percentage in the company, a car of the make and model of my choosing, a new office, a second assistant, two additional weeks of vacation time. At a certain point, the sheer accumulation of perks became hyperbolic and even threatening: it was like they were subtly daring me to leave. But because, in all negotiations, one must yield something, I conceded a single point: instead of quitting definitively, I proposed that we call it a sabbatical year. They declined. They promoted one of the associate creative directors to my position. The day before my birthday, I worked until the usual hour and went directly from the agency to the restaurant.

Regrettably, the third and most significant change in my life — the exhausting, ineluctable advance of the divorce proceedings — was outside my control. If it were up to me, we would have scheduled the hearing with the judge for the day before my birthday, thus intensifying the sense, deceptive though it may have been, that a new beginning was unfolding before me, that I was starting with a clean slate. Paula and I had signed legal separation papers ten months before — although we were still living together at the time — as well as an agreement laying out the terms of our divorce, stipulating a categorical parting of our financial seas: there would be no alimony or other compensation. This was due in part to a slight asymmetry in Paula's favor with respect to her family's financial stability. As one of the lawyers (hers) pointed out to us while we were waiting our turn with the notary, the whole business was made much simpler because we didn't have children. This spared us from having to worry about educational expenses, child support, visitation schedules and any number of other complications. I glanced at Paula and her eyes met mine for an instant, but she said nothing. She merely nodded. The corners of her lips curved in what wasn't quite a smile, acknowledging the paradox: had there been children we wouldn't be there. Or would we? The first family court hearing was scheduled for a month after my birthday. Paula was going to have to come all the way from Madrid. It seemed she was planning to stay there, even though she hadn't yet found a job. Her sister Mariana had built a life there that she didn't want to give up: she worked at a photography gallery and had just paid off her apartment near the Chueca neighborhood, and she'd invited her half-sister to stay with her indefinitely. I was looking forward to Paula's impending visit, though perhaps not for the right reasons. I had to admit that now, three months after her departure for Spain, I was starting to miss her terribly.

I made myself a strong cup of coffee in the new coffee maker. I walked silently through the apartment, checking that everything was in order. I settled in an armchair in the living room, facing a window overlooking the street, a diamond of morning light filtering through the pane. I had no plans. I had decided to replace my birthday with a sort of simulacrum of my birthday, a play performed without an audience or for an alter ego, a part of myself that doubled as a silent, neutral observer. And this meant an emptying out, a minimization so that I could start over at zero. No special events. It was literally the first day of my new life, and I would have to improvise, just as, at some point, I would need to decide what to do with my freedom and my future. I had received two informal offers from other agencies over the past two months. It was clear to me that two decades devoted to advertising were more than enough, but those offers were like a safety net in case of a free fall, a last resort. I had enough money for one sabbatical year, maybe a bit longer. In the short term, I needed a few weeks of rest. My only plan, still vague, with no fixed destination and no departure date, was to travel. Maybe to India, Turkey or Morocco. I was hoping that travel would lessen (or even eliminate) my episodes of amnesia.

Sitting in the armchair, through an intricate and random association of ideas sparked by the amnesia, I thought of

Fernanda Soto, a model I'd met while filming a commercial a year ago and then run into again by chance a month earlier at the gym. The neurologist had ordered me to start exercising. Moderate physical activity would benefit my health in general, he said, and the condition of my nervous system in particular. I joined a gym in Vitacura. In two months I'd only gone three times, after work, to walk on the treadmill. As soon as I arrived, even before I'd changed into my workout clothes, I'd start counting the minutes until I could leave. The exercise was the least of it. Once I'd broken through my inertia, my body would adjust to that different rhythm and it became difficult to stop. But I hated the atmosphere of the gym, the exhibitionism, bodies exulting in themselves, the stagnant smell, the harsh lighting, the insufferable music, the televisions playing all the channels simultaneously like in a control room, the summation of repetitive movements that merged, for me, into a single, discordant dance. It was possible that the place was beneficial for the majority of my body, but not for my nervous system. The morning I went in to cancel my membership I noticed Fernanda running on one of the treadmills. I walked in her direction until she saw me, and she waved, smiling. I returned the greeting from across the room. I turned and walked out. Now, sitting in the armchair, the image of Fernanda and her buoyant ponytail refused to leave me. I told myself that it was contrary to the spirit of the day, that, among other things, I ought to be promoting the illusion of self-sufficiency, of answering only to my own autonomy, even as I went down to the street and walked to the corner facing Santa Lucía hill to hail a taxi.

I arrived at the gym around ten, fearing that I was too late. The main exercise room was almost empty. Also no trace of Fernanda in the smaller room, a mirrored cubicle enclosing the weight machines. I ran into her at the exit. In my daze, I didn't even go to the trouble of pretending that I'd gone there to exercise. I invited her for a coffee, pointing to a café across the street. She accepted, surprised, clarifying that she only had a few minutes because she had to go shopping with her boyfriend. She had cut her black hair above her shoulders. She was wearing a long-sleeved t-shirt and sweatpants. She was shorter and more solidly built than I'd remembered. She seemed taken by surprise. And I was too. Why her? Why today, on a day in which, no matter how hard I tried not to, I suspected, in every detail and expression, an enigmatic significance, a deep, ulterior relevance? I didn't know her at all. She was one of many models who'd flirted with me — perhaps just a nod to my rank more than out of any true interest — during commercial or photo shoots over the years. Were my friends right? Did my unpredictable, erratic behavior the last few weeks indicate the onset of a midlife crisis? Was Fernanda the first in a series that would inevitably turn pathetic?

We settled into a couch on the empty second floor. I asked her about her life, of which I knew nothing, pretending I was getting caught up. At twenty-one, she'd finished a program in advertising at an institute that had once offered me a teaching position, which I'd declined. She was radiant with happiness and pride because she had just been cast as a model on a television show. They were in rehearsals now. Her boyfriend, to whom she referred somewhat unenthusiastically, was one of the producers. They'd met in casting. I knew who he was. He'd had a run-in with the law for small-scale coke trafficking at his previous job with a different television channel, a fact I abstained from mentioning, though I suspected she was well aware. A pair of women appeared at the top of the stairs and went to sit in the opposite corner of the room. One of them put a white laptop on the little round table in front of their chairs. Fernanda lowered her voice to a complicit whisper.

"And you, Tomás? What about your life? How are things at the agency?" she murmured.

We were still sitting a certain distance apart on the couch. It was ten-thirty in the morning. I was about to tell her I'd quit yesterday, told them all to go to hell, but her cellphone rang. The sound attracted the attention of the two women, who looked up from the computer screen and observed us with cool curiosity. Fernanda answered:

"Hi, love. Would it be okay if we went tomorrow? I got held up. I'm just now getting to the gym. I'm going to turn my phone off now but I'll call you later. See you on set. Bye."

She hung up and gave me a little smile of apology, which also included an acknowledgement that she's just lied to her boyfriend.

"It's just that Nico gets super jealous," she said, a bit irritated. "Where were we? Oh, right. How are things at the agency?"

"Do you want to go back to my place?" I said too loudly, surprising myself as much, or maybe more than I'd surprised her. I hadn't even tried to get near her, to touch her. I couldn't believe my clumsiness and the fact that I was putting myself in such a vulnerable position on this of all days. Now the course of my perfect day depended on her.

Fernanda looked me in the eye for a moment, serious. She dropped her gaze. She allowed a pause.

"Okay," she whispered.

We left. I raised my hand too late to hail a passing taxi.

"You don't have a car?"

"I'm not allowed to drive," I said casually, enduring her look of surprise. "I have episodes of amnesia."

Lately, everyone looked at me as if I were going crazy, as if they understood with total clarity some obvious thing about me that I was unaware of. A taxi stopped.

We scarcely spoke during the drive. The taxi driver was listening to tropical music at full volume. Fernanda looked fixedly out the window. I couldn't decide whether to touch her hand, which rested on the stained upholstery between us. I was afraid she'd change her mind when we got to my building, that she wouldn't get out of the taxi. The super was watching the entrance, leaning in the doorframe, holding a broom and talking to another woman. I walked by her without looking up. In the elevator, Fernanda kept her distance, tense, head down. But once we were inside the apartment, her attitude relaxed and she smiled in relief, I think, at the relative normalcy of the place, the half-empty spaces, the minimalist decoration, in contrast to my awkwardness and eccentricities. As if she'd been afraid she'd find something anomalous there, something that confirmed her worst suspicions.

"I love it like this, so empty," she declared, walking across the living room's parquet floor.

"I still need to buy some furniture."

Fernanda took a book from the shelf (a Bilal comic) and started to leaf through it.

"How long have you lived here?"

"Since today."

She gave me a perplexed look.

"Seriously?"

"Seriously. I've been renting it since the beginning of the month, but I officially moved in today. This will be the first night I've slept here. Would you like something to drink?"

Fernanda shook her head. She walked out of the living room and into the bathroom adjoining my bedroom. I waited for her outside the door. She startled when she opened the door, but forced a smile. I kissed her.

"Do you mind if I take a shower?"

"Sure."

I sat on the edge of the bed. The sound of running water had a calming effect on me. It struck me for the first time (until that moment it hadn't occurred to me to connect the two events) that this radical rupture — divorce, move, sabbatical year — was actually a second rupture and that it was possible that they occurred in more or less twenty-year-cycles. The first had occurred when I was twenty-two, the second, at forty. Did that mean I could expect a crisis of similar magnitude around the age of sixty, and another, with luck, at eighty? It was amazing to me that I had almost forgotten what, at the time, had seemed the most important and most drastic event of my life, the pivot upon which my destiny turned.

In those days, my parents were still married and living in Vitacura, not far — now that I thought about it — from the gym and the café. My father was turning fifty and had decided to go all out. It was a Friday night at the end of October. A tent, an orchestra, over two hundred guests: an event as big as a wedding. I was in my fifth year of Law at the Catholic University. I remember that I got drunk and tried to kiss my seventeen-year-old cousin Loreto, who threatened to tell my girlfriend, Ximena, whom I was planning to marry after finishing my exams. At some point during the party, in an alcoholic stupor, I remembered my secret childhood refuge, a hollow inside a dense hedge. I crept inside it and lay on my back, my arms outstretched. The mossy ground rocked delicately beneath me, as though I were resting in a boat on a lake.

I fell asleep. I awoke to nearby voices. Two men had sat down on a wooden bench, not three feet from my head.

"Loreto is furious."

"It's no big deal, viejo."

It took me a few seconds to recognize my Uncle Rafael and my father.

"It was all Mirta could do to convince her not to tell Ximena."

"Come on," said my father, who also seemed a little drunk, "the kid had a few too many pisco sours and that's that. He should be allowed to blow off some steam, right?"

"He's undisciplined," Rafael declared after a pause.

"No, I was exactly the same. Remember when I got thrown out of the National Institute for punching that guy during oral exams? What was his name?"

My uncle didn't respond.

"That's how the Ugartes are," my father went on. "We go full tilt when we're young and then later we correct course."

"You think? If I were you, I'd be seriously worried about Tomasito, what with the drinking and the marijuana and who knows what else."

My father whispered something and they both laughed.

"Viejo, I'm sorry that happened to your daughter, I really am. But don't worry about Tomás."

"I know it's none of my business…" Rafael conceded.

My father dropped a cigarette butt on the ground (I remembered it with absolute clarity) and crushed it beneath one of his black shoes.

"He's in his last year of law school," he said, "and he's started studying for the final exam. He's no genius, but he'll pass. I'll make sure of it. And he's going to marry Ximena. I haven't told him yet, but I've already found them a house in Las Condes. It's small, but if he wants a bigger one, he'll have to pay for it by the sweat of his own brow. The brat says he doesn't want to be a lawyer, that he's only getting the degree to make me happy, but I'll bet you anything we'll have him at the firm by this time next year. Mark my words, viejo. Marriage will settle him down. And kids even more so."

Rafael's silence was a tacit agreement with my father. Deep in my gut, I felt again the physical effect of his voice (not his words, which were nothing more than his typical harangue in my defense): his condescending, nonchalant tone was, in and of itself, a betrayal. I remembered the tone my grandmother, his mother, used when I was a child whenever she referred to me in my presence, the way she would tell trivial stories about me to other adults as though I were invisible. I didn't know which of those voices I was reacting to. He added:

"Ximena's the key. He got lucky there. At first, she didn't want anything to do with him, but she's come to see that my son's a much better bet than that other loser."

"Is it true that you gave her a little push?"

"Who told you that?"

"Or, rather, a few pushes?"

They both burst out laughing again.

"How could you even think such a thing?" said my father, feigning indignation. "You're talking about my future daughter-in-law, the future mother of my grandchildren."

"If only it were so simple," Rafael said after a minute.

"Viejo, you can always count on survival instinct. Young people can walk backwards as much as they want, but they're on a conveyor belt and they don't even know it. Over time, they run out of room to maneuver, just like anybody else…"

I didn't listen to the rest. I crawled out of my hiding

place. I wandered around the party like a zombie, considered escaping to my room. I ran into Ximena, who hugged me and flitted off again. I headed for the pool. I climbed onto the diving board. I walked out to the edge. I noticed that this stirred up some attention, people already delighting in anticipation of the predictable lark of jumping into a pool fully clothed at a party. I needed to pee. I unzipped my fly, planning to pee off the diving board. I registered several disapproving or warning looks. In that moment, I made a decision. The break would be free of dramatic gestures, I told myself, but profound, with no concessions, carried through to its ultimate consequences. I took a step forward.

Over the next two weeks, I broke up with Ximena, quit law school — without even bothering to officially withdraw — and went to live in an ex-classmate's house in El Arrayán. Pancho had left the law program a few years back and was now studying music. I lived in a guest room for four months without his parents — who saw me there all the time but never managed to connect one encounter with another — ever realizing or caring. In fact, Pancho's stepfather worked in an ad agency and found me a three-month internship, at the end of which they hired me as an editor. I choose advertising, in part, because my father despised it. I didn't see him for over a year and, after that, our relationship was never again more than distantly cordial. Around that time, the firm hired a former classmate of mine, Marcela Acuña, who more or less stepped into the position that had been meant for me. My father, Tomás Sr., ended up leaving my mother to marry her. Until the day he died, he never understood my stance, although he must have suspected that I'd overheard his conversation with his brother-in-law, a conversation that had reduced me to a ghost, a mere projection, a puppet he secretly manipulated to his own purposes. I think I wounded him deeply, a wound impossible to stitch back together and which only grew deeper over the years, but I never regretted it or considered a compromise. I never took one step back from the edge of the diving board. During the first year of my repudiation, he sent me dozens of recriminatory messages by way of letters or through my mother, and he even tried — when I rented my first apartment and started at my second ad agency — to secretly help me, with money and contacts. I was fueled by the acute sense of determination inherent to any struggle for independence, a process inextricable from violence and ingratitude. I even considered going by my middle name, Ignacio, or my mother's last name, but didn't in the end. Perhaps with even greater force because he was my namesake, Tomás became — in an impersonal way, disassociated from his attributes and individual circumstances — *the* enemy, the model against which I should trace an inverse map of my life, the photographic negative through which my own identity would be revealed. Except for a tendency to discredit the duplication or superimposition of experience, a certain impatience in seeing someone make the same mistakes from which he'd already learned lessons long ago, it was to be expected, given his social class and position, that he'd set out to mold his only son in his own image and likeness, and had wanted to smooth the way for him. In the same way. it was to be expected that I'd decide how to live my own life. Over time, I understood that I had used certain categories or attributes against Tomás Sr. — a heightened sense of embarrassment, a low threshold for indignation, a propensity for melodrama — that I'd internalized from him. It could be considered a subtle revenge of fate — or of genetics

— that, at forty, the process that had slowly been transforming me into his spitting image was now complete. Sometimes, caching sight of myself out of the corner of my eye in a shop window or in the window of a parked car, I thought I was seeing my father, at the age he was in my childhood memories, before he gained weight and his hair turned suddenly white, and before his new beginning (his midlife crisis at fifty) in the arms of Marcela Acuña.

Fernanda emerged from the bathroom, wrapped in a towel. She fell onto the bed. I moved the towel aside. With one finger, I traced the lines of a tattoo in the shape of a mandala on her hip, just below her navel. She closed her eyes and arched her back. Although it hadn't been my original intention, I decided to take it slowly, not rushing through the preambles. Fernanda, her face buried in my new pillow, held her breath for long stretches. I think I was trying to compensate in some way for my brusqueness, my ineptitude earlier that morning.

"Do you have a condom?"

I had bought a box at a pharmacy the previous afternoon: a prerequisite for life as a bachelor. I found it in the nightstand, relieved not to have to get up and go look for it in the bathroom.

"But it's not strictly necessary," I said.

"It's not?"

"I can't have children. I'm sterile."

"Better safe than sorry..."

She tore one open and skillfully put it on me. Then she straddled me. The bedroom was as unfamiliar to me as a hotel. I lay flat on my back, determined to prolong the moment — the perfect centerpiece to an inaugural and prophetic day — as much as possible. At one point, I caught her glancing at the clock on the nightstand.

"Do you have to go?"

She nodded, embarrassed.

Fernanda went into the bathroom. She took another shower. She came over to the bed and kissed me, scattering cold drops of water across my chest and stomach.

"Where are you going?"

"To the gym and then into the studio," she said, already on her way to the door.

"Do you want me to go with you?"

"No, thanks."

"Leave me your cell number. I'd love to…take you out. We could go to a movie one of these days."

"I'd better not, Tomás."

"Because of your boyfriend?"

She nodded.

"We've been together for three months and he's already cheated on me at least once, with some girl from the show… But I love him."

"So this was revenge?"

"No…not at all," she said, uncertain.

That loser doesn't even deserve the honor of retaliation, I thought, but I refrained from saying it. More than revenge, I told myself, in sleeping with me (with anyone) she was trying to reestablish some measure of balance, a symmetry.

I got up and, wrapped in a bathrobe, walked with her to the door.

"I'm not with the agency anymore, but call me if you need anything, a contact or…"

"Did you change agencies?"

"No, I'm taking a sabbatical year."

She gave me a quick kiss goodbye on the cheek.

"Today's my birthday," I confessed when she was already heading down the hallway toward the stairs, in too much of a hurry to wait for the elevator. She turned around to give me one last, perplexed, awkward look.

"Happy birthday," she said, and went down the stairs.

Faced once again with my complete freedom, I considered going out for an early lunch in one of the cafés on José Miguel de la Barra or Merced. Instead, I made myself a late breakfast: toast, scrambled eggs and yogurt with fruit. I needed to go grocery shopping, but I was going to leave that mundane task for the following day. I ate sitting in the living room, forcing myself to act naturally so as not to invest every small gesture and circumstance with symbolic value.

I went back to the bedroom. I stretched out on the bed and inhaled Fernanda's scent with a twinge of nostalgia. I closed my eyes and fell asleep. In the darkness, I had a notion of the flat plane of the bed, and of my consciousness floating a few meters under that surface, in an impossible space that did not necessarily correspond to the apartment below. I realized that I'd stopped breathing and in that instant something or someone above me took a breath and I saw the contraction of their ribs, a double grid of parallel lines of light in the darkness, and I began to ascend toward my own body. I awoke tangled in the bathrobe and the sheets, bathed in sweat. I saw that I'd been asleep for almost two hours. I decided to take a bath. As the bathtub was filling, I walked through the apartment to familiarize myself with it in the light of that time of day. I sank into the hot water, the bathroom illuminated only by a gap where the door was ajar. My eyes grew accustomed to the dim light, until I could make out the tongues of rising steam skimming the surface of the water. The second half of my life was getting off to an auspicious start, I thought. The phone rang. I listened to my own voice on the answering machine, recorded a few days earlier, and then to Paula, who was calling from Madrid to wish me a happy birthday.

It happened a few minutes later. Suddenly, I was an old woman and I was struggling to advance a few steps across the gravel of a plaza. I was wearing slippers. Gravity pulled me down. Right away, I noticed the abrupt change in the water temperature and a more subtle alteration in the shaft of light coming from the bedroom. One of my absences, I told myself, discounting the indisputable fact that I'd just had a dream. An episode within an episode. It seemed less strange to me that I'd accepted that experience as authentic, the certainty of having been — for a few seconds — that woman, than the fact that the sensation of verisimilitude didn't disintegrate upon my return. Unlike the memory of a dream, which, upon waking, mutated and distorted like the wail of a siren passing in the distance, the images and feelings held their consistency. Though it was ridiculous, I was possessed by the intimate certainty that — in some way, on some plane — the transformation had truly occurred.

Shivering, I emptied the tub. I stood for a long time under the shower, trying to get warm. I got dressed quickly. I decided to change the sheets. Spending my first night surrounded by Fernanda Soto's scent would only have highlighted the other side of the coin of my recently conquered autonomy: solitude. It was 3:25. I calculated that the episode had lasted no more than forty minutes. I went through my email. I counted four birthday greetings, including one from Paula in which she said she'd left me the message on my answering machine. How was the new apartment?, she wanted to know. I closed the computer. I was struck by the absurd temptation to call the agency, my ex-assistant, to ask where things stood with yesterday's urgent matters. I left the apartment. I did not run into the super. I started walking in a zigzag through the neighborhood. I walked up to Lastarria. I walked down Merced to Bellas Artes and then along the park toward Fuente Alemana. One of the few areas of the city with some soul, I thought, since the other neighborhoods — the affluent suburbs — made me think of a bad imitation of Canada. Manuel had told me that this was another symptom of a midlife crisis: the bachelor pad in a "bohemian" neighborhood, a fantasy most particular to ad men and creatives. "What are you going to do now?" he'd asked after knocking back a few cups of sake the night before, "write poetry?" I walked for a long time, to clear my head and tire myself out. My attention had become attuned by that strange dream (or whatever it was) and for long stretches I seemed only to come across people living on the streets. I wondered if the plaza I'd seen had been the Parque Forestal. I tried to recognize the precise spot among the gravel paths. I looked for an old woman wearing slippers. Every once in a while, someone came up to me to ask for money or to say something incoherent. I didn't find her.

I came out on Alameda and walked downtown. I considered the possibility of going into a movie theater to kill a couple of hours. I decided against it. Inactivity was proving uncomfortable, but I told myself again that this was as it should be. I needed the change. As much as it had been triggered by Paula, by her decision to leave me, I needed to see it through to its ultimate consequences, just as I had done eighteen years earlier, standing at the end of the diving board at my parents' house. I paused outside a travel agency and looked at the washed-out posters of Caribbean destinations. I was planning to leave in a month, after the Family Court hearing. When I got back to "my" neighborhood, I stepped into a café. I ordered fried empanadas and a beer. I returned to my apartment before eight. Other birthday messages had accumulated on the answering machine. During the previous days, I had vaguely planned to go out that night to the local bars, walk around on my own, meet some people, get a little drunk and open myself to whatever chance had in store for me. Now, however, the expectations for that day had begun to weigh upon me. I was unsettled that the most trivial incidents could project outward into incalculable consequences, which was, strictly speaking, true of every day. I decided to stay in, resigned to the insomnia that would result from my two-hour nap. I opted not to watch television or open my computer or listen to music. I uncapped a beer and settled down once again in the gray armchair in the living room. I stayed there listening to the sounds of the neighborhood, watching as the light faded and was replaced by the glow of the streetlights, no longer expecting anything more from that foundational day, the first day of the second half of my life.

TWO

THE next morning, I called the neurologist's office. The receptionist informed me that an appointment had opened up for that afternoon and I took it. Bald, pale, with feminine hands, Doctor Briones nevertheless wore a permanent, invisible mantle of authority. His mask of bonhomie transformed into concern as soon as I told him why I'd come in. A new episode. In fact, I told him, this one made four since my last check-up.

"Do you have any idea what caused it, Tomás?"

"No."

"Any strain or shock?"

"Like what?"

"Intense physical exercise, immersion in hot or cold water, sexual activity, stress at work…"

"Immersion in hot water and sexual activity," I said. "It happened in the bathtub."

"How long beforehand had you had sexual relations?"

"Two hours…two and a half."

"It's more likely that it was the hot water," he determined, "though the other could have contributed. Have you had headaches?"

"No."

"Nausea, vomiting, dizziness, tremors, excessive sweating, feelings of panic or shortness of breath, chest pain, neck pain, altered vision, tachycardia?"

"No."

"As I've explained to you before, Tomás, we don't know the exact causes. We think it could be a narrowing of the vessels carrying blood from the brain to the heart, and we know that the episodes are almost always accompanied by powerful emotional or physical experiences."

The doctor checked my pupils, my reflexes, had me walk an imaginary line from one end of the exam room to the other, balance on one foot. He had me try out what looked to be a child's toy, with two twisted wires, to check my psychomotor coordination. He asked me my name, the date, our present location, the names of political figures and soccer players. He made me memorize a brief list of words.

"Everything seems normal, Tomás," he concluded, scribbling an order, "but I'm going to ask you to do an EEG and a CT scan just to be sure. My feeling is still that it's transient global amnesia, that we're not looking at something more serious, like a tumor, a brain hemorrhage or some other physical injury. Have you hit your head since the last time we saw each other?"

"No."

He held out the order for the exams.

"The only strange thing about your case," he added, "is the persistence of the episodes. It's a rare thing and rarer still for it to happen more than once. And you've had fourteen or fifteen episodes in one year. Have you been seeing a psychotherapist?"

"No."

"Forgive me for insisting, but please remember that one of the most serious effects of TGA is the anxiety and disorientation that it causes. And if you add personal problems and work-related stress…"

"Doctor, I had a dream during the episode yesterday."

He looked at me in astonishment.

"What do you mean?"

"I had a dream. I dreamt that I was an old woman and I was walking across a plaza."

"Tomás, that's impossible."

I shrugged.

"What's happening is that you're functioning normally until, because of a small vascular occlusion, you experience a lapse in your short-term memory. It doesn't have anything to do with sleeping or dreaming."

"I had a dream," I insisted.

The doctor held my gaze for a moment with a tired expression. He made a note on his pad, tore off the page, and laid it on top of the order for the exams.

"Doctor Rojas is an excellent psychiatrist. Tomás, I really do suggest that you go see her. If I were you, I'd be worried about my stress level, which can have much more serious consequences than transitory amnesia."

"Thank you," I said. I folded up both sheets of paper and stood to shake the doctor's delicate hand.

The first episode had occurred a year earlier, as I was preparing for a trip to New York. My friend Sebastián had written to let me know that his small studio in Flatbush would be vacant for a while — the student who'd been renting it had left school suddenly — and he offered it to me for a week or two to rest and get some distance from the crisis with Paula, which by then seemed a lost cause. I had just stepped off the metro in Providencia and was on my way to exchange some money and go to the post office to mail a certified letter. In the next instant, with no transition whatsoever, like in a damaged film reel, I found myself in the post office, standing at the counter, holding the letter in my hand. I was frozen in place.

"Sir, how can I help you?" the woman behind the counter was saying with obvious impatience. "Sir?"

"Sorry," I stammered. I stumbled out to the street. I couldn't breathe. The surface of the sidewalk vibrated beneath my feet. The sunlight blinded me. I leaned against the doorframe. In the back pocket of my pants I found a wad of dollars and the receipt from the money exchange office.

A doctor friend of mine recommended Doctor Briones. His diagnosis was immediate: transient global amnesia. He cleared me to travel, even though he wouldn't see the results of my tests before my departure. If there was anything to worry about, he'd email me. He told me not to worry, that, apart from the natural anxiety and disorientation, this was a relatively harmless phenomenon and that it would most likely never happen again.

Sebastián had been right. The change of scenery and language, getting away for a few weeks from the pressures of work, had a beneficial effect, especially during the first few days, during which time I gained — with respect to the long and torturous process with Paula — an unprecedented sense of clarity. I understood that I still loved her and I decided I'd exhaust all my resources in order to save my marriage. Unfortunately, the separation had the opposite effect on her: it gave her a taste of what it would be like to be free of me.

I didn't see Sebastián during my nearly two weeks in Brooklyn. Actually, his offer hadn't been completely selfless. He needed to show the apartment to potential renters but had a conference in Hawaii and a series of commitments at the university in California where he taught that he couldn't get out of. Sebastián had gotten his Ph.D. in literature at NYU. He'd bought the studio in Flatbush with a Dominican girlfriend who worked as a librarian at a museum in Brooklyn. Now he was an associate professor at a mid-level university in the Central Valley, a rising academic star.

The first person to visit the apartment — a Korean-American student encased in an enormous parka who arrived early, before I'd had time to make the bed and tidy up — asked me if I was also Mapuche.

"To a certain extent," I said, "all Chileans are."

She nodded, not particularly convinced.

"But I'm committed to the cause," I added, striking a false note, eager for her to like me, without exactly knowing why.

"It's a disgrace," she said, dead serious, eyeing the studio from the threshold, perhaps surprised at my ability to create disorder from such few elements: a futon, a pillow, a sleeping bag and an open suitcase.

In his first year at NYU, after breaking up with Elisa, Sebastián found his niche in the history of Mapuche literature. He had grown increasingly involved in the conflict, raising funds for legal counsel, writing articles for university publications and organizing symposiums. Every year, he would take advantage of his visits to Temuco to see his ex-wife and son, to tour the disputed lands, once even being detained under suspicion of terrorist conspiracy, which earned him a hero's welcome upon his return. Elisa was Mapuche, a Spanish professor and a poet. I had never been able to appreciate her poetry, which had been quite successful, particularly in North American academic circles and largely due to Sebastián, tireless champion of his ex-wife, editor of two bilingual collections published by university presses (translated from Spanish to Mapudungún, rather than the other way around, as he once confessed to me). The student brought to mind a conversation I'd had with Sebastián on his way through Santiago a few years back. He just attended a talk in Arizona given by a curiously blond, blue-eyed Native American documentarian. Except for a multi-colored vest and his long hair worn back in a ponytail, he said, nothing about him signaled that he belonged to an Indigenous nation. He was involved in a documentary series focused on the reservations and native communities in the Northwest. At some point in his talk, he had referred to his own genealogical tree and to his Coeur d'Alene great-grandmother. Sebastián had silently calculated that he had a larger percentage of native ancestry than the presenter. He had never in the least tried to pass for Mapuche. I don't think it would have crossed his mind. Or was this student's question evidence of something I didn't know about? In southern Chile, the fact of his whiteness, that he was a huinca, was never in question. But in the north, in the cloisters of academia, which employed a cruder standard of authenticity and a sort of binary ethical and emotional code that separated the acceptable from the aberrant, the orthodox from heresy, Sebastián paradoxically occupied an ambiguous space and appeared to be transitioning — not of his own volition, but rather due to the gravitational pull of his passion — toward a new cultural identity.

Three more potential renters came to see the studio, but the matter didn't get resolved during my stay. I spent my days visiting museums and galleries, seeing movies, buying books on advertising and design, but, above all, walking the streets and thinking about Paula. I remembered my first trip to New York (courtesy of my father), in the mid-'80s, and I was struggling to superimpose the present city over the city I remembered, permeated with a sense of danger, of imminent disaster, a now-vanished roughness: graffiti on the subway, deranged people babbling on street corners and entire neighborhoods that seemed to have been colonized by the Third World. *That* New York, which I was spiraling toward via a cyclical route. On that first visit (and on the two or three after that), I moved through the streets intoxicated by my own euphoria at being there. My emotions rubbed up against my surroundings and propelled me like a wind-up car. Later I would link that forced enthusiasm with the period of time when I flirted with the affectation of becoming a film buff, a cinephile, with an excessive fervor for certain directors that I liked, but actually liked less than I had decided I ought to. Over time I became disenchanted with New York, brandishing a pedantic and conservative resistance to the radical changes in most of its neighborhoods (for a mere tourist, an absurdly possessive nostalgia for the hard times). My pilgrimages to the Mecca of advertising and nearly everything else became less and less frequent, especially after Sebastián left. That stay in the studio in Flatbush was my first time back in six years. My previous visit had been with Paula. Now, as I walked, my only goal to reflect on our marriage and on fatherhood, I was beginning to fall into sync again with the city's wavelength, to feel at home.

During my walks, without intending to, I found myself studying children in an almost ethnographic way. I spent an entire morning sitting on a bench in Central Park watching them ice skating and building snowmen and making snow angels, affecting a sufficient level of nonchalance, exaggerating and projecting true harmlessness so as not to awaken suspicions of pedophilia. I'd always been indifferent to children, no matter how hard I tried to convey the opposite to my friends. Their world and mine did not mesh. By contrast, Paula felt drawn to them, which she demonstrated — in restaurants, in public squares, on airplanes — with a zeal that verged on embarrassing. Now I observed them in light of the possibility, contemplated for the first time, of living with another person's daughter. (Paula always insisted that it would be a girl.) Circling in my mind was something Sebastián had said to me in that same studio apartment one evening as he was making pisco sours in a fit of distance-inspired criollismo: that having children was to engage in a temporal paradox, summed up in a verse by an English poet: "The child is father of the man," which did not refer, he said — himself flush with nostalgic sentimentalism — to the sappy commonplace that the-children-are-our-future, but rather to the idea that we were the evolutionary past of something glimpsed in the child, something that would fade before adolescence and from which we were exiled. Fatherhood marked the entry point into a circular time, he added, in which we return to being our parents, like in a play where the actors have to exchange roles. I didn't really understand what he was talking about. I remember I considered using the concept, the child is father of the man, for an ad campaign I was struggling with, but I ended up scuttling the idea as too cryptic.

Paula was on the pill for the first five or six years we were married. Then, in a rather casual way, she went off it. We weren't in a rush to have kids; our careers in advertising and photography were well underway, we had no financial problems, and our relationship, with the usual ups and downs, was solid. We decided to leave it up to fate. But after a year, Paula mentioned, in an offhand way, that she was surprised she hadn't gotten pregnant yet. In short order, infertility would become the central drama in our lives and would open an abyss between us. From the very first tests it became clear that the problem lay solely with me, though they weren't able to determine the cause. I remembered the humiliation, not of having to masturbate in a narrow bathroom used by the office staff, but of the nurse averting her eyes as she handed me a plastic container and a couple of tattered issues of Penthouse. In any case, it was something I'd end up getting used to. In addition to the semen analyses (which immediately revealed the virtual absence of sperm cells), I had to endure a testicular biopsy, ultrasounds, hormonal tests, genetic and antibody studies and a vasography. All the tests confirmed what the doctor had suggested from the start: it wasn't possible to determine the cause — it could have been due to an infection as a teenager or to some environmental factor, contact with pesticides or radiation, or even stress — and that there was no cure. Our options were assisted reproduction, using a sperm donor, or adoption.

In retrospect, my refusal to adopt was the death knell for our relationship. Or, better yet, the scapegoat for everything that had seemed to work but didn't, and the visible punishment for the most arduous aspects of married life: domesticity, routine, disenchantment, tedium. I didn't fully understand the reasons for my own obstinacy. For me, fatherhood was inextricably bound to a sort of unconditional surrender to the mainstream, to the common valuing of rituals (Easter eggs, Mother's and Father's Days, school plays, Christmas decorations), not for their actual content, but rather for the mere fact of being rituals, which gave a certain air of distinction to the inability to break vicious cycles: the vast majority of my agnostic or atheist friends — Sebastián, for a start — had baptized their children to appease a grandmother, children who, in turn, would be agnostic or atheist and would end up baptizing their children to please a future mother-in-law or those very same friends growing progressively less agnostic as they aged. These people's fascination with their children was egocentrism, pure and simple, in the same way that my father had considered me, for all intents and purposes, a mere extension of himself; they shut themselves up inside their families (in houses, in cars, like airtight capsules), giving themselves over to a centripetal force, ignoring the dysfunctional fate awaiting them, the hell-that-was-other-people, incapable of glimpsing — in babies, in the little girls taking their first steps, in the adorable children gliding across the ice in Central Park — the adolescents and adults and elderly people who would be taking their places in the blink of an eye, conned by the most basic of evolutionary ruses. I wasn't opposed to the idea of children, just to the obligation of having them, the absurd conviction, to which Paula clung with all her might, that by their mere existence, they would magically reestablish a lost wholeness. One of the pretexts that I wielded to justify my reticence was an oppressive lack of time, the never-ending obstacle course of life that left no room for children. Paula, possessed by an irrational and unbridled frenzy, by the certainty that her time was running out, promised to leave her job and focus entirely on the little girl, but by that point the argument had taken shape as a competition in which each of us strove (or at least I did) to score the most points. The outcome of this contest was less surprising than the fact that it went on for so long.

The second episode of amnesia occurred the day before my return. I was sitting on the futon in the studio, about to put on a pair of thick, wool socks. The next second I found myself in Central Park, on a paved path that wove among continuous rows of benches. A wave of terror swamped me, the feeling that the ground beneath my feet had disappeared for a fraction of a second. I spun around, trying to get my bearings, startling a woman who was jogging toward me, exhaling faint clouds of steam. I sat down on a snow-covered bench and forced myself to calm down. My feet hurt after walking, I supposed, a long distance, and I needed to go to the bathroom. I was also overcome by an irrational impulse to look at myself in a mirror, to make sure there wasn't anything in my appearance that betrayed what had just happened. I was wearing my parka and I had on my wool hat, a scarf and gloves. In a pocket of the parka I found my cellphone and determined that four hours had passed. I searched for receipts or any indication of what I had done during the lapse. Despite my exhaustion, I had most likely taken the subway. I didn't think I was capable of walking from Brooklyn all the way, if my calculations were correct, to Seventy-something Street.

I continued walking along the path until I came to Fifth Avenue, the need to empty my bladder becoming dire. I crossed the street and studied my reflection in the window of a parked car. I was surprised by my anxious grimace, but there was nothing strange about my appearance. I walked away from the park, looking for somewhere I could use a bathroom. With difficulty, taking short little steps, bent over from the sharp pain in my low belly, I made it to the corner of Madison Avenue. I saw a Mexican restaurant across the street, half a block down. As I was waiting for the light to turn green, a tall, red-haired man with freckles, dressed in an elegant dark suit, long overcoat and scarf, emerged from a funeral parlor on the corner and stopped alongside me. He took a phone from the pocket of his overcoat and made a call.

"Martina, hi, it's Juan Pablo. I just spoke with the Dutch. They want to postpone the meeting until tomorrow at four. Everything's ready, right?"

He not only spoke in perfect Spanish, but had a Chilean accent. His tone was at once authoritative and personable.

"Try to find Jack and ask him if he's available in the morning. Move everything else to Thursday or Friday. Thanks, sweetheart. I don't know what I'd do without you."

He hung up. He noticed me watching him and gave me a quick warning glance. Don't mess with me. I was tempted to identify myself as a compatriot, but I didn't. Nothing was in worse taste than the forced camaraderie among Chileans abroad. The light changed. The man strode across the street and climbed into the back of a limousine. The distance separating me from the Mexican restaurant seemed insurmountable. I decided to try my luck in the funeral parlor.

The place was empty. At the back of the dim room I made out a coffin illuminated by four wax candles in tall candelabras. I scanned the side doors and, on one, found the longed-for word: restroom. Once inside, I asked myself if I'd bought an extra large green tea to go at the spot on the corner of Flatbush Avenue or if I'd opted for an orange juice in some café in the Village. I strained to imagine both scenarios in an attempt to summon the memory, but it was no use. I looked at myself carefully in the mirror. Everything seemed normal. When I came out of the bathroom I walked over to the closed coffin and paid my respects in silence. On my way to the exit, a tall man dressed in black stepped up and urged me to sign the guest book. I had no choice but to acquiesce.

The funeral director led me to a small table lit by a bronze lamp. He handed me a gold fountain pen. The book was blank.

"Didn't the other man sign?"

"What other man?"

"He was on his way out when I came in. A tall guy, red hair…"

The funeral director shrugged.

"I went into the office for a minute. I didn't see anyone," he noted with contained brusqueness.

Under his vigilant gaze, I scrawled a terse phrase, the date and my signature.

"Please, include your name and address," he commanded.

"Why?"

"So we can send you a card," he explained firmly.

"Of course," I said, obeying. The man either failed to notice the irony in my voice or decided not to let on.

That night, the evening before my return flight, I called Paula to tell her about my latest episode. She answered in a sleepy voice and I remembered that it was two hours later in Chile.

"Did I wake you?"

"It's okay."

"I'm leaving tomorrow. I'll be there Monday."

"Yes, I know. Do you want me to pick you up from the airport?"

"Well, have you had time to think?"

"Yes, Tomás."

"And?"

A pause. Not a good sign.

"Let's talk when you get back."

Another silence. I wondered whether to tell her about the episode.

"Tomás, I was planning to call you," she added with unexpected enthusiasm, "to tell you something surprising. You're not going to believe it."

I said nothing. She went on: "I have a sister!"

One of the things that had connected us in the beginning, aside from sexual chemistry and work (the creative director and the photographer, the photographer and the creative director), had been that we were both only children. This was an intimate betrayal, undermining the foundation of our complicity, I thought with a knot in my stomach.

"Her name is Mariana," she said reverently. "We're actually half-sisters, on my Dad's side, obviously. Mariana is the daughter of a woman Pedro was seeing after he separated from my mother and before he married Sonia. We were both born in the same month: June of '72. Mariana is eleven days older than me. Apparently, my mother never knew about her, but Mariana's mother, who went into exile in France after the coup and now lives in Holland, in Rotterdam, she found out about me. Mariana lives in Madrid. She's a photographer, just like me, though she's a fashion and design photographer and doesn't really do anything in advertising. She uses her mother's last name. Mariana," she went on, her voice breaking, "has known about me all these years and I had no idea, I had no idea…"

Sitting on the futon in the dark, surrounded by the nocturnal hum of Flatbush Avenue, I listened to Paula sob gently.

"I'm sorry, Tomás, I still haven't quite taken it all in…I feel on edge, sort of shaken up."

"Don't worry about it."

"I talked to the lawyer today and asked him to postpone the appointment with the notary until April. Is that okay with you?"

"Sure, fine. We have time."

Paula blew her nose slowly. She murmured another apology.

"How did she contact you? Through social media?"

"No, she's had my contact info for a long time, but she didn't dare reach out..." Paula choked up again. "You know," she went on, "she looks a lot like me. From what I can see in the photos she sent me, she's a blonde, slightly thinner version of me. We could be twins."

"A blonde and a brunette. Sounds exciting."

Another pause.

"So now what," I asked.

"She's coming to Chile next week."

After my return from New York, the processes that had been gradually gestating and accumulating were immediately set into motion, unfolding at an alarming rate. The revelation of the existence of Mariana — whom Paula refused to let me meet in order, as she put it, "to avoid mixing two phases of her life" — acted as a catalyst. At least it did for Paula, shifting her center of focus and allowing her to concentrate on the future, filing down the sharp edges of our break up and making our divorce — initiated by the signature of the notary after Mariana left to go back to Madrid — a mere formality.

On the way home from the airport I informed Paula, somewhat pompously, that I had made the decision to adopt a baby girl. I even had a few names picked out. (I wasn't at all enthusiastic about the idea, but it was a price I was prepared to pay in order to keep her.) To my surprise, she told me that this — the millstone that had meticulously broken down and pulverized our life together — wasn't the point. With her eyes fixed on the highway, she said harshly that I still didn't understand anything, that the topic of adoption was a symptom, not the underlying problem.

"Please, illuminate me. What is the underlying problem?"

"Your selfishness."

She added that even at that very moment, in bringing up adoption — which, by that point, felt like a cruel joke — I didn't seem convinced, that my tone was that of a person who had finally decided to yield in a negotiation.

After that, I gave up. Paula wanted to postpone the separation until after Mariana's visit. I understood that Paula had reached a decision long before and that I was the only one pushing against the tide, assuming that we were both trying to salvage what remained of the shipwreck. I understood just how arbitrary our truce had been — built on the sum of our transactions, marital tugs of war — how, no matter how natural and necessary that truce had seemed throughout the years, it was an equilibrium in a void, one that either party could topple with a single well-aimed blow. I also sensed that, by ceasing to struggle, I could avoid, to a large extent, the pain and sense of failure. No big deal, I told myself. After all, half of marriages end in divorce. Nothing was forever. Everything vanishes into thin air. I'd never considered myself a sentimental person and I was surprised by my own attitude in recent months. I'd allowed myself to be swept along by assumptions that suddenly seemed foreign to me, expecting, like most people, too much of marriage. Just like Paula's lawyer had pointed out in the notary's office during the signing of the legal separation papers and divorce agreement, the absence of children made things easier, the problem would become its own solution.

Paula and Mariana became immediate "best friends." They had lunch together. Paula didn't tell me where. I couldn't repress a jealous, sarcastic comment, witnessing the anxious pains she took in dressing and primping for that first meeting. She left before 1:00 on a rainy day at the end of March, and didn't return until midnight. The connection with her sister had been instantaneous. In so many ways, she declared, pacing overexcitedly around the kitchen and living room, they were like twins, and not just because they'd been born less than two weeks apart or because of their physical resemblance. It was a much deeper connection. In addition to photography, they shared endless traits, peculiarities, skills, gestures, aesthetic and political opinions, tastes in food, and an affinity for the same books, movies and TV shows. More than anything, they were connected by a kind of telepathic link; on several occasions throughout the course of their conversation, they were able to read one another's minds, to guess what the other was just about to say. In addition, Mariana was in the process of ending a long, live-in relationship with a man who, based on her description, sounded remarkably similar to me.

The fourth or fifth time they got together, this time at a restaurant in Nueva Costanera, I decided to spy on them. Lucky for me, they sat at a table near the window overlooking the street. I walked around the block so that I could approach them facing Mariana. I couldn't make her out clearly, as the light from a streetlamp was reflecting off the window, hindering my view. I didn't dare get very close for fear that Paula would sense my presence and turn around. But from what I could glimpse, the resemblance was astonishing. A beatific smile played across Mariana's face, a slightly more angular version of Paula's. They gazed at one another, enraptured. I strained to see, in the light of the candle on their table, if they were holding hands. When I'd come within about thirty feet of the window, Mariana glanced at me without much interest. Lacking a plan of action, I couldn't think of anything to do except move quickly out of her field of view, pressing myself up against the metal grating of the neighboring house. I tripped over a wire and fell face first into a patch of shrubbery. It was for the best, I thought, crawling on elbows and knees until a row of paving stones forced me to get up. I left, retracing my steps, hunched over, walking across driveways and the rectangles of grass that bordered the sidewalk, weaving in between hedges, activating motion-sensor lights, until I was sure I was out of her range of vision.

Paula, whom I'd always considered a reasonable and mature person (much more so than me, certainly), as well as constant and stable, capable of navigating the most difficult situations without losing her poise and composure, a person of ineffable elegance, was abandoning herself to Mariana with a sort of fanaticism, revealing a tendency to obsessively anchor her life to external factors, as she'd first done around the concept of motherhood. I was concerned about her ecstatic zeal over the discovery of Mariana, who appeared to have been dropped into the world with the sole purpose of satisfying every one of her half-sister's needs. I even wondered if there were some sort of magic spell involved. I had never before seen her profess such idolatry for anyone. (As far as I can remember, it wasn't that way with us. We'd succumbed to a gradual, mutual enchantment.) I'd never seen her so in love.

Over the course of Mariana's visit, I was witness to another of my wife's traits, projected in an unexpected direction. In every situation, Paula drew people to her. At the end of an interview, a trip or even just a photo session, she'd be inundated with an avalanche of people wanting her attention and her time, if not her outright friendship, and Paula found herself obliged — in her charming but firm way — to draw a line, to maintain her personal space as a refuge from the invading hordes. I used to tell her, from the very beginning, that if we ever broke up, the suitors would descend upon her like a plague. Apparently, that's how it had been before I came on the scene. Now, though she was still living with me in our apartment in Pedro de Valdivia Norte, she had begun to draw that dividing line with me. I scarcely saw her for a few hours each night and, in any case, she'd only stayed because a move would have required time and energy that she preferred to dedicate to Mariana instead. During those weeks, in which her plan to go to Madrid was already beginning to take shape, it wasn't jealousy that hounded me, but rather the sense that I was losing her even as a friend. More than anything, it was her distraction that wounded me.

After Mariana left, we officially began divorce proceedings and we separated. The original idea was to immediately sell the apartment, which we'd already nearly paid off. Paula's stepfather was going to help her buy a new, smaller apartment in the same neighborhood. But she decided, in light of her plan to go to Spain, to move in with her mother for a few months. Busy with work at the agency, I stayed on, purely by inertia. Finally, as my fortieth birthday approached, I turned the apartment over to a real estate agent who sold it in less than a week. During those winter months, I went out with two or three women, including (serious mistake) an executive at the agency. She invited me to dinner to talk about a problem with a client. From the restaurant we went to a bar and, after a couple of hours and numerous rounds of vodka, to a motel. I never took anyone back to the apartment. Paula and I continued to make love once or twice a month, until she left for Spain at the end of November. Freed from the tedium of cohabitation, daily pressures and the anguish of infertility, those furtive lunch-hour encounters in the apartment brought back a sexual fulfillment we'd lost years before. It was a convenient arrangement, especially for her: known territory. In between, I didn't see her much. Our relationship seemed to have completed a circle, coming back to our bodies.

During this time, in the midst of a particularly hectic period at work, when it seemed as if fires were erupting and multiplying by spontaneous combustion, I returned to New York for a few days. I received an envelope from Sebastián that turned out to be a letter addressed to me that had been forwarded from the studio apartment in Brooklyn to California. It was from a New York law firm. It informed me that a woman named Phyllis Anna Carstensen had died, leaving no heirs. As stipulated by the deceased in her will, because I had attended the wake and signed the guest book the previous February, I was to receive a portion of her estate. I called the lawyer who'd signed the letter and, after explaining the situation to a receptionist, was put through. In a serious, courteous and formal tone, he confirmed the ludicrous information contained in the missive. Despite all appearances to the contrary, it was not a scam or a joke. I asked him who Phyllis Carstensen had been and he replied that he knew little about her, only that she'd lived the last fifteen years of her life alone and in apparent poverty, in a small apartment facing the Queensboro Bridge, and that they had been unable to locate a single member of her family. She had made arrangements with the funeral parlor and signed her will a decade ago. The neighbors were relieved to be rid of her. I asked him how many people had signed the guest book, and he replied that he was not at liberty to disclose that information. The amount was considerable; it equaled, more or less, a year of my salary. He informed me that I'd have to sign a series of documents and offered to send them to me by mail. I told him I wasn't interested in the money. That would involve signing a different series of documents.

I decided to take a few days and resolve the matter in person. I found the idea of accepting the money unsettling, not knowing whose hands it had passed through, how it had been amassed. But I also had no real reason to refuse it. By that point, I'd already begun thinking about taking a year abroad after my upcoming birthday, and it seemed like a lucky coincidence that the sum lined up with the amount it would take to carry out that plan; it confirmed that it was a good idea, though technically — between my savings and the recent sale of my car because of the amnesia, plus the equity on the apartment — I didn't need it. This time I stayed in a hotel. I met with another New York attorney, this one a specialist in tax law. I went back to the funeral home on Madison Avenue in a vain attempt to gather some information about Phyllis Carstensen. At her apartment building, the only thing that became clear was that her neighbors hated her for her lack of hygiene. A man sweeping the dark entryway informed me, his voice barely audible over the din of traffic on the bridge, that the health authorities had been unable to find one of her cats, which continued to prowl about the building. To emphasize the point, he pushed open the door, stepped out onto the sidewalk and pointed to a ledge six feet up on the side of the building, crowned with razor wire, I suppose to prevent people from dropping down to it from a section of the bridge's overhanging structure. An enormous, feral-looking gray cat rested on the ledge. He watched us with a grim, severe expression from his impregnable post, as if he knew we were talking about him.

In the days after my birthday, I began to settle into a routine revolving around my apartment and my new neighborhood. The relaxation had a restorative effect.

I did all the tests ordered by Doctor Briones and asked for the results to be sent to his office. The receptionist told me that, according to protocol, they would contact me only if there was anything abnormal. They didn't call me. My brain was in perfect condition, just as it had been a year ago, when the episodes had first begun. On my walks around Lastarria and Bellavista, I was hounded by a silent anxiety about the imminence of my next lapse. At times, I was conscious that every step could transport me, to put it one way, to another dimension. I wondered where I would turn up, after having done what, though, so far, I didn't appear to have done anything abnormal or violent during my absences.

I started planning for my trip. I booked a flight to Paris with a return in a year. My plan was to travel overland through Spain and onward to Morocco. Other possible stops included Egypt, Jordan, Turkey and India. The only thing I knew for sure about the adventure was that it wouldn't end up looking like my initial plan. The idea was to improvise, let one thing lead me to the next, maybe settle somewhere for a bit if called to by circumstance or inspiration. I considered calling my landlady and offering to pay her the rent for the entire year in a single deposit. My state of mind was one of subtle and agreeable disintegration. As the days passed, I felt validated in my decision to dismantle my life. I felt no impulse to construct a new one, or establish any long-term plan. If this was a midlife crisis, as my friends maintained — with a dose of envy, as is always the case when one criticizes anything about anyone — I didn't care at all. I felt the tides had shifted in my favor.

I went to the gym, but I didn't see Fernanda. The manager refused to give me any information about her. I went back the next day, an hour earlier. I spotted her on one of the machines. When she recognized me, her focused expression turned to alarm. She straddled the treadmill, placing her sneakered feet on its motionless edges.

"Hello, Tomás," she said icily. She was panting.

"I was in the neighborhood and I thought I'd stop by and see you."

I tried to smile. She remained serious. She took a sip of water from a plastic bottle and put it back in a holder on the machine. She was wearing tight sweatpants and a tank top. I noticed that she had small, half-moon shaped sweat stains beneath her arms.

"I have no other way to find you," I said.

"I know."

I dropped my gaze to the conveyor belt, eagerly churning away on its own. Fernanda pushed a button and the machine stopped.

"I didn't mean to interrupt you. How about I wait for you and we can go get a coffee?"

"Tomás, Nico is coming to pick me up in half an hour."

"You're still with him then?"

"I'm still with him."

In one of the mirrors that covered the walls, I saw that a trainer — in a t-shirt with the gym's logo on it — was watching us, waiting for the slightest sign from Fernanda that something was wrong.

"Well, take care," I said, and walked away from her. I passed the trainer. I glimpsed Fernanda's reflection in the mirror. She was watching me in surprise, still motionless atop the treadmill.

As the date of Paula's visit approached, my life settled into a rhythm of waiting, not so much for her as for the divorce hearing, at which the date of the second hearing a month or two later would be set, after which I'd be able to travel. Not even the brief setback with Fernanda had managed to undermine my serenity and sense of purpose, whose energy derived from its lack of objective. The tabula rasa I'd decided to effect after my fortieth birthday (the number was, of course, arbitrary) required sustaining that absence of plans as much as possible. I didn't know what my intentions had been with Fernanda, but whatever they were, they would have meant an attachment, a dent in my freedom, in the plasticity of the future I had before me. This was confirmed to some extent by the sudden disappearance of the recent past, which now seemed segmented into discrete entities, enclosed like bubbles: the agency, my life with Paula, our old neighborhood.

The agency, which, up until a few weeks before had dominated my time and mental space, was rapidly sinking into memory, becoming unreal. Everything there seemed to have happened to a different person. I missed the intensity, the urgency, the constant exercise of certain skills that would, from that moment on, begin to atrophy inexorably. My great talent was not as a professional persuader. I was better than average at the art of breaking down the barriers of public cynicism erected by the constant media bombardment; at the art of indirect indoctrination; and of complicity through irony and the stimulation of varying degrees of good taste. And I had surrounded myself with even more skillful subordinates. My genius lay in recognizing the invisible people in every meeting and in giving each of them their due, in exactly the right way, at exactly the right moment. Both within the agency and in client relations, I wasn't concerned — despite appearances to the contrary — with the content of ideas, but rather, with the type and level of attachment to those ideas among the parties involved. The fuel that drives every company, including the agency, is the ego of the person in charge, whom I was in the habit of detaching and treating as a double, as if another individual were present in the room, turning every negotiation or presentation into a game with more players than it appeared. More than selling products, I was selling my ability to sell them. As the symbolic threshold of forty approached, I had begun to feel too old for the business and it became harder for me to keep pulling rabbits out of my hat. My style started to feel predictable to me and I could see a moment, not too far off — though before my partners and my team would see it — in which I'd start overselling myself. The idea of a sabbatical year was nothing more than a euphemism. I had exited in full command of my skills. There is also such a thing as the art of escape.

I found myself at ease in the midst of the decisions I'd made. I wasn't expecting a great deal from Paula's upcoming visit, or even from the trip that was starting to take shape or, more specifically, to gain momentum inside me. I gave myself over to the languid uncertainty that everything I began from that moment on would also be transitory, that even that period, the beginning of my new life, was doomed to be embalmed in memory.

Then — three days before Paula's arrival and five days before the first divorce hearing — it happened.

THREE

SUDDENLY, with no perceptible shift, it's happening again. An episode, I tell myself. I'm aware simultaneously of myself and of the hallucination surrounding me, in the same way you know, in dreams, that you're dreaming. But this certainty tends to be fleeting, it's the prelude to waking, or part of the waking process itself; perhaps, as they emerge into wakefulness, certain areas of the brain manage to alert other parts that what they are seeing and feeling is not real. But that's not what's happening. Both the vision and the awareness of experiencing the vision persist, superimposing themselves one over the other. Just a moment earlier, I was walking from one spot to another in my kitchen on Rosal Street, from the refrigerator to the microwave, holding a plate of lentils covered in aluminum foil. Now I'm outside on the street. Once again I'm this old person, this woman. After an initial moment of alarm, of vertigo, a strange calm comes over me. I'm trudging arduously around the edge of a vacant lot. Every five or six steps I have to stop to catch my breath, leaning up against a cinder block wall where someone has scrawled, in huge red brush strokes: ROT IN HELL, PERUVIAN DOG. In the distance, I can see the leafy green of trees. In my hand, I hold a crumpled bill and some coins. The change from a taxi, I think. Instinctively, I head toward the plaza.

The first thing I notice is the exhaustion. I want to simply stand up straight and shake it off. The late-summer sun hits me full on and, even so, I'm cold. I make it to the corner. One more block to reach the plaza. A short block. I hear the sound of the buses on the next street over and the thud of a heavy bundle being dropped to the pavement from the back of a truck. Against the silhouette of the church, I can make out the shapes of cranes at a construction site. I cross the street. I see a bicycle coming toward me from a long way off. A young guy with tattoos on his legs overtakes me well before I manage to reach the other side of the street, and he makes a subtle maneuver to avoid hitting me. In contrast to his movements, so fluid and natural, I move as if in slow motion. I step onto the sidewalk. I clutch a concrete post with both hands. Blood beats in my temples from the effort of crossing the street. I stand staring at a segment of wall covered in a collage of posters. Someone has torn off three identical posters from the top layer, exposing the faded layers beneath. I need to rest. I decide I'll sit down on the curb, but as soon as I try to bend over there's a stabbing pain in my back, and my legs tell me if I allow myself to fall down there (because I would have to collapse from this height) I won't be able to get up again without help. I should cross the street and head west. Get out of the beating sun. But the opposite corner is heaped with piles of garbage bags and it would be hard for me to get past them. The distance separating me from the plaza, from the dense shade of the trees, seems insurmountable. Why didn't I get out of the taxi there? So they wouldn't see me arrive? I'm outraged at the weakness and inefficiency of this wretched carcass, reduced to a system of rigidity and pain. I don't want to accept the weight of my body, the enormity of the challenge inherent in walking a single block.

I have to skirt around another vacant lot, its perimeter ringed by a chain link fence. From there I can clearly make out — eyesight seems to be the only thing not failing this woman — the palms and araucarias standing out among the other trees, and, above the used-book stands, the sycamores obscuring the front of the church. A brownish stray dog with one leg missing passes me by. It comes to the corner of the plaza, sniffs the air, turns right and disappears behind the booth at the entrance to a parking lot. The dog is familiar to me. I've seen it somewhere before. Is that my memory or hers? I also think I recognize the vacant lot, the rectangle of dry grass strewn with plastic bottles and yellowed newspaper pages fluttering in a barely perceptible breeze. In the middle of the lot stands a refrigerator with no door filled with rusty tin cans and potato chip wrappers. I notice that I'm dragging my right foot, encased in a pink sneaker. Every ten or twelve steps I stop to rest, grasping the chain link fence with my twisted fingers. My head hurts. The sun burns the nape of my neck and the spotted backs of my hands. I clear my throat and say out loud: Okay now, that's enough! My voice is raspy, but surprisingly firm. Wake up, huevón! I say, but I do not wake up. I yank on the fence, with a wild sensation that it's locked me in, that I'm on the other side. I understand that there's no way out. I am no longer Tomás. I am this other person. What is her name? Should I remember it? This is what has been gestating over the past few months, I think. The other episodes were nothing more than an embryonic version of this, the definitive one. A part of me refuses to accept it. I sense that full awareness of my situation is about to come over me suddenly like a physical assault, and then, a collapse. It can't be, I mumble, it can't be. I open my eyes wide and convince myself that I'm on the verge of returning to myself, that the length of the dream is also deceptive. I scream, clutching the fence, but nothing happens. I'm still here. A woman walking down the adjacent street carrying a shopping bag throws me a furtive glance through the fence. Crazy old lady, her look says. I hold her gaze and she picks up her pace. I tell myself that perhaps I've traversed a threshold. That instead of heading toward the plaza, I should turn and retrace my steps. If I go back to the corner where I got out of the taxi (should I walk the last stretch backwards?), maybe I'll be transported back to my kitchen on Rosal Street and find myself holding a plate of lentils that I'm about to uncover and put in the microwave. But I don't have the strength. I have to rest. It's only twenty or twenty-five more steps to the plaza. I let go of the fence — my hands had started to seize up — and keep going, limping even more heavily, determined to cover the distance in one push.

I cross into the shade. Walking carefully over the uneven cobblestones, I head for the nearest bench, which is missing two slats on the seat and part of the backrest, and I collapse onto it, panting. I'm facing the street I've just come from. I turn around and study the plaza. I make out, behind a row of rusty flagpoles, an equestrian statue facing an empty fountain in the shape of a cross. I see a playground, couples stretched out on the grass, plastic bins in various colors chained together and the traffic moving along on the other side of the park. I'm certain that somewhere in this plaza is my spot, (that is, her spot), but I can't recognize it. I try to organize my thoughts. What surprises me most is that the sensation of being her differs so little, aside from the physical hardships, from the sensation of having been Tomás Ugarte. I wonder if knowing yourself to be someone —

this intimate certainty — is the same for everyone or if I'm experiencing it like this because I'm still myself, but trapped in the body of this old woman.

I fall asleep. My head tips back and, at the last moment, I tell myself with infinite relief that, of course, naturally: this is the way out. It's obvious. When I come to, I'll be in my apartment again, in my life. I open my eyes. I'm still on the bench. A truck loaded with gas canisters passes in front of me. A guy sitting in the truck bed is banging the levers of one of the canisters with a screwdriver. I think I heard that ringing in my dreams. A wave of desperation washes over me and I struggle not to cry. I do, however, notice that the brief rest has restored my energy. I see a man approaching along a gravel path. He makes a detour so as not to step on the grass and passes by my bench. He also seems vaguely familiar. Something about his particular gait, slow and springy, as if he were stepping on a spongy surface. I'd guess he's about fifty years old. He's wearing white sneakers, dirty jeans, a black T-shirt, and his longish, graying hair is slicked back. His eyes, two bloodshot slits, dominate an impassive, sunburned face. The man stops abruptly in front of me. I'm overcome by panic, but I try not to let on: in this body, I'm defenseless. The man smiles and his eyes narrow even further. He's missing three or four teeth. Inesita, he says sweetly, I didn't recognize you in those clothes. My name is Inés. It's true. I'm surprised that I didn't know it until just now. Inés. Inés Escobar. I shrug. I run a hand over the purple fabric of the pants. I'm wearing one of Paula's tracksuits and it's incongruous with my age and circumstances. Where did you get it? the man wants to know. Someone gave it to me, I reply. You don't say, he remarks, looking at me in disbelief. He rubs his cheek. You're not gonna get much business in that get-up. I smile. I guess not. Where were you? We've been missing you. We thought something bad had happened to you, he adds; there's a trace of sarcasm in his friendliness. I was over there, I wave my hand vaguely, past the church, with a relative of mine, a nephew. Ah, we thought you were alone. We? I think. Well, now you know. And did your nephew just ditch you here? I shrug. Well, at least you're all cleaned up and you have some new clothes. A pause. Your nephew didn't happen to give you any money, did he? No, sorry. The man takes a step back. Well, good to see you. Stop by anytime you want, when you feel like wetting your whistle. The man laughs, his dark tongue poking through the hole between his teeth. He gestures goodbye. I watch him walk away with his floating steps and suddenly I remember his nickname: Flaco.

I walk around the plaza looking for my spot. The inappropriateness of my outfit attracts a few glances, quickly distracted away by the utter invisibility and anonymity intrinsic to old women. I wander around the plaza's central esplanade for a while, happy to have recuperated a bit of energy during my nap, although my back hurts a little and I'm dragging the edge of my right sneaker. I turn around. From this angle, I feel like the plaza is on the verge of dovetailing with another, truer version of itself, a version held fast in Inés's memory. As I walk, trying to go from one shady patch to another, fragments of images and feelings gather in my mind. The memories rise to the surface of my consciousness like bubbles, surprising but undeniable, provoked by concrete details: a trash can, a graffiti mark on the plinth of the equestrian statue, the pigeon shit on the lamp posts, the shadow cast by a palm tree. I've been here, with this light. I recall (and are the memories, therefore, now deformed by the evocation?) two or three times when, in revisiting a place or reencountering a person nearly forgotten with the passage of time, my memory seemed to expand and multiply with each new random stimulus, every hidden corner and expression filling me with the disquieting suspicion that I was assembling the past with material taken from the present. In a sense, this is what's happening now: the plaza before me is no less illusory than the memories that it summons.

I sit on an intact bench in the shade of a poplar. I doze for a while. I open my eyes. A man and a woman, dressed in old overalls and rubber boots, clean the tiles of the empty fountain with mops and a hose. Nearby, a trio of young street artists rehearses an intricate routine revolving around a green hat that passes among hands and heads in a single continuous wave. They're wearing brightly colored vests and pants cut off at the knee. Their manner is jovial, carefree. One of them has a small accordion hanging across his chest. Every once in a while he emits a few random notes whose relation to the routine I can't figure out. They repeat the movement of the hat over and over again. Beyond them, on a strip of grass still in the sun, facing the construction site, I see Flaco. He's sitting with his back against a tree, chatting with a man and two women. Next to them rest three filthy dogs, panting in the heat. I recognize the brown one with the missing leg. Nearby, two other men and one woman sleep in unselfconscious poses. The woman's face is buried in the grass and a short skirt rides high up on her thighs. I know they're all part of a group: the winos. That's what the neighborhood shopkeepers call them, I think. Now another memory surfaces, not about Flaco, but connected to the fear that overcame me a little bit ago, when he stopped in front of me and during the entire length of our brief exchange. A cold, dark room in which I lie naked on a table (a younger version of this woman) gapes before me like a pit. Terrified, clutching the bench with both hands, I struggle to clear it from my mind. To the left of the winos, apparently unrelated to them, I see a row of benches piled with old plastic bags, sleeping bags and articles of clothing that I know belong to them. Among the bags, next to an old mattress propped against a water spigot, I see various empty cartons of wine and juice. I remember the winos. I can even recall some of their names. What's the brown dog's name? But I'm not sure about my relationship to them. I should really try to figure it out, I can't afford the luxury of making mistakes. I could go over there and strike up a casual conversation. But something tells me it wouldn't be a good idea.

A young guy walks by my bench. He recognizes me with a surprised expression, but then looks away without speaking to me and walks quickly away. He can't be older than thirty, but he looks sick, not just because of the bandages covering both legs and one arm, but also because of his pale, gaunt complexion, dirty hair plastered to his cheekbones, which jut out, revealing the shape of his skull, his crumbling teeth. Where's your girlfriend?, I want to ask him as he passes by, but I bite my tongue. He moves swiftly away from me. In his backpack is his walking cast for his right leg and a set of disassembled crutches clattering together. He's still wearing the dirty scarf around his neck that he uses as a sling for his arm. His name is Aníbal. Aníbal and his girlfriend beg at the side entrance to the church, one on each side of the door. That's their territory. They're only pretending to be crippled and the parishioners know it, but they give them coins anyway, even though they're suspicious about what they spend them on. The performance is confined to the stone steps that lead to the postern door inside the main door, but everyone sees them coming and going, walking just fine on their own two feet. The real problem is the shouting and fights that the priests or cops have to break up. Aníbal, inevitably, tries to hit his friend, even with one of his crutches, but she's stronger than he is. They shout whore and motherfucker at each other, trading looks of contempt from opposite sides of the staircase, but they never abandon their posts, their territory.

Which makes me think of my territory, my spot. I have to look for it, defend it from usurpers. They're not going to take away what little I have. I comb through most of the plaza, trying to jog my memory. Other, more distant memories come to me, and almost all of them have to do — in tone more than in content — with that dark room, they seem drawn to it as to a black hole. I'm just about to start searching the rest of the plaza, which stretches out to the west. Suddenly, it occurs to me that this is an absurd endeavor. Instead of worrying about someone taking over my spot and my belongings, which won't be any better than the winos' things, I should devise a way to appropriate Tomás' things. I decide to focus my memory on that other space and I find that I can recall easily, and in great detail, the apartment, Paula, the agency, a photograph of my father. But the most recent period — the past days and weeks — are much blurrier. I'm flooded by the dizzying sensation of having forgotten something in this very moment. It's almost within reach, but it's irretrievable. And what if, as Inés's memories emerge, they begin to replace Tomás' memories? I can't pinpoint any concrete part of Tomás that has faded away. I can envision countries he's visited, restaurants where he's eaten, movies he's seen, but I feel as if his presence is losing ground inside me. I wonder if maybe reversing the process is not up to me. Clearly, his circumstances are preferable to mine.

I check the pockets of the tracksuit. (Paula bought it, along with another one, in an off-white color. For some reason, as far as I can remember, she never wore this one. It hung in her closet — I can see just where — for a couple of years with the tags still on. I don't know, however, how it came to be here.) I go through the pockets and find nothing except the change from the taxi. It's not enough to get to Rosal Street. I could take a bus, but I don't know the routes. I don't think I could manage the steps with these legs of mine. Or go down to the metro. The most sensible thing to do would be to get as close as I can by taxi and walk the rest of the way. It must be about twenty blocks. I know his bank account numbers and I think I could forge his signature. I need to get into his apartment, get hold of his credit cards, his checkbook. I could even live there for a few days, pass myself off as his grandmother. I have more than enough information. I could even write down the most important details as a hedge against forgetting. But I don't have a key. I can get into the building easily enough, but the apartment? And what if Tomás is dead? It's possible that he dropped dead there in his kitchen, a plate of lentils in his hand. Is this reincarnation? Shouldn't the soul return to this world as a baby (or fetus) and not in a withered old body like this one? It could be that this is a rare case, a cosmic error. Maybe fate or God plays tricks on some people, cruel pranks. If Tomás is dead, going back there could be risky. Aren't I wearing his ex-wife's tracksuit and sneakers? But no one's going to notice. He could have given them to me. I don't think I'm guilty of anything. He would have died of natural causes.

I decide to get as close as I can on foot and, when my legs give out, take a taxi the rest of the way. Hopefully, the taxi driver will take pity on me and leave me right at the door. I start walking, crossing the plaza diagonally toward the corner where the church is. The winos watch me pass by. Flaco waves at me and I return the greeting and keep walking until I've left the plaza behind. At this time of day the traffic is heavy. Up ahead, a cacophony of honking. I walk slowly, sticking close to the build-ings, pausing before every doorway so the people going in and out of the shops won't sweep me aside. Even so, a fat man — wearing dark glasses to hide a patch over one eye — almost knocks me down coming out of a gro-cery store. I'm hungry. I decide to spend a little bit of the taxi money. I go into the store. The cashier, a woman with hair dyed a dirty yellow color, smiles at me. Doña Inés, where have you been? I'm so glad to see you! But how stylish you look! You had us worried. In a whisper, the woman offers to let me use the bathroom and I ac-cept. I follow her out to a back patio edged with adobe bricks and partially covered by an eave made of rusty zinc sheeting. Is this my spot? A winter refuge? I don't remember which is the door to the bathroom and the woman is surprised. The light doesn't work and I feel for the toilet in the dark. I'm in the dim room again, lying down, naked. I push the door open a crack. I'd rather they saw me. I have to hold onto the sink to sit down. From my waist down, I feel nothing but varying tones and degrees of stiffness, discomfort and pain, but once seated on the toilet I realize just how badly I needed it. A little boy runs by but doesn't stop to look at me. I think I fall asleep for a little bit. I go back into the store. Marta (that's her name, of course) offers me a glass of water. I accept that too. I buy half a marraqueta and a strawberry yogurt. I ask Marta for pencil and paper. I write down the address and Tomás' ATM PIN number; I scrawl a trembling version of his signature. I thank Marta. I walk out onto the sidewalk.

I keep walking close to the storefronts, which are covered by striped awnings. The foot traffic is heavy. I tell myself that I'm in a different, slower dimension of time, in which everything appears to flow around me at a rapid pace, like in fast-forward, and slightly ridiculous. I would like to cross the street and sit down at a bus stop to eat the yogurt and bread, but the sun is still beating down over there. I'm not cold anymore. The exercise has warmed me up. I come to the entrance of a garage. Inside, I see stacks of plastic drums, rolls of wire, a Ping-Pong table, a ladder leaned up against a wall and the frame of a car from the 1940s half-buried under a mound of bundles. I remember that here, hidden off to the right, there's a water tap. Further down the street, a woman watering the rectangle of sidewalk in front of her rubber stamp shop waves at me. I open one corner of the yogurt and start to sip it. A young guy wearing a bicycle helmet passes by, followed by a woman in a blond wig, with huge fake breasts jutting out of her tiny tank top. I know they're fake not just because of their shape and size, but, more than anything, because of the way she displays them, ostentatiously, as if cashing in on an investment. It makes me aware of my own breasts, pendulous and, fortunately, small, hidden, despite the fact that I'm not wearing a bra, by my stooped posture. I finish the yogurt and put the container on the lid of a metal garbage bin, full to overflowing. I chew the bread with my back teeth. I pass by a tricycle cart selling mote con huesillos. I look the woman in the eye but she doesn't seem to recognize me and I get the impression I've crossed an invisible line. I would like a little of that peach nectar. The bread is going to make me thirsty, I think. But I have to save my money for the last stretch. I distract myself by looking at some towels in a shop window, printed with portraits of Marilyn Monroe, Che Guevara and other people I don't recognize. My right sneaker, which I'm dragging behind me a little, catches on a board covering a hole in the sidewalk and I almost fall face-first into a tree well. A car attendant in a yellow uniform catches me. Do be careful, señora, he says sarcastically, the comment clearly meant for the benefit of his two companions. I sit down to rest on the high ledge of a shop window. A unicycle hangs over my head. I focus on chewing the bread. On the other side of the street I see a door walled-off with bricks and, further up the street, still illuminated by the sun, a thick concrete tower framed in the gap left after a demolition job, next to the exposed beam framework of an adobe wall. I understand that this tower is a stairwell, the only thing left to be demolished. I fall asleep with the bread in my hand.

My head falls forward and I wake up. Judging by the light, I'd say not more than ten or fifteen minutes have passed. I start walking. On the next block, surprising myself, I stretch my hand out to a woman. Any spare change? I murmur. The woman sidesteps me and shakes her head, looking away from me. I repeat the gesture. I exaggerate my limp a little and try to hunch over even further, but it hurts my back. On the fifth or sixth attempt, a man stops and digs his hands into his pockets. We're in front of the door to a Chinese restaurant. He gives me fifty pesos. I want to thank him but he's already walking away. I notice that the majority of passersby are irritated, they feel they're being invaded. I should set myself up someplace, I think, let them approach of their own volition. But you can't simply occupy any old spot. My begging, in fact, has attracted the attention of the vendors in the newspaper kiosks, and in the shoe, book and food stands. A young guy in shirtsleeves and tie, holding a bottle of perfume in each hand, offering samples, takes a few steps backwards and hides his treasures behind his back. I'm tempted to go up to him and offer my wrists for him to spritz, but there's no time to waste.

I notice that the line of sunshine is rising up the face of the buildings across from me. When I reach the corner, I cross the street. I don't make it across in time and the bus in the far right lane has to wait for me. The first horn blare scares me so badly that I drop the bread. I hesitate a moment, but I know I can't pick it up. Another blast of the horn. The crowd waiting at the bus stop stares at me with a unanimously blank expression. The driver pulls forward before I've even made it up on the curb, missing me by millimeters. The nearly intact roll is lying in a pool of oil on the pavement. I count the coins I've amassed and decide to buy another one. I pass by a taxi stand. The one at the head of the line signals, trying to enter the line of stopped traffic. If I want to take a taxi, I tell myself, I should wait. I turn into a covered arcade. The dimness of the tunnel is scarcely relieved by the sky-lights and the fluorescent bulbs hanging from chains. This wouldn't be a bad place to sleep, I think, but a few yards from the street I come to an open metal gate on wheels. The arcade echoes with the interwoven rhythms of print-ing press machinery, creating a harmonious counterpoint. This place is familiar to me. I study the faces of the printers working away in the shops or walking down the hallway — where leaflets, reams of paper, folders of invoices and cardboard boxes are stacked up — but no one seems to recognize me. That vague memory summons other, more distinct memories, though I don't know whose memo-ries they are, and also that other one that persists, like a constant baseline, which I need to banish from my mind.

At the same time, I'm aware that I'm slowly losing vast regions of Tomás. I can direct my mind to his father or his ex-wife, for example, but I can no longer see their faces, I have only a sense of their nearness, of their voices. I have no doubt that, before, I was Tomás, but his presence is being snuffed out inside me. The idea of usurping his life (like he's usurped mine?) has begun to fade, to lose coherence; it now seems crazy to me. Finally, I remember my spot in the plaza. It's a hollow in the privet hedge that separates the vacant lot from the parking lot. The attendants let me hide some of my things there and rest there at night. I never sleep more than a few minutes at a time. I should go back, I think. Reclaim what's mine. How long's it been since I slept there? They won't have forgotten me.

I come to the back of the arcade and see that the hallway curves around here in a dogleg. I turn left and then right. Several large, empty tables block the hallway here. There's a chair beside one of the tables and I sit down to rest for a minute. In front of me, on the floor, I see the rusty remains of a metal shutter. From my pocket, I pull the scrap of paper with Tomás' information written on it. His PIN number, 2099, means nothing to me. Why would he have chosen those numbers? I crumple up the paper and toss it in the direction of a garbage can. I miss. The owner of a photocopy shop, to whom this table and chair must belong, along with a row of flowerpots arranged on the linoleum floor, looks up from his work and scrutinizes me with distaste. One of my legs has fallen asleep and I massage it, trying to bring it back to life. I stand and move on, feeling suddenly very tired. Tracing the shape of an S, the arcade opens onto a side street. I'm surprised to see that it's already growing dark.

The dim room closes in on me again and I don't have

the strength to push it away. I'm very cold. My butt and the backs of my thighs are wet. I'm grateful for this position because it's restful. My ears hurt. So do my wrists, knees, the soles of my feet, my fingernails, a bruise on my throat. When they come, I go far away, vacating everything beyond the exact boundaries of pain, but in the intervals, I try to keep my body company, surprised that it's still there. I'm mindful of the unhurried beating of my heart, the gentle swaying of my stomach with every breath, although this also means being conscious of the pulsing in my temples against the blindfold, tied too tight. This is how I want to remember it, it's to these intervals that I return if I have no choice but to return, but I'm also aware of the breathing of the other women and the stealthy movements of rats across the cement floor and the rustle of cockroaches, the terrible anguish of waiting. There's one interval in particular, longer than the others, when they leave us alone for several days without food or water. We lie in our own waste and it's a relief.

I stand for a while in the arcade's entrance. I'm reluctant to leave the murmur of the machines. My legs tremble slightly. I can't seem to recall the reason for this venture. Why did I want to go to Tomás' apartment? How was I planning to get in? And what if Tomás is home, watching TV or reading a book or sitting at the computer? What would I do then, ring the bell? And what would I say through the intercom? That he should let me in because I was once him and now I'm this old woman? No, Inesita. Best to go back to the plaza and to your spot before they forget about you and let someone else have it. Couldn't you just be getting confused? Couldn't you have just come across that young man somewhere, passed him on the street? Couldn't you have heard some story about him and you got some stupid idea in your head that you know him from personal experience? Couldn't you have dreamed that you were him? For a while now, your mind's been playing tricks on you. I decide to go back. I'm no more than five or six blocks away from the plaza, but that distance now seems insurmountable to me. My legs can barely support me, my stomach contracts with the beginnings of nausea. Exhaustion weighs me down like a stone. I would happily stay in the arcade. I saw three or four good spots in the hallway as I came through, but the shops are closing up and any minute they'll turn off the fluorescent lights and lower the grate at this end. I set off south, toward the plaza. The blinds in the shop windows are lowered and I can see two or three stoplights changing in unison at the next intersections. I walk past the metal grate of a bank. In the glass box of the ATM, I see, behind the machine, a small space where it would be possible to lie down to rest (and to use the grate to pull myself back up). I wait.

I wait for more than half an hour, leaning against the hood of a parked van. I cry a little from sheer fatigue. I comfort myself with the thought that the sparse traffic at the ATM means that, once I'm inside, I'll be left alone. The street is nearly deserted. On the wall separating the bank from a video arcade, a flyer reads, in rain-smudged letters: "…needed." The rest is illegible. I see faint lights in the plastic bag-covered windows of the large house on the next corner, apparently in ruins and dominated by a photo of an already-elected political candidate. The cone of light from a streetlamp reveals a mural in which two robots or astronauts battle it out in space suits. Finally, a taxi double parks, puts on its flashers. The taxi driver enters the ATM vestibule. I see him put his money away and I get ready, calculating the seconds it will take me to push open the door before it closes behind him. But I don't make it in time. My legs don't respond at the moment or at the speed I need them to. The taxi driver holds the door open without looking directly at me. I reach the door. I'm inside. Standing in front of the keypad, I wait for him to walk away. I try to remember the PIN number, but I've already lost it. It doesn't matter. I study the empty space, which is covered in dust and wrappers and ATM receipts, but nothing really disgusting. Carefully grasping the grate, I manage to sit and then to lie down, pulling my legs up into a ball so as to attract the least possible attention. I doze. I move in and out of a disturbed dream. One part of me remains alert, aware of the raw, flickering fluorescent lights and the few passersby out on the sidewalk who, no matter how tightly I scrunch up my aching legs, can see my pink sneakers. In my dreams, I see unfamiliar faces and traverse imaginary cities, perhaps pieced together from that young man's experiences.

Someone enters the vestibule. A fat man. He seems nervous. Before opening his wallet, he glances out on the empty street. I can see his reflection in the glass side-window, which looks into the bank. One of my legs starts to cramp up. I try to bear it, but it grows more intense and I have to move my leg slightly. The man notices the movement and he startles. I hear him yelp in surprise. Our eyes meet in the glass. The man leaves. After a few minutes, he comes back in. He leans out decisively from behind the machine to observe me. I pretend to be asleep. I'm scared. The man moves in front of the keypad and withdraws money. He leaves. I'm alone. I should sleep a little bit more, gather my strength for the journey back to the plaza. I close my eyes, but can't settle into sleep. I need to go to the bathroom. I hold it for a long time. My gut twists. I fold into a fetal position, run through with pain, until it passes. I have no choice. I don't want to have an accident. It's happened to me before. That's why the edge of the parking lot is my spot, because I can escape quickly into the vacant lot and cover my waste like a cat. I gather up a few ATM receipts and sit up, clinging to the grate, afraid the effort will cause my bowels to empty. First I sit up, and I use one foot to push the sneaker off my other foot. I stand up. I try to open the door that goes into the bank, but it's locked. I open the door to the sidewalk. I drop the sneaker so that it holds the door ajar. The sidewalk is empty. I head for the nearest tree. I wait for a passing car to be gone. I lower my sweatpants and underwear. Delicate underwear, a young woman's underwear, which must also belong to that young man's wife. What was her name? Grasping the blackened trunk of the tree and leaning against the rear bumper of the van, I squat down as far as my back and trembling legs will allow. Please, please, don't let anyone come right now. I stain my pants a little bit. I can't help it. I hear voices. A group of young men. I raise up a little and I see them through the van's windshield. They've just turned the corner with the astronauts and they're headed in my direction, on the other side of the street. Two or three of them are holding liter bottles of beer. I crouch back down and lower my head. With a little luck, they'll pass by without seeing me. I wipe myself with the receipts the best I can and I wait. The young men pass by and start to walk away. They're talking in shouts. I have the impression that they're exaggerating their drunkenness. Suddenly, one of them, shirtless, with a shaved head beneath a baseball cap, runs between the cars and snatches my sneaker that was holding the door ajar. He goes in. He pauses for a moment in front of the keypad. With the skilled moves of a martial artist, he starts to kick the screen, but he can't manage to break it. The kid glares defiantly into the security camera and spits at it. As he's leaving, he puts the sneaker back in its place. Then he sees me. He grins mockingly. Crazy old lady, he says and runs off to join his friends who are already moving in the direction of Alameda.

I stand up. With difficulty, I pull up my underwear and sweatpants. Luckily, I haven't gotten myself too dirty. The street is empty. In the next block, beyond the big house with the mural and a new building, I make out a group of young people tacking up posters on the wooden wall of a construction site. I'm trembling from fatigue and cold. And it's still summertime. I should start heading back to the plaza, I think. But better not to abandon this refuge. Tomorrow I'll ask Marta to invite me for a cup of tea. I can buy the tea bag and she can make it for me. Let's wait a little longer and see if we can get some good sleep. I enter the vestibule. I put on my sneaker without bending over. I lie down in my place behind the ATM machine. Exhausted, I fall asleep instantly.

I awake terrified. I can only move my eyes and turn my head. The rest of my body seems to have been buried in sand. I'm paralyzed! No, Inesita, you just slept a long time. Two or three hours. It's the longest you've slept in a single stretch in… ten years? And your body isn't used to it. You'll feel better soon. You need to move your arms a little. That's it. Now your legs. Bend them and stretch them out. Loosen them up. Take your time. That's good. Well, don't go overboard. You needed the rest. I close my eyes again. I hear voices, whispers. I sit up a little and see a couple outside the vestibule. They enter. The vestibule fills with the scent of perfume. They kiss. They realize I'm there and they don't care. The man withdraws some money. They leave. They walk off arm in arm, heading south. I watch the door as it slowly closes. At the last second, when I think I've already heard the click of the lock, someone runs up from the opposite direction and grabs the door, wedging his fingers in the gap to keep it from closing.

All I can see is his blurred reflection in the glass and he has his back to me, but I recognize the naked torso, the baseball cap. Come on, motherfuckers! he shouts. Silence. I hear the sound of something metallic (a chain?) clanging on the pavement. Laughter. Fuck, man, with that shitty aim we're gonna be here all night, says another. Another silence. Then there's something like a dull crackling noise and everything goes dark. Not just in here, but the entire block. A blue security light, far off, comes on inside the bank. Now they're inside the vestibule. Four or five of them. I close my eyes and curl into a ball. They grab me by the legs and drag me into the middle of the floor. I try to sit up but one of them puts his boot on my stomach. I stop moving. Crazy old lady, the one with the baseball hat says to me, we're going to give you a bath. They all laugh. I notice that one of them is holding a jerrycan. Leave me alone! I admonish in a calm voice, surprising myself. I haven't done anything to you! Some of them seem to hesitate. The one with the baseball cap takes the jerrycan, uncaps it and pours the liquid all over me, from my sneakers up to my face and my hair, until the can is empty. You're going to be clean as a whistle. The liquid gets into my nose and mouth. The smell and taste are so intense that, at first, I don't recognize it. I choke. I was expecting something foul. It's gasoline. I spit. I scream. I know that I'm screaming, but I can no longer hear myself. I'm naked again on the table, blindfolded, listening to my own breathing, aware of the hidden beating of my heart, reverberating through my damaged body. A match illuminates the faces of the five boys. They share a stunned expression, hypnotized, as if they were all about to jump together into a well. The small, luminous capsule floats between us. Then it brushes against my hip and the vestibule fills with a sudden coppery brilliance. I see them backing up, entranced, disgusted, incredulous. One of them shoves open the door. The smell of burning clothes and hair reaches me. I wave my arms in a reflexive attempt to free them of the glowing, delicate substance that covers them. The pain takes me by surprise. It begins at my ears and cheeks and, in a few seconds, envelops everything, fills the vestibule and suffocates me. It explodes over me like a wave and after that I don't care anymore. I see myself from a certain distance, off to the left. It takes me a moment to recognize my reflection in the glass. I imagine that it's happening to someone else, that it's not my own body laid out, screaming, writhing in a placenta of light.

FOUR

I TRIED to scream but I didn't seem to have lungs or a mouth. I concentrated an enormous effort into uttering an inarticulate howl, using the sound to tear through what felt like layers of darkness. I opened my eyes. I was standing in line at the supermarket. The woman in front of me — paralyzed in the act of unloading her groceries onto the conveyor belt — the checkout clerks, customers and baggers stared at me with frightened expressions. I understood that I had just roared at the top of my lungs. A glance at my own cart revealed that I had been filling it with the usual items, just as I had planned that morning (if it was even the same day), when I was debating whether to do the shopping that afternoon or leave it for the following day. I mumbled an apology and walked away from my cart, into the depths of the grocery store, which, though moderate in size, seemed unfathomable to me. My heart pounded. I gasped for air. My legs moved slowly and not quite correctly. I was overcome with fear as I blundered through the rows of multicolored bottles, cans, jars and plastic packages, harboring the harrowing suspicion that their precarious equilibrium was in some way related to mine. The too-sharp light overwhelmed me. I had to get out of there, but at the same time I had to get away from the phalanx of checkers and baggers with their scrutinizing gazes. My hands and neck were sweating, drops of perspiration ran down my ribs underneath my shirt. The full aisles and shelves undulated gently, as if I'd just come to in the middle of an earthquake. I stepped carefully, trying to stay in the exact center of the aisles, my arms held out to measure the distance separating me from the rows of products and to keep them at bay. Above all, a single, inescapable thought haunted me: that this was the definitive loss of control, that I was going to drop dead at any moment or that the end had already been set into motion. A panic attack, I thought, it's just a panic attack. I repeated the words "panic attack" to myself and tried to regain my sense of calm. I told myself that it was only natural, considering what I had just experienced: transforming into another person and dying, no less. But this did not prevent a new wave of fear from swamping me. Fear of the panic attack itself, that it could only be a harbinger of the imminent end, the collapse. I managed to find the aisle leading to the store entrance and I stumbled toward the door. I met a security guard dressed in a gray uniform and cap.

"Are you all right, sir?" he asked, his tone authoritative. "Is there a problem?"

I doubled over and vomited. The guard had to leap backwards in order to spare his shoes and pressed uniform pants. Lentils. The last thing I remembered was being about to put a plate of lentils, leftover from the night before, into the microwave. That meant it was still Thursday. I hadn't postponed my shopping until the following day. Slipping on my own vomit, I headed for the door. The guard did nothing to stop me. I felt a little bit better. My head hurt and I was still bathed in sweat, but I was breathing easier and my heartbeat seemed to be slowing down. I decided to walk the five blocks to Rosal Street, despite the heat. I was afraid to be inside an enclosed taxi. My gait was unstable and passersby gave me a wide berth, the same way you would do with a drunk. When I arrived at the building, my shirt was dark with sweat. The super commented that I was as white as a sheet. I mumbled something and walked toward the elevator, trying to straighten my stride.

I washed my face and brushed my teeth. I decided to wait until I was in a little better shape before taking a shower. I poured myself a whiskey and dropped, exhausted, onto the living room couch. Despite everything, I felt happy to be myself again. I calculated that my absence had lasted, at the most, a couple of hours, though my dream or vision had stretched for nine or ten. It hadn't been a dream. You didn't remember dreams with that wealth of detail. But, then, what had I just experienced? A hallucination? Maybe the amnesia opened up an empty space in my mind, susceptible to being filled by something. But by what? Another person's memories, captured by chance out of the air like someone tuning into radio waves? Had I ever seen that woman out on the street? Maybe she'd asked me for money once and now my brain, in a moment of imbalance, had used those few seconds to construct a mise-en-scène centered around her? Had I read in the crime reports about a homeless woman killed in that way? I couldn't remember. The verisimilitude of the experience was striking. And what if that woman actually existed? For an instant, I felt once again the weight of her body, the intimate recognition of a nucleus that remained intact while the organism that contained it broke hopelessly apart. I recognized Plaza Almagro, stretches of San Diego and Arturo Prat. Should I look for her? Look into her story? Or, if I had been granted a glimpse of the future, warn her about what was coming? What connected me to her?

I remembered finding, during the move, some of Paula's belongings in the storage room of the apartment on Pedro de Valdivia Norte. Now they sat in my closet, awaiting her arrival the following Saturday. I pulled out the boxes and lined them up on the bedroom's parquet floor. In the first box, I found a pair of pink sneakers. At the bottom of the second box, I discovered the purple tracksuit. I laid both parts of the tracksuit out on the bedspread, and placed the sneakers at the bottom of the legs. Together, they traced a vaguely disturbing outline, a map of Paula's absence. I dragged the boxes back to their place in the closet, beneath my jackets, shirts and overcoats, but I left the sneakers and the tracksuit on the bed. I don't remember having seen the tracksuit since Paula bought it, along with another one in white. As far as I knew, she never put it on except in the dressing room at the clothing store. In fact, I had completely forgotten about it until my vision. Even so, it seemed to corroborate the idea of an assemblage based on miscellaneous memories: Paula's tracksuit, some news item (though I still couldn't call it to mind), an old woman I'd casually crossed paths with on the street.

After a shower, I went to look for the phone number of the psychiatrist among the mess of papers on my desk in the living room. I found the number, but I couldn't bring myself to call her. What was I going to say? So far, all of my decisions had been in response to a real need for change, which, after a time, seen in retrospect, might reveal a coherent course, an internal growth line punctuated, from the outside, by a string of incongruous milestones, apparent eccentricities or whims. I didn't yet know where it was leading me, but I had no doubt that I needed to keep moving forward. Its hidden logic would become manifest in due course and, when it did, it would be less relevant than my current blind determination to press ahead. My friends' criticisms, sarcasm and concern seemed more and more tinged with an undertone of envy. But this was different. Psychiatric treatment for hallucinations? Checking myself into a clinic? No. I was going to have to get through this on my own, no matter what.

Driven by curiosity (how could I have such a detailed memory of a neighborhood I hadn't visited in at least fifteen years?), I went down to the street and hailed a taxi. In less than ten minutes I was standing on the same corner where my journey had begun. The similarity was astonishing. If memory wasn't deceiving me, molding secretly to what I saw before me, the street, the vacant lots and the trees in the background replicated exactly the ones in my vision. I noticed a single difference: on the last corner before the plaza, on the other side of the street, I saw three garbage bags around a post. When I'd passed this place in Inés' body, I'd noticed a mountain of bags that spilled out into the street and blocked the sidewalk. The plaza looked different due to the change in the light, but everything matched what I'd seen through the old woman's eyes: the graffiti on the plinth of the statue, the deterioration of the benches and the playground, the rust on the flagpoles, the location and size of the fountain, the pigeon shit on the lamp posts. Facing a construction site, two cement trucks with their motors running blocked the street, the huge cylinders turning slowly. A pair of workmen were filling some red plastic barriers with sand. I told myself, vertigo setting in, that I had, without question, been there before. I walked all over the plaza looking for Inés. I headed for the place that she remembered as her spot, on the border between the parking lot and one of the vacant lots. On the benches facing the statue of Pedro Aguirre Cerda, I found the winos' mattress, bags and clothing. But I saw no trace of them.

I walked down Paseo Bulnes and sat down to rest on the low concrete wall bordering the grass. Then I saw her, halfway down the next block, coming in my direction. An old woman, tiny and stooped, limping and dragging her right foot behind her. She moved in a zigzag among the couples or groups sitting on the benches or on the low concrete wall, holding her hand out for coins. She advanced so slowly that some, seeing her coming, had time to stand up and move out of her range. She wore a pair of shabby slippers. The right slipper had split along the edge where she dragged it. She wore a stained dress that had once been black, a filthy, formless, vest, full of holes and too heavy for this time of year, and a wool Chilote hat. Her black, determined eyes contrasted with the devastation of her dirty face, marked by deep clefts, her lips sunken inward from a lack of teeth. I was struck by her attitude as she begged, a little defiant, even ironic. I was aware of an internal distance which, curiously, I hadn't noted from inside, perhaps because, when I'd first extended my hand, I'd already begun to lose myself in her. No one gave her anything along her route. Before she reached me, she sat down on the edge of a fountain. She leaned forward with difficulty. Supporting herself precariously on one hand, she dipped the other hand into the murky water, in which floated plastic bottles and wrappers, and washed her face. She rinsed her mouth and spat. She stood up with enormous difficulty. Her eyes came to rest on me and she began walking towards me. I walked out to meet her.

"I don't give out money," I said, "but if you'd like, I'll buy you something to eat."

She scrutinized me seriously. My offer seemed to

make her uncomfortable. She'd lost her forward attitude, her defensive wall, and she seemed timid and caught off guard.

"Okay," she decided, "why not?"

She pointed to the next corner and started walking. I went with her. One step. Pause. Another step.

"What happened to your leg?"

"I fell."

I resigned myself to silence until, tracing a diagonal course, we made it to the corner. Inés focused all her attention on the effort of walking. I offered her my arm in support, but she refused. A jumble of thoughts crowded my mind. Inés existed. That mere fact was incredible. At her side, as I synchronized my pace to the rhythm of her uneven steps, I became convinced: I had been, in some inexplicable way, transported into her. For a few hours, I had occupied her place, that broken down body that I knew more intimately than any other woman's body. The only incongruence with my vision was her clothing: Paula's purple tracksuit and pink sneakers.

"Do you live near here?"

She glanced at me sideways.

"Yes, of course."

We went into a small store on a side street.

"Inesita, how are you?" the fat man sitting behind the cash register greeted her in a booming voice.

Inés' acrid stench filled the narrow, dark space, though the shopkeeper didn't seem to care. She limped toward the shelves in the back, not bothering to explain the situation. She picked out a small bottle of water and a yogurt.

"Do you have marraquetas?"

The clerk, an old man swathed in a blue apron, put half a roll wrapped in a green plastic bag on the glass countertop. Inés put the yogurt and water in the bag and walked toward the exit. To all appearances, she found my generosity unpleasant, but she had no choice but to accept it.

"Don't you want anything else?" I asked.

"No, thank you," she answered, without turning around.

"You can get whatever you want."

"Thank you," said Inés, already crossing the threshold on her way out.

I paid and caught up with her out on the sidewalk.

"Inés. Do you mind if I call you Inés?"

She shook her head, her breathing labored with the effort of walking.

"How can I help you? I'd like to help you."

Inés stopped and looked up at me. She studied me carefully, at close range. The water from the fountain had smeared the grime on her cheeks and neck. Her wizened features shaped into a grimace of surprise.

"Osvaldo?"

"No, my name is Tomás. Tomás Ugarte. Who is Osvaldo?"

"My nephew. He lives down south," she said imperiously. "Are you sure you're not Osvaldo?"

"I'm sure."

"You look just like him. Exactly, just exactly like him. I didn't notice before…"

For some reason, I took out my wallet and showed her my ID. She held it very close to her eyes with a twisted, spotted and trembling hand that I knew well. She gave it back to me.

"You look just like him," she said again and started walking toward the Paseo. "Even in the photo."

"How can I help you?" I insisted.

"Why do you want to help me? Did Osvaldo send you? It's about time that ingrate remembered his great aunt."

"I don't know," I said.

We came to the corner of the Paseo. She turned in the direction of the plaza.

"Would you like to have dinner?"

"No, thank you. This is plenty for me. Now I need to rest a little."

"Lunch tomorrow?" I asked.

She stopped. She studied me again up close.

"Okay," she said and turned away from me.

I didn't follow her.

I walked back home. As I walked, and for the rest of what remained of that afternoon and evening, which I spent sitting in the dark in the gray armchair in the living room — the spot I'd come to think of as my anchorage inside the apartment — I couldn't shake the memory of her for a single instant, as if the roles had been reversed and now she were inhabiting me. I poured myself glass after glass of whiskey, but the alcohol did nothing to quell my unease. I told myself over and over, gazing at the faint light from the window reflecting in my ice cubes, that things happen for a reason and my job was to figure out what that reason was. The episode in the bathtub on my birthday had only been a warning. I thought again of what had happened to me in terms of a displacement of liquids: during the episodes of amnesia, something inside me emptied out, creating a space capable of being filled by something else. The repeated episodes suggested a series, a process taking shape. I felt affirmed in my decision not to call the psychiatrist. The straightforwardness of the extrasensory perception (is that what it was?) was disarming: I could observe it, but not explain or communicate it to anyone else. Up until then, my experience had been limited to coincidences or minor symmetries. I would be walking along the street and, for no reason at

SERGIO MISSANA

all, someone I hadn't seen in years would pop into my
head, and then I'd run into them in the next block. I was
in the habit of taking an afternoon nap — another way in
which I was turning into my father — and I would very
often wake up just a few seconds before the phone rang.
I remembered, for the first time in a long time, a scene:
the two-year-old daughter of one of Paula's cousins, in
pajamas, her hair wet from the bath, asked me to read
her a book and I thought of the title of a children's book.
The little girl looked at me quizzically and declared impa-
tiently that they didn't have that book, repeating the title
that I hadn't said out loud. I also remembered wondering
which of the two of us was exercising telepathy, me or
the girl. I decided it was her. These things happened to
everyone, I thought.

But this thing with Inés was different. Under the circumstances, the panic attack seemed justified. It had
been a result, not of the episode, but rather, of the abrupt
transition, which offered me the measure of my fragility.
With every step, I could fall into a well. And even without
moving, even here in the armchair, relaxing and sinking
deeper into its welcoming concavity, I could be descending into another world. But I didn't care. Wasn't it like
this for everyone? Each breath could be the last, always.
No, I didn't need the help of a psychiatrist. I needed to
unravel the reason. I refused to accept that it was nothing more than pure chance. There had to be some link
to Inés, communicating vessels. I thought back on the
discrepancies between the vision and reality; the garbage
bags, Paula's clothes. Suddenly I understood: my experience was prophetic, I had been given a glimpse, from the
inside, of Inés' future. My duty was to prevent it. That
was the reason: I had to save her, intervene in the course
of events that led to that terrible conclusion. Maybe I had

already done so, by the mere fact of crossing her path. I wanted to pour myself one last whisky, but I was too tired or too drunk to get up. I fell asleep in the armchair.

I got to the plaza past noon. It took me about ten minutes to find her, walking down San Diego, head bowed. I walked up to her.

"Doña Inés, good afternoon."

She didn't appear to recognize me.

"We spoke yesterday. We agreed to have lunch."

"Osvaldo?"

"No, my name is Tomás."

The old woman made as if to continue on her way back to the plaza. I had just seen a little café on a side street, with round plastic tables set out on the narrow, uneven sidewalk.

"Come on," I said, taking her by the arm.

She seemed frightened, but she didn't resist. She didn't have the strength to resist. Her body, half hidden by the bulky vest and the skirt on her dress, was very frail. I knew it all too well. Her arm seemed like nothing more than bones hinged together. Her clothing, even out in the open air, exuded an unbearable stench.

All five tables were unoccupied. I led her to the one furthest from the door. A waiter approached us, but stopped halfway there. He retraced his steps and disappeared inside the café. After a minute, he appeared in the doorway alongside another man, who must have been the owner. They conferred for a moment. Finally, the waiter came over to the table.

"I'm sorry, sir, but you can't be served here," he said nervously.

"Why not?"

The waiter gestured slightly at Inés.

"You can't. If you want, you can speak with the owner."

"No, don't worry about it."

I helped Inés to stand up. We trudged back to San Diego. I would have to buy provisions at a store and eat in the plaza, I said to myself. Without pausing to think about it, I hailed a taxi. I offered to pay triple the fare on the meter if he took me to Rosal. He accepted. It took me a great deal of effort to get Inés settled into the back seat. We opened all four windows and, even so, the reek was dreadful. The driver, an older man, remained silent for twenty interminable blocks.

He let us out on the corner. Inés looked extremely tired. She breathed laboriously as we walked the brief span to my building. One step. Pause. Another step.

"Where are we going," she asked during one of those brief pauses, seeming disoriented.

"To my house."

The super saw us coming and didn't take her eyes off us until we arrived at the door to the building. Her expression of suspicion and repugnance turned to alarm when she understood that I intended to go inside with Inés.

"Mr. Ugarte, you can't…"

"This is my aunt, she's very ill," I managed to say, making our extremely slow way to the elevator.

"Disgusting!" she grumbled.

I had to hold my breath in the elevator. The journey from the elevator to the door to my apartment also seemed to last an eternity. Luckily, none of my neighbors appeared. My goal had been to invite her for lunch, but first things first. I half led her and half pushed her into the bathroom. Her body tensed in a gesture of refusal. I turned on the tap in the bathtub.

"We're going to have a bath," I announced.

Inés didn't say anything. She remained still, her eyes fixed on the tile floor. I squeezed bath gel under the stream of water to make bubbles. I went to the kitchen to look for a trash bag. I tried to take her vest off, but she resisted. I sat her on the edge of the tub and took off her slippers, putting them in the bag. She let me. I turned off the water. I understood that she was not going to be able to get into or out of the bathtub on her own.

"Doña Inés, you need a bath."

She remained still, tense, her eyes lowered.

"This is what we're going to do," I insisted, as if speaking to a small child. "You can bathe in your clothes. We have to wash your clothes anyway. Okay?"

She didn't reply, but she allowed me to take off her vest. I lifted her by the armpits and sat her in the water, surprised at how little she weighed. She was still wearing the wool cap. I took the bottle of bath gel from the niche in the wall and held it up in front of her, then set it down on the edge of the tub, within easy reach. I left the bathroom. I spent the following minutes ventilating the apartment. Her stench was concentrated in her clothing, in the wet dress. What was I doing? Maybe Manuel and the rest of them were right and I had a screw loose. This was a much more worrisome symptom than my absences, even than a meticulously detailed hallucination. I waited in the bedroom, sitting on the edge of the bed. I looked at Paula's tracksuit, which I had tossed onto a chair that morning after waking up in the living room in a hungover stupor.

I knocked gently on the bathroom door. There was no answer. I opened the door a crack. The old woman was still sitting in the bubbles, wool cap on her head, motionless. Her dress floated up around her like seaweed. Something came over me: a blind impulse born of a combination of indignation at her filthiness and a strange urge to impose, upon myself, a degree of rigor or discipline. I yanked off her cap. Her dirty, thin, white hair was plastered to her skull, revealing a large bald patch. She objected when I tried to take off her dress. She screamed. Scratched my face. She crossed her arms so that, when I tried to pull the dress up over her head, I lifted her whole body up inside the bathtub. I managed to subdue her, taking her by the elbows, half in the water myself, until I managed to get the dress off her. I quickly lifted her with one hand, supporting her around her back, and used my other hand to pull off her underwear, a pair of men's briefs, much too big for her and long since stained with shit and urine. I was amazed that her tiny, frail body could still be functioning; her skin clung to her skeleton: a human marionette. By the time I finished undressing her, I was as drenched as she was. I sat her back down in the bathtub (she was unable to do so herself). Tears of rage ran down her cheeks. I put all of her clothes in the trash bag and tied it with a knot. I took off my sneakers and kneeled down next to her. She hid her face with soap-covered hands and wept.

"I'm sorry, Inés," I murmured, "but we have to have a bath."

I lathered my bath sponge with gel and scrubbed her shoulders, back, armpits, breasts, arms, legs and feet. The water and soap bubbles turned chocolate-colored. I emptied the tub and filled it again. I washed her sparse hair. I detached the showerhead and used it to rinse her head and then I massaged shampoo into it again. She allowed herself to be washed, but within her passivity there remained an unalterable note of unyielding internal resistance, indignation, hatred. I stood her up in order to wash between her legs, her buttocks. I had to scrub hard to strip off the crusts of shit. I kept stubbornly at it until she began to bleed a little. During the entire operation, she looked me straight in the eye. Finally, I rinsed her with the showerhead. Then I wrapped her in a towel and dried her hair. I looked through Paula's clothes and found a pair of underwear and socks. I helped Inés put on the underwear and the purple tracksuit. I bent down to tie up the sneakers, which were only a little too big for her.

"Now we're all done. See, was that so terrible?" I said, trying to cheer her up, surprised by my arch, paternal tone. "Now you'll be so much more comfortable. Are you hungry? Why don't we have something to eat?"

Inés didn't respond. She looked a little ridiculous in a young woman's clothes.

"My hat."

"I'll buy you another hat... and dresses and vests and whatever you want," a hint of anxiety echoed in my voice. "Your clothes are too dirty to..."

"I want my hat, huevón."

"I'm sorry, Inés. I really am."

I steered her into the kitchen. I sat her on a chair. I gave her a glass of milk that she drank straight down, holding the glass with both hands. I made scrambled eggs, mashed avocado and instant mashed potatoes. Soft food. While I was cooking, a cat jumped down from a ledge and balanced for a moment on the frame of the window overlooking the courtyard. The sudden movement startled me and I almost dropped the skillet with the eggs. To my surprise, Inés let out a dry cackle. I turned around and smiled, but she looked away. She hated me. She would never forgive me for my affront. If she had the strength, she would stab me in the kidneys with a kitchen knife. The gray cat arched its back and looked me in the eyes for a moment. I saw him calculate his next move and disappear with a leap.

Inés ate happily, taking big mouthfuls of food, but she

wasn't able to finish her plate. It was a lot of food for her, she said, resting her hands on her stomach. I asked her if she wanted to rest and she nodded. I put her on my bed and she fell immediately asleep. I covered her with a blanket. I changed clothes and went out to buy a wool cap.

I headed downtown. In a shopping mall, I found a hat almost identical to hers. I walked quickly back, even running at certain points, reliving in memory the horrendous end of my vision, which had been, I was certain of it, premonitory. If I left her alone for too long, she might escape, only to end up in that ATM booth. It was conceivable that this represented only one of several possible futures, I thought, and that my intervention had already nullified it.

Inés was waiting, sitting quietly at the foot of the bed. She only slept for brief stretches at a time. She received the hat with no reaction whatsoever. Her inscrutable gaze reminded me of the cat's.

"Were you able to rest?" I asked with a big smile. "That's great!"

The condescending tone of my voice disgusted me, but I couldn't help it. I was treating her like an adorable little old lady, trying to force her into that role, in large part, because she wasn't.

"Would you like to watch TV?"

She didn't answer.

I piled the pillows up against the headboard, picked her up and deposited her against them.

"Are you comfortable there? Perfect."

I turned on the TV and gave her the remote control, which she held in her hands, along with the wool cap. She stared at the device, hypnotized. In the living room, I opened my computer and checked my email. Nothing from Paula, who would be arriving the following morn-

ing. I tried to surf the web for a bit, searching, like I usually did, for information about places I was thinking about
visiting — Essaouira, Petra, Varanasi — but I couldn't
concentrate. Every so often, I would poke my head into
the bedroom to spy on Inés. Her attention was fixed on
the screen, utterly absorbed, as she slowly changed the
channels. She had turned the volume way up. She fell
asleep at regular intervals.

As evening set in, the landlady called on the phone.

"Tomás, dear, how is everything?"

"Fine, thanks."

"Forgive me for bothering you, but Elsa told me that
you took a homeless woman up to your apartment."

"She's not a homeless woman, she's my Aunt Inés," I
lied. "She's been... sick."

"Tomás, you're going to cause problems for me with
the other tenants."

"There's no problem. I'll speak with Elsa tomorrow
and she can come up to meet her."

"Will she be staying long?"

"A week. Two at the most," I improvised.

A pause.

"Okay, Tomás, I'd appreciate it if you spoke with Elsa.
She's quite upset. She called me and also the building
manager."

"Don't worry," I said. "I'll take care of it."

I made dinner. While I was cooking, the gray cat walked
haughtily back and forth on the window ledge, on the
other side of the glass. He wasn't wearing a collar. Did
he live in one of the neighboring apartments? I'd noticed
a few cats in the courtyard and on the corrugated metal
roof of the parking lot visible between the two wings of
the building, but I hadn't paid them any mind. I didn't
like cats. I turned on the bedroom light. I switched off the

TV. I led Inés to the kitchen and sat her down at the small table. After watching several hours of television, her eyes were bright and unfocused. I served her a modest portion, which she devoured hungrily. She looked a little bit more at ease.

"Doña Inés?"

She raised her eyes to mine, her entire body a knot of suspicion and distrust.

"You told me that you have a nephew in the south, Osvaldo..."

"Osvaldo and Aurelio, grandsons of my late sister."

"Where do they live?"

"In Temuco."

"Do you have any way of contacting them, a phone number or an address?"

She shook her head. After a moment she added:

"Did I tell you that you look exactly like Osvaldo?"

"Yes."

"He's a bit darker, but you're like twins."

I found this idea unsettling. Inés finished her plate.

"Would you like more?"

"No."

I felt relieved at even the slightest sign of ease in my presence. Or at least of resignation. It was undeniable that she was not there of her own volition, that she was a prisoner. I told myself that, after a life of hardships and indignities, not only would she grow accustomed to these comforts — the soft bed, hot food, clean bath, cable TV — but that, soon enough, she wouldn't be able to live without them. I wanted to ask her about her previous life, the journey that had led her to the plaza. I hoped to gain her trust, little by little.

"I'd like to rest awhile," she announced.

I led her to the bedroom. I took off her sneakers. I put

her in bed, still dressed in Paula's tracksuit. She fell asleep.

I settled onto the sofa with a pillow and blanket.

Something woke me in the middle of the night. I opened my eyes and found Inés, sitting in the armchair a few feet away from me, motionless, observing me with a maniacal intensity in the dimly lit living room. I stood up in fright.

"Inés… What's going on?"

"Why are you helping me, huevón?"

I rubbed my face with both hands, still muddled with sleep.

"Yesterday I had a sort of dream. I dreamed that I was you in the plaza."

Inés said nothing. I continued:

"And then I found you. And I thought that it hadn't been a coincidence that I dreamed of you."

"I can take care of myself."

"That isn't true, Doña Inés. How many years have you been living in the plaza?"

"Eleven."

"It's time for you to have more comforts in your life, medical care…"

Even in the dark I could feel her penetrating gaze, her powerlessness. I had no right to usurp her life, no matter how miserable and squalid it seemed to me. It was hers. Her sole possession. Given her fragility, her physical defenselessness, shielded only by the tenuous wall of general indifference toward an indigent old woman, she was at the mercy of the first person who'd decided to interfere in her affairs. Why would anyone decide to concern themselves with her? My answer to this question (having seen her in a dream) probably didn't help much. The only thing that mattered was my undeniable determination, from which she couldn't escape. She was in my hands, subject to my will. I think that, in part, she felt forced to accept that, for her, the possibility of turning back no longer existed. She could, and certainly would, regain a degree of independence, of sovereignty over her own decisions, but to go back to wearing rags, to her spot in the vacant lot, to digging through trash bins? Soon enough, I told myself, she would come to think of this captivity as a rebirth, a last chance, and her resentment over the required violence was bound to subside sooner or later.

I took her back to the bedroom and tucked her in like a little girl. She cried quietly. I stood leaning against the doorframe until I could be sure she'd gone to sleep. For better or for worse, I thought, I had assumed responsibility for her and there was no turning back. More than her life, in reality I was taking charge of her death, which I couldn't allow to occur in the way I had foreseen in my vision. Although I sometimes imagined a silent observer, en eye registering my actions from the corner of each room, giving me its tacit approval, I was conscious that I was taking refuge in that approval, bolstering myself with it, at least in equivalent measure to its most apparent opposite. The duty to take care of her, to take responsibility for her felt undeniable, but at the same time, it gave me a foothold, a trajectory to follow, something to occupy me, a distraction from my own vulnerability. At any moment, everything in front of me, including her, could vanish into thin air like a magic trick. In some way, Inés' eventual disappearance forecast my own. If, through acts of compassion, we were almost always seeking to save ourselves, if those acts accomplished a therapeutic function — through the mere fact of deflecting attention from our own problems onto other people's problems— wasn't it even more true in this case of a literal doubling, of having found myself incarnated as her?

Paula called early the next morning to say that she was going straight from the airport to the beach with her mother. We would see each other in family court on Monday.

At around ten I took Inés out for a walk. I calculated the time so as to ensure we would cross paths with Elsa, the super, who only worked in the mornings on Saturdays.

"Doña Elsa, I'd like to introduce you to my Aunt Inés. She's going to be staying with me for a few days.

"Nice to meet you," said Elsa stiffly, flustered, not sure whether to touch Inés.

It took us more than an hour to walk around the block. Inés, who walked with her arm in mine, had to stop every ten or twelve steps to rest. She told me that she was cold, so at the intersection of Luis de Valdivia, we crossed over to the sunny side of the street. I tried to ferret out information about her life, but all I got were a few disjointed sentences about the plaza, the garbage cans, the winos, the territorial disputes and truces, the neighborhood systems of shops, the type of people who gave out money: webs of relationships invisible to busy passersby, inside which her memories appeared trapped as in a labyrinth. When she talked, she grew short of breath and had to stop more frequently. After a certain point I took over the talking and summarized the recent changes in my life: quitting my job, the divorce, the move. Inés smiled sweetly, showing her gums, and, her gaze fixed on the sidewalk, declared in a new tone of voice, one of a much younger self, that she remembered very well her fortieth birthday, in 1966, that those had been the good times, when her daughter was still alive. I asked about her daughter, but she came back to herself as if awaking from a trance, her eyes went blank, that other speaker disappeared, replaced by the sullen, reticent old woman I knew. I remembered the dark room, her naked body laid out in the darkness. I struggled to recuperate what I had known then. Was her daughter the reason for her detention? I restrained my curiosity. I went back to talking about myself, about my family, watching her closely, but it didn't happen again. Even as she was an enigma to me, I felt a greater degree of intimacy and mutual understanding than I'd ever felt with my parents or even with Paula; if incapable of actually reading her thoughts, I was able to feel and gauge in her the most minute mood changes. The memory of having merged with her, of having gradually lost myself within her, stayed with me. Though it amounted to a loss of my own self, I didn't relive it with a sense of anguish, but with a measure of relief, an almost voluptuous abandon. The story of my family garnered no reaction from her. She looked exhausted. When I mentioned my father, I was assailed by an uncomfortable thought that I tried hard to sweep from my mind: in taking responsibility for Inés, I was in some way reproducing Tomás Sr.'s overprotective compulsions, his suffocating attention. It could be in my genes, I supposed, maybe that was the reason I'd been denied fatherhood: in order to break a vicious cycle.

When we got back to the apartment, Inés announced that she'd like to lie down for a while. She fell asleep immediately. I spent a large part of the morning in front of the computer, gathering information about rest homes. Inés woke up and wanted to watch TV. By noon, I had narrowed my search to three alternatives: establishments not dominated by religious fervor or the feel of a correctional facility. I would have liked to keep her nearby, but the best homes were in Providencia, a neighborhood that had filled up with the elderly. They were expensive, more than my own rent, but they included medical, physical therapy, nursing, nutrition, lab, pharmacy and ambulance services. I called one to ask if it was possible to check someone in who wasn't immediate family and they suggested that I speak with the administrator on Monday. On Monday I had the divorce hearing; I made an appointment to tour the place with Inés on Tuesday. I decided to spend the inheritance from Phyllis Carstensen, which I was keeping in a special account in the U.S., on the rest home. I'd still have sufficient funds for my trip. I liked the idea of a symmetry between the two old women, whose lives had come to an end under analogous circumstances, and that I, who had crossed both of their paths by chance — or by a coincidence too complicated for my limited understanding — would serve as nothing more than the conductive material.

Over the weekend, we settled into a routine of naps, meals, walks and television, during which I saw myself as a sort of Pygmalion, striving to mold Inés into the adorable little old lady that she was not and never would be, a routine that was, in truth, the result of an implicit transaction, a middle ground between irreconcilable positions. Inés agreed unenthusiastically to visit a couple of rest homes on the following Tuesday. On Saturday afternoon, I went out, at last, to do the grocery shopping. When I returned, I was relieved to find her in her usual place in bed, absorbed by the television screen. (It would also have been a relief, I said to myself with a stab of guilt, if she had escaped.) She was unwavering in her silence about her past, her family. I didn't even manage to get the last name of her nephews in Temuco out of her. From among Paula's clothes, I selected a few items that would work for her, but she never changed out of the purple tracksuit. Insisting that she needed some new clothes, I suggested that we go shopping later in the week, after our tour of the rest homes. She agreed with a shrug. On Sunday, I forced her to take another bath. I sat her in the empty tub, dressed in a t-shirt and underwear. I squeezed bath gel onto the bottom of the tub, turned on the water and left, so she could bathe alone. Then I extracted her from the tub, dried her off and helped her get dressed, trying not to look at her. She submitted to my care and ministrations with no hint of gratitude. She didn't resist physically, but I recognized in her eyes an internal flight — with the sole exception of her comment about her fortieth birthday and her (murdered?) daughter — a withdrawal to a distant place.

On Monday, she said she was too tired for our morning walk. She dozed for a while and spent most of the morning glued to the television. After lunch, she took a long nap. I dressed in a suit and tie and woke her before leaving. I told her I would be gone for a few hours, but that I wouldn't be far away. The family court was just five blocks away. I wrote my cellphone number on a piece of paper and left it on the nightstand. She felt around in the folds of the bedspread, looking for the remote. I handed it to her. She took it in her gnarled hand and turned on the TV without thanking me. I was seized by a new feeling: Who do you think you are, you ungrateful old woman? With everything I've done for you, you could deign to thank me at least once, at least one goddamned time.

I repeated my cell number for the super. She looked it up in a tattered notebook and confirmed that she already had it. I asked her to let me know if she saw my Aunt Inés leave. I arrived at the family court, on San Antonio Street, a few minutes early. Inside the building, crowds of people were crammed into the maze of hallways and waiting rooms. I ran into Paula's lawyer. He didn't look me in the eye.

"Where's your witness?"

"What witness?"

"Didn't Paula tell you?"

"No," I replied, alarmed.

"Usually, the witnesses are present during the second hearing, but since the divorce is by mutual agreement and all the financial considerations have already been resolved, the judge can admit the witnesses and resolve the divorce immediately."

I called Manuel. He was just finishing a lunch meeting. He agreed to come right away.

Paula arrived, accompanied by her mother. We hugged and that asshole of a lawyer commented that this was unusual in a divorce proceeding. Alejandra gave me her most saccharine smile, asked me about my new apartment and my life post-advertising. Our mutual hatred had only grown over the years. I hadn't thought of it until just that moment, but that was more than enough reason to justify the divorce: ridding myself of her. It was not unlikely that this would be the last time I would have to tolerate her hypocrisy, her vampirism, her strange wit that threatened to turn against every interlocutor the second they walked away. With her daughter, they played out an old, circular routine of inescapable dynamics. Despite everything, Paula looked beautiful, tanned after her weekend in Rocas de Santo Domingo, alert, full of energy. I knew right away that it was due to her time in Spain, which I could already hear in her accent. That was what I needed as well, I told myself, as soon as the divorce was final: a change of scenery.

The hearing was without surprises. Manuel and my lawyer arrived at the same time. The judge — a middle-aged woman with badly-dyed hair who observed us from the depths of a bottomless boredom — carried out the formalities at an astonishingly slow pace, a trick to reduce her workload, surely learned and perfected over the course of many years. She reviewed the final divorce settlement and its conditions, confirming the end of the marital relationship. She asked us if the divorce was by mutual agreement and if either of us wished to propose any requirements that would modify what was recorded in the document. She wanted to know the date, reasons and circumstances of the separation. Paula lied about the date and I corroborated her statement. The judge questioned Manuel and Alejandra. Do you know Tomás Ugarte? Where is he? How do you know him? What is his marital status? Who is his spouse? After this process, the judge reviewed all the documents again. I had the impression that she wasn't reading them, but simply allowing time to pass. At last, she determined that a second hearing wasn't necessary. She assigned us a date within one month's time to receive the final determination, but the lawyers assured us that the divorce was approved. We could travel without any trouble.

Paula and I walked up Merced Street and went into a café on José Miguel de la Barra. She wanted to see my new apartment, but I said no. I'd decided to have it repainted, I lied. It was a disaster. She wouldn't see much with all the furniture and the floors covered in plastic. And it reeked of fresh paint. I'd love to have her over in a week or so.

"Mariana says hello," said Paula, stirring her espresso.

"But she doesn't even know me."

"She saw you that time at the restaurant, when you were spying on us."

"I have no idea what you're talking about," I said.

"She recognized you from photos. I didn't see you, but she said you dove into the bushes." She looked up and met my gaze. "She told me that's what made her like you.

You won her over with physical comedy."

We were silent for a few moments.

"How are things going with her?"

"Amazing. Her flat…her apartment is lovely."

"What are you going to do for work?"

"I already have a couple of options. Mariana, obviously, has tons of contacts. The most difficult part is getting residency. I have to stay there illegally, register myself and go through a whole long, annoying process. Compared to that, divorce is child's play."

We stayed at the café long enough for the clientele to turn over several times, which, combined with the light outside, slanting and changing color and finally fading, transfigured the café, as though it were traveling through the city and not just through time. Paula told me in great detail about her adventures over the past few months, her adjustment to Madrid, which she found welcoming and fascinating and full of life, in contrast with the toxic atmosphere of Santiago; her trips through Spain, Portugal and Morocco. Living with Mariana was working out well, though she imagined that could change if either of them started seeing anyone seriously. She didn't rule out living alone, though rents were very high. Listening to her, I told myself that our conversation was the model of the stated ideal for all couples at the end of their relationships: remain friends. I also thought that we were clinging gently to one another out of fear of the unknown and that this harmony and complicity were transitory and, for that matter, not real, that distance and the appearance on the scene of other actors would come to destroy it. For her part, she asked me about my new life in that neighborhood and post-advertising, and about my travel plans. She wanted to know if there had been any women and I told her just one, on my birthday.

"Did you take her back to your apartment?"

"Yes."

"And you won't have me over," she said, with exaggerated disappointment.

"I can't."

"Come on, no one's buying your paint story. But it's okay. It's your new life."

"Why don't we go to a motel?"

Paula looked me in the eye.

"I'd love to, Tomás, but...no."

"Why not?"

"We have to stop at some point, right?"

"At some point, but not necessarily now."

She smiled. I tried to take her hand, which was resting on the table, but she pulled it away.

"We just had our divorce hearing," she said. "And we haven't fucked in two months. It's like quitting an addiction..."

"You're moving to another country anyway."

"It's better if we stop intentionally, don't you think?"

Paula raised her hand in a casual gesture, signaling for the check. It was nine o'clock at night. We'd moved from coffee to herbal tea to wine, we'd eaten cheesecake and quiche. For the first time in hours, I thought of Inés, who was waiting for me a few blocks away. I needed to make her dinner. I paid the bill. I was already starting to miss Paula.

"Tomás, I almost forgot," she said as we were finally about to get up from the table. "I need to ask you a huge favor."

"What is it?"

"I have so many loose ends to take care of..." she sighed. "I need you to help me sell the car. I have two weeks, but I've been offered a job up north, in the desert.

I need to take the Suzuki and I won't have time when I get back and I don't want to turn it over to a used-car dealer. I'm sorry, I know it's a hassle."

"What job?"

"I've been asked to take some stock photos for a film."

"A feature film?"

She nodded.

"Who's the director?"

"I don't know."

"Are you doing the still photography?"

"No, this is preliminary… They need photos of architecture and landscapes for the production design."

"No problem," I said.

"Obviously, you don't have to drive the car. I'll leave it at my mother's house. She says to please forgive her, but she's just useless when it comes to this sort of thing."

"If there's anything I have plenty of right now, it's time," I said. "I just have one small condition."

"What?" she said, alarmed.

"That we go to a motel right now."

Paula burst out laughing.

"I'm serious," I insisted.

"I need to sign an authorization form so you can sell it. Could we meet tomorrow morning at the notary on Apoquindo?"

"I can't tomorrow."

"How about in the afternoon?"

"I can't do that either," I said. "Let's do it on Wednesday."

"At ten thirty?"

"Okay."

We went out to the sidewalk. Paula hailed a taxi. She kissed me on the cheek.

"Are you sure you're not hiding something from me?"

she asked before getting in the taxi.

I shrugged.

"Like what?"

"I don't know. Something," she said. She gave me another kiss and got in the cab.

When I got back to the apartment, I stuck my head around the doorframe of the bedroom and confirmed that Inés was asleep. I took off my shoes. I studied the contents of the refrigerator. There were a few things I could reheat in case Inés woke up. The cat appeared from somewhere and its silhouette balanced on the narrow sill of the closed window. It meowed softly. I poured myself a whiskey and sat down at my desk. I read my emails and the news. I shut off the computer. I called Manuel to thank him for the favor that afternoon. Fifteen years ago, we'd been a dynamic duo at our agency. It was almost two years since his own divorce. The answering machine picked up and I left a message. I stretched out on the sofa and replayed my entire conversation with Paula. I was free to travel. I decided that I would buy the tickets that very week. I fell asleep.

I startled awake. When I stood up, I knocked over the glass and a pool of water spilled across the parquet. The voices and laughter that had woken me up echoed down on the street. I stumbled to the kitchen to find a rag. I saw that it was eleven thirty. I cleaned up the puddle. I peered in through the bedroom door. Inés lay perfectly still, in the same position she'd been in a few hours earlier. I tiptoed toward her and switched on the bedside lamp. The bed was empty. I understood immediately that Inés hadn't been there two hours earlier either, when I'd come home from the café. In the dim light, I'd been fooled by the wool cap resting on the pillow and the tangle of sheets still bearing the shape of a body.

I turned on the bathroom light. I searched the entire apartment, including the living room, in case she'd been stationed in a dark corner, spying on me as I slept. Down on the first floor, I headed toward the super's door, but, just before knocking, I changed my mind. She would have told me if she'd seen Inés leave. It wouldn't do any good to bother her. I hailed a taxi on the corner of Merced. The driver was blasting reggaeton at full volume. He turned it down to listen to my instructions — Plaza Almagro and Nataniel — then turned it back up. As we moved through the tunnel and headed down Carmen toward Curicó, I was overcome with the growing certainty that my eyes had not deceived me: when I got back to the apartment, I'd seen Inés (or her double or a ghost) lying on her side in my bed. The taxi headed west along Tarapacá. As we crossed Arturo Prat, I thought I glimpsed a brief flash of light. I shouted at the driver to stop, but he didn't hear me. I touched his shoulder. He dropped me off on the corner of San Diego. I handed him a bill that was more than double the fare and, without waiting for my change, I took off running toward the corner of Arturo Prat. I turned and headed north. What I had seen was the flashing of emergency lights which — as I ran as fast as my legs would carry me, ignoring the strange whistling noise coming from my lungs and the stabbing pain in my side — were steadily multiplying, pulsing dissonantly. Amid the chaos, I made out two fire trucks, several police vans and cruisers, an ambulance and a police barricade behind which a small crowd of onlookers was gathering.

FIVE

Elderly Homeless Woman
Burned Alive in ATM Vestibule

Five criminal delinquents, who were quickly appre-
hended, doused the victim with gasoline and set her
on fire, resulting in her death.

An elderly homeless woman sleeping in an ATM
vestibule on Arturo Prat Street in downtown Santiago
was the victim of a vicious attack carried out by five in-
dividuals who soaked her with gasoline and ignited it.

According to the Criminal Investigator, the incident
took place last night around 11:30pm.

An off-duty police officer passing by the location
alerted authorities, and four perpetrators were intercepted a few blocks away as they attempted to flee the
scene. Another eluded the initial police roundup. After
a heated pursuit, he was captured near the Plaza de
Armas.

The woman, who has not yet been identified, was
taken to the emergency room at Posta Central Hospital, where she was pronounced dead on arrival.

All of the perpetrators are minors. The cause of this
brutal assault is not yet known.

I WAS the cause, I said to myself, closing the computer.
If it hadn't been for my rash, harebrained intervention,
Inés would be alive or, if her time had come and she had
to die because God or fate or her own biological collapse
had so decreed it, she would have had a more dignified
end, free of the pointless martyrdom which I had foreseen, for the sole purpose — I knew this from the very

beginning — of preventing it from happening. Every step of the way, I'd done nothing but contribute to that atrocious denouement, even by means of Paula's tracksuit. If I had hidden the tracksuit and sneakers it was possible that things could have gone a different way. I realized now that, at least unconsciously, I was molding my actions to the vision, that is, to the future. Strictly speaking it would have been enough to have behaved differently at any point: I could have not intervened at all, or put her immediately into a rest home or gone home straight after the divorce hearing or locked her inside my apartment somehow or turned on the lamp in the bedroom when I got home. Maybe the course of events had been decided in more subtle moments: a gesture, a sentence, an uncomfortable lull during one of our walks, a scene in one of the television shows she'd watched. My mind refused to go near the circumstances of her death. Instead, I saw her naked body, no larger than a child's, her hunched back accentuating the bas-relief of her spine and ribs. I imagined hugging her, comforting her. But the truth is that the real Inés had opposed me with a constant, implacable resistance. My attentions — not only scrubbing away the layers of filth from the delicate skin of her buttocks, from the insides of her thighs, rubbing so hard the sponge came away tinged with blood — had been, for her, a sustained form of violence. I can take care of myself, she'd said from a vast distance, from a sum of experiences irreconcilable with my own.

The prisoner had planned her escape, I thought, in part by pretending that she no longer was one. She told me that morning that she was too tired to go for our walk; what she was doing was conserving her energy to flee. If I had realized it in time, if within half an hour she'd seen me coming across the plaza (in the vision, she didn't fear this happening because it wasn't her, but rather me, trapped inside her body), would she have screamed, asked the bums and the drunks for help? At the same time, I was amazed at the continuity of my experiences the previous afternoon: the hearing, the walk with Paula, the conversation in the café. In my vision, I found myself suddenly in Inés' body, and my trajectory was, at first, governed by my impulse to go back home. As she began to take over, she grew disoriented, her determination flagging, until her steps led her to the ATM. Where was I at that point? Shouldn't I have suffered one of my absences? But the temporality that ruled those visions did not correlate to the life they were interrupting. During the first crossover with Inés, in the bathtub on my birthday, what had lasted just a few brief seconds had required a memory lapse of more than half an hour. And further, in the longer vision, hadn't I found myself transported to another time, to the future? Aside from that dark place, her naked body on the cold, hard table, other diffuse memories were surfacing — a courtyard of bare earth between stables, the shade of a willow tree near an irrigation ditch, an iridescent lizard on the edge of a cinder block wall, a dark-sand beach on a cloudy, windy day — that could be hers. That was all that remained of her, aside from the impression she'd left on her relatives, on the other homeless people in the plaza, and on me, from the outside. Her relatives — I would need to find some way to contact them. It was likely that, with the news of her death — when her body was identified — at least one of them would come forward. Her nephews in Temuco, for example. There must be some secret connection, something in her past that would explain why we'd changed places. It was possible, of course, that simply having been the protagonist of my vision was precisely the point of contact, the link I then took upon myself to intensify and prolong.

I went to the notary. Paula looked exhausted, overwhelmed by the tasks required to dismantle her life. This was one more of them, though it would mean transferring a burden from her shoulders to mine. She said she'd decided to postpone her trip north for the following week. I offered to go with her. She declined. Signing the car paperwork was just a checkmark on a list in which the items seemed to multiply by spontaneous generation. The most draining task was the rounds of visits to family and friends. During this visit, she'd decided to nurture her extensive network of contacts, which meant three or four get-togethers per day, a full schedule. The same scene kept repeating itself: she'd meet a college friend for lunch or for a coffee and, when the check came, she'd ask, anxiously, if there would be time to see each other before Paula left. Wasn't that what they'd just done? Paula would be obliged, once again, to draw a dividing line, to erect a barrier against the invading hordes. Her mother had decided to throw her a goodbye party on the night before her departure (to which I was not invited), but the idea of only seeing each other there had offended many of her acquaintances. Finishing up at the notary, I resisted the impulse to invite her out for a coffee. In any case, she'd already arranged to have coffee with a cousin of hers and then she had a lunch date afterward.

I bought my ticket to Paris and made the reservation for within the month. My lawyer suggested that I wait until the final divorce determination. I decided to give up the apartment, now indelibly linked to Inés. It didn't make sense to pay a full year's rent. My vague original plan had been to build a new life in that space and then to embark on an adventure. But, in reality, what I was shaping instead was an anti-life, a routine defined by the negation of what had been before and which constituted nothing more than a preface to the trip, a phase of my farewell. I would have to sell some pieces of furniture, loan others out, put my books and films and some of my clothes in a storage unit. Emulating Paula, I made a list of to-do's: renew my passport, bank transactions, visas and vaccinations, give notice on my lease, relocation, storage, sell Paula's car.

I didn't attack the list right away. I approached it calmly. I was surprised by my own capacity for idleness; it was new for me. During the past eighteen years, since the break from my family, I had never once let up in terms of my ambition or work ethic. The truth is I missed work, not the agency in particular, or even advertising (which, from this very slight distance, now seemed like a simulated world in which everyone had agreed to consider certain things important, to respect, for example, the urgency of deadlines), but rather my own competence. The exercise of muscles that were already beginning to atrophy. I should have plunged into my list as a way to distract myself from Inés. But it was to precisely this that I devoted the days following the murder: to thinking about her, reliving the features of our time together and of the vision, searching for the key. I felt accompanied by her memory at all times. I continued to sleep on the sofa, unable to bring myself to reclaim the bed. I felt indebted to her. Mixed in with my feelings of guilt, grief and failure — sharper and more urgent than I'd felt about the divorce, which, at the end of the day, had been a public collapse and, in part, its own punishment — was a dose of relief at the fait accompli.

One afternoon, as I was preparing lunch, the cat returned to the narrow window ledge and meowed urgently at me. I opened the window. The animal hesitated for a moment. Then it jumped inside and rubbed up against my pant leg. I had to resist the impulse to back away or kick it. The contact with its warm, elastic body sent a wave of revulsion through me. She (I was beginning to suspect that it was a she) proceeded to explore the rest of the apartment, room by room. Her steel-colored fur seemed to change subtly in tone against different backgrounds; her paws gave off a metallic luster as though emanating their own light. Every once in a while she would look up at me to study my reactions and to confirm that she had the right to stroll through my home. She leaped up onto the bed and lay down, curling into a ball on the bedspread. No, I said in an authoritative tone, as if I were speaking to a dog. She ignored me. She remained in her spot, purring, her calm green eyes fixed on me. I took a step towards the bed and she jumped to the floor. She continued her reconnaissance mission: the bathroom, the living room — where she repeated the experiment of settling into the armchair and the sofa — and finally back to the kitchen. I pointed to the window. No response. I picked her up, again stifling a feeling of disgust. The idea of throwing her into the void crossed my mind briefly and she, apparently reading my thoughts, tensed her body. I deposited her on the windowsill and closed the window. She remained there, meowing. I knew I had made a mistake. I couldn't take responsibility for an animal just before leaving on a trip, but I also told myself that it wasn't up to me. She had chosen me. I opened the window. I poured milk into a saucer. She lapped it up, purring loudly. When she finished I put her out again. I left my lunch half-cooked and went out to eat instead.

I started with the easiest thing: renewing my ID and passport. I decided I'd cross one item off the list each day.

But the list, just like Paula's, kept growing longer by at least one task per day. I bought a round trip ticket, London-Bombay. My idea was to travel overland, via Spain, from Paris to Morocco, then head to Egypt, cross over to Sicily and return to London, all in two months. I thought I'd spend at least half a year travelling around India. I also hoped to visit Nepal and Tibet, flying to Lhasa from Kathmandu. My plan consisted almost entirely of the absence of a plan. My method would be intuitive caprice and improvisation, always leaving open the possibility at any point of settling for a while along the way.

Not far from my apartment, I saw a pet food store and veterinary clinic that, until then, had been invisible to me. I even went so far as to ask if they'd recently opened, despite the fact that the place showed obvious signs of deterioration and was permeated with the smell of countless patients. Fifteen years, a kid in a white apron who couldn't have been much older than that himself, told me from behind the counter. I bought cat food and two metal dishes. I told the kid about the cat that had adopted me and said that she visited me twice a day to drink a saucer of milk.

"Don't give her milk."

"Why not?"

"It's bad for cats. What they're trying to do is hydrate, and water's best for that."

"Okay, thanks."

"You should bring her in," he added as I was heading for the door. "Cats get illnesses that are harmless to humans, but they can also have parasites that can be very dangerous to us."

The kid's innocent expression made me suspicious. I knew better than anyone that you should always be wary of advice from interested parties.

"We recommend deworming them every three months," he insisted.

"And how do you do that?"

"You give them a pill or you put drops on the nape of the neck."

"Do I have to bring her in for that?"

"You can buy the medicine and apply it yourself. But it would still be a good idea for her to have a checkup."

"And how do I bring her in?"

"A cage is the easiest," he pointed to a tower of new plastic cages in various sizes. "Or you can use a box. Do you live far from here?"

"Three blocks, near the intersection of Rosal."

"You could just carry her in your arms, though sometimes the traffic scares them."

"I'm moving in a month," I replied, "and I'm going on a trip. I can't take care of a cat."

The kid shrugged his shoulders. I bought the antiparasitic drops.

The next morning, the cat, whom I'd christened Lola, jumped down to the kitchen floor and discovered a bowl of food and another filled with water. She came over to me and rubbed up against my legs. Then she devoured the food and lapped up every last drop of the water. When she finished, instead of embarking on her retreat, she headed for the living room and settled into the armchair facing the window, watching me for a reaction. I sat down on the sofa, from which I no longer bothered to remove the pillow or sheets.

"I should warn you that this isn't going to last long, Lola," I said. "I don't know if the next occupants are going to accept you. Or if you'll accept them."

Lola listened attentively as I spoke. After a minute of silence she relaxed her body, rested her head on her front paws and closed her eyes. Talking out loud to a cat made me feel like an old bachelor. What would Manuel say? Or Paula? Were pets even allowed in the building? I read through the rental agreement, but it didn't say anything on the subject. I noticed a clause that I hadn't paid any attention to before: I had committed to leasing the apartment for at least one year; if I left sooner than that, I would be required to pay the remaining months' rent. I called the landlady. She asked after my aunt and I told her that she was no longer staying with me, that the situation had been resolved.

"I'm glad to hear it," she said.

"I'm calling about something else."

"What is it, Tomás?"

"An incredible professional opportunity has come up," I improvised. "An offer I can't refuse..."

"And...?"

"It's in Spain."

"When are you leaving?"

"At the end of next month."

Silence.

"You're going to owe me nine months' rent."

"That's why I was calling. Might it be possible to come to an arrangement?"

Another pause.

"Let me think about it, okay? I'm busy right now. I'll call you back."

She hung up.

I attacked my list with a vengeance. I got my visa at the Indian Embassy, hired a moving company, bought clothes and gear for the trip. The landlady called with a proposition: she'd put the apartment on the market. I would have to pay until it was rented and be willing to show it to potential renters while I was still in Santiago. I ac-

cepted. Lola staked out the living room and the kitchen
as her territory. She didn't stay the night with me, but she
showed up every morning to eat and drink. At first, she
bolted her food, but after a few days she began to ration
it. She would eat a little, chewing loudly, head for what
was now her armchair, covered with gray fur, rest for a
while, go back to the kitchen, eat a little more. And so
on, for most of the day. Her comings and goings followed
a regular pattern. She liked to go out into the courtyard,
that dark, quiet, closed-off world delimited by the back-
side of the buildings and the parking lot. The moment she
passed through the window she'd disappear, as though
entering another dimension. She would grow impatient
and meow insistently if she found the window closed, so
I was obliged to go in to open or close it at regular intervals. Aside from these moments and the early-morning
feeding ritual, for which she showed her appreciation
by rubbing against my ankles before attacking the dish,
she paid very little attention to me. She moved haughtily, proud of her own elegance, conscious — it seemed
to me — of the subtleness and fluidity of her body. Every
one of her postures exuded nobility. A queen. Or, better yet, as she was still young, a princess. More intense
contact would have annoyed me, but she maintained
her distance and her independence, tolerating my company as a necessary evil. I grew accustomed to the feel
of her warm body against my legs, to the constant trips
to the kitchen to open the window and to her apparent
ubiquity: sometimes I would leave her presence in one
room to go into another, only to find her already there.
A few months before, the idea of living with a cat would
have sounded ludicrous, but now I was adapting to her
in an oddly natural way. Sometimes, when I was sitting
in front of the computer, Lola would walk past me and

settle into her spot in the armchair without giving me so much a glance, flagrantly ignoring me, but there was a subtle rapport between us, a curious harmony. I think she could sense the admiration and fascination that the metallic glow of her ears and paws, her intelligence and self-sufficiency, aroused in me. I told her again and again that ours was a temporary arrangement, that she shouldn't get used to it. At times, an internal voice would admonish me for the crude psychological trick I'd deployed in adopting Lola: you're using her to exorcise the memory of Inés, you need to take care of someone (or something) as a way of taking care of yourself or as a protective barrier against your own circumstances. The truth was that she had chosen me, though it was undeniable that her presence was, in some way, counteracting the old woman's. Once that chapter was closed, I would remember that apartment as Inés and Lola's.

I continued to scan the news. After a few days, there was no more mention of a homeless woman cruelly murdered by drug addicts in the middle of downtown. In the follow-up stories that appeared in the tabloids, there was no mention of her name or whether her remains had been claimed by family. Then there was silence. Inés' battered body was buried beneath other events worthy of public attention. I kept searching for more than a week, secretly hoping there wouldn't be anything and I could consider the matter closed. I could go to the plaza, I thought, talk to some of the protagonists of my vision, but that would mean, if not implicating myself, at least making known a link between me and Inés that would be difficult to justify without raising suspicions. In the face of the evidence that there was no longer anything I could do about it, my curiosity began to wane.

As the date of my trip approached, my life in the apartment began to recover some of the lightness of the early days as I cast off the burden of routine. The apartment's spaces once again became mere way stations. I went to the international vaccination clinic at the Hospital Salvador. Walking home through Parque Balmaceda, I decided also to get the cat vaccinated, even though our separation was imminent. I called Paula. I was starting to feel pressured to sell the car, as there were only three weeks left before my departure.

"Hi, Tomás."

"How did it go up north?"

"I'm leaving tomorrow," Paula said. "I've been stuck dealing with a million things, but everything's taken care of now. The only thing left to do is this job."

"Is it still worth doing it?"

"It is…and anyway, they already paid me."

"Do you have time? You're leaving in less than a week."

"If everything goes well, I think so. I'm calculating a day and a half to get there, one day there, and another day and a half to get back."

"You'll just barely make it."

"I'm sorry about the hassle of the car."

"Don't worry about it. Will we see each other when you get back?"

"Of course.

I found Lola dozing in her armchair. I picked her up and carried her to the kitchen. She allowed me to put her in a cardboard box, but she protested when I tried to close it. We fought and I won. But when I set the box on the floor, she lunged against one side with all her strength, destroying the box. She leapt up on the dishwasher and, seeing that the window was closed, ran and hid under my bed.

I went to the veterinary clinic. I bought a plastic cage. Lola had returned to her spot and, to my surprise, allowed me to put her inside the cage without a fight. She meowed in terror for the entire three blocks to the clinic. The kid in the white apron took the cage and led us to an adjoining room, leaving the door that led to the shop open. He lifted Lola from the cage by the nape of the neck and placed her on a metal table. She was indeed a female, he said. She'd been spayed. He listened to her throat and abdomen, checked her mouth and eyes. He said she was young. Judging by her teeth, he calculated between two and three years. She appeared to be in perfect health. He injected her with the triple feline vaccine. He mentioned the illnesses it would prevent, information I was unable to retain. He did a test and announced that it would also be necessary to vaccinate her against leukemia and rabies, as well as a booster of the triple feline vaccine, but that it wasn't recommended to do all the immunizations at the same time. I explained that I was leaving and that the cat would probably not have an owner within three weeks' time. He shrugged.

"Bring her in next week and we'll do the leukemia vaccine, and the week after that for the rabies."

The kid opened the door to the cage and Lola went inside, this time on her own.

"Is it normal for a cat to appear like this, out of nowhere?"

The kid nodded, pushing the cage toward me.

"She appears to have been well cared for and she's used to living with people. It could be that her owner died and she ended up with nowhere to live."

"Would it have been someone in the neighborhood?"

"Probably, but I've never seen her before."

Lola meowed less vigorously on the way back home. An image kept forming in my mind, a dark apartment with heavy curtains, cluttered with old furniture. The vague silhouette of an old woman. The third in a series that included Phyllis and Inés. I let the cat loose in the kitchen, with the window open. She gave me a disdainfully patient look and opted for the gray armchair in the living room.

That night I finally returned to my bed. At five in the morning, the phone rang.

"Tomás, I'm sorry to call at this hour," said Paula's voice.

"Is everything okay?"

"No. It's not..."

For a few minutes, I listened to her sob on the other end of the line.

"I'm sorry..." she stammered. "I needed to tell someone."

She let out a sort of howl, which gave way to a new round of sobs. I sat up in bed, my own distress still muffled by sleep.

"It's Mariana," Paula finally managed to articulate. "She's dead."

"What happened?"

"I'm sorry, Tomás. Forgive me..."

She started crying again, uncontrollably. I waited silently as she poured out her grief.

"Are you still there?"

"Of course," I said.

Paula took a deep breath and exhaled into the telephone.

"She was rear-ended on the M-30," she said in a neutral tone. "There was an accident up ahead and several cars had to slam on their brakes and the guy behind her didn't realize it in time or else he was going too fast. Mari..." her voice broke. "Mari was wearing her seatbelt, but the impact was..."

She broke into another wave of tears.

"Are you at home?"

"Yes."

"And Alejandra?"

"Sleeping."

"Wake her up."

"I don't think I can. She took a sleeping pill."

"I'm coming over," I said.

"You don't have to, sweetheart. I'm fine. I just needed someone to talk to. I needed to cry. I hadn't been able to cry."

"I can be there in twenty minutes."

"No, really, it's best if you don't. I'm going to try to sleep."

"Wake your mother up. I don't want you to be alone."

"It helps me to hear your voice," she said.

We were silent for a moment.

"How did you find out?" I asked.

"Her mother called me."

"When did it happen?"

"Last night."

Paula sounded a little better, more grounded.

"Are you going to be okay?"

"I don't know if I'll be able to sleep. I have to wait until nine before I can call the airline."

"Are you leaving tomorrow?"

"If I can get a ticket."

"You called me 'sweetheart.'"

Paula laughed quietly.

"I know. A slip."

"Are you sure you don't want me to come over?"

"I'm sure."

I waited until ten in the morning and then called her cellphone, but it was turned off. Alejandra answered the house phone and informed me that Paula would be leaving that evening and that she was asleep.

I wasn't able to reach her on her cell that entire morning. Around noon, I headed to Alejandra's house in Ñuñoa. Before ringing the bell, I noted that the Suzuki wasn't in the space in front of the garage. The housekeeper came out to the street to tell me that Paulita had gone to the airline office and to buy some euros. Doña Alejandra was resting. I walked around the neighborhood for an hour, but finally gave up. Why this near desperate desire to see Paula? It was possible that, more than a wish to comfort her, to reassure myself that she was okay and would come through this catastrophe, more even than jealousy (which I knew would continue to rankle me, even after Mariana's death), I was motivated by the same blind need shared by all her friends and family: I wanted to claim a fragment of her attention, of her time.

I went back to the apartment and sat down to read in the living room, to wait for her call, my cellphone and the landline both within easy reach. I couldn't concentrate on reading so I opened my computer. I searched mechanically through the news, looking for any mention of Inés. Nothing. I stretched out on the sofa. I tried to sleep. The telephones remained silent until six-thirty, when my cell rang. It was Manuel. He told me he was single again and up to his neck with work at the agency. He had a date later that night and he'd thought of me. It would be no problem for his date to invite a friend. I told him that Paula was leaving for Spain and I was going to the airport to see her off. We agreed to meet for lunch the following week. When I hung up, I heard Lola meowing in the kitchen. I was about to get up to go open the window for her when I saw her cross the floor with something in her mouth. A mouse. She let it go. The rodent, who looked stunned, in shock, remained motionless for an instant. It tried to flee to a corner and the cat caught it easily, immobilizing it with her paw. She bit it carefully on the neck, lifting it up. The mouse started squeaking, then seemed to resign itself to its fate. Lola brought it over to me, let it go again and meowed boastfully. The mouse waited a few seconds before trying to escape in the opposite direction, leaving a trail of blood on the hardwood floor. Lola caught up with it and put her paw on its tail. When she had it between her fangs once again, I picked her up by the nape of the neck, like I'd seen the veterinarian do, and carried her to the kitchen window, which I closed behind her. She looked at me in surprise. Wasn't I impressed with her skill as a hunter? The mouse, taking advantage of her tormentor's momentary distraction, tried to drag itself along the window ledge, and Lola, with a casual gesture, knocked it into the void with one swipe of her paw. She gave me one final recriminatory meow and disappeared from sight.

I waited until the time they would have been leaving for the airport, but Paula showed no signs of life. The irrational and superstitious desire to see her one more time before she left overwhelmed me. Too late, I went out to find a taxi. Out on the street, I was met with a blast of warm air. The clouds seemed to have sucked up all the smog and the air was unusually clear. Even in the light from the streetlamps, the façades of the buildings and the hillside beyond seemed to have developed new details, refined their contours. Before I'd gone ten paces from the door of the apartment building, it started to rain. A few drops that grew immediately into a downpour. Luckily, I found a taxi fairly quickly. It pulled up in front of me and a woman got out. I walked around the taxi and climbed into the back seat while she was still paying. I was drenched from head to toe. It was the first big rain of the year and the streets were instantly flooded with murky water. It took the taxi more than twenty minutes to travel the few blocks to the highway tunnel.

I ran into the airport dripping wet, like in a bad movie, thinking not about Paula, but about how Hollywood tended to use rain to emphasize a character's pitifulness when everything seemed to be going against him. There were only a few stragglers still at the airline counter, weighing their luggage. There was no sign of Paula or Alejandra this side of the international security checkpoint. I tried to call her for the umpteenth time. Then I saw her, in the opposite wing of the terminal, beyond security, pulling a carry-on bag. Her serious, thoughtful demeanor reassured me. From what I could make out from that distance, her outward appearance did not betray the blow she'd just received, projecting instead a high level of composure. I waved my arms. Then I stood still, waiting for her intuition to alert her to my presence, for something to force her to turn her head toward me. But she didn't. She kept walking until she moved out of sight behind a handicrafts shop.

On the way back home, before hitting the tunnel, I called Manuel.

"Compadre. I'm on my way home from the airport. Does your offer still stand?"

Manuel said something, but I couldn't hear him. The taxi driver was barreling at top speed though the downpour.

"Sorry, I didn't hear you."

"She couldn't make it, something came up," shouted Manuel. "But I'm going out with the friend."

"Oh, okay."

"If you want, I'll ask if she has another friend."

"No, that's okay. I'll see you on Wednesday."

Stuck in traffic inside the tunnel, I thought that during my time in my new bachelor pad, I'd withdrawn involuntarily into a strange isolation, a retreat into myself — due partly to Inés — that seemed odd to me only now. From the start, Paula and I had been a social couple. Dinners, parties, barbecues, going to the movies and out with friends were things we took for granted, facilitated, certainly, by our lack of children, the fact of which had also meant we'd begun unintentionally hanging out with progressively younger couples. Had Paula-the-irresistible been the secret engine of that rich social life? Was it also linked to working at the agency, to establishing and greasing networks that combined work and socializing? Was a vein of misanthropy revealing itself after the separation, or was this retreat part of my midlife crisis, nothing more than the need to be by myself for a while at the fork in the road? If my current situation weren't temporary, I would have made more of a conscious effort to break out of my isolation, I thought. But traveling on my own was going to provide ample opportunity for contact with new people.

I took a long shower to warm myself up. I got in bed and turned on the TV. The rain and the wind grew more intense. The power went out. I felt around in the kitchen for a flashlight. I left the window ajar to allow Lola to come back in. I opened a beer and stretched out on the living room sofa.

The doorbell woke me. It was still raining hard outside. The tiny green light on my computer charger told me that the power had come back on. I turned on the hall light and stumbled to the intercom.

"Hello?"

A shrill woman's voice answered.

"Tomás, is that you? I think I may have woken one of your neighbors. Or maybe two."

"Who is this?"

"Fernanda. Sorry it's so late. I need…" she trailed off for a few seconds, "to talk to you."

I pushed the button. It took her a long time to get to the door, which I opened just as she was about to knock. She was so drenched it looked like she'd jumped in a pool fully clothed; the water in her shoes made a sound like suction cups. She moved unsteadily. It made me think of a novice actress pretending to be drunk. She kissed me passionately. Her rough tongue tasted of a mixture of alcohol, including wine and rum.

"Have you missed me?"

"Very much," I said in a guttural voice.

She pulled away from me and walked purposefully into the apartment. She got tangled up in her own legs. She wobbled. I had to hold her up so she wouldn't lose her balance.

"Wow, this place is moving like a boat… in a storm."

I led her to the kitchen.

"Don't turn on the light."

"Do you want some coffee?"

"Probably not a bad idea."

Even in the semi-darkness I could see that she had a cut on the side of her mouth and the entire side of her face was begging to swell. She was shivering with cold.

"What happened?"

"It was Nico."

"Did he hit you?"

She nodded, ashamed.

"He cheated on me again," she said in a thin voice. "I got mad and that son of a bitch told me to fuck off and gave me this as a souvenir."

She touched the wound with the tips of her fingers.

"Did you break up?"

"All men are assholes. Except you, of course."

"Of course."

"We went to a bar near here," she said, slurring her words, her eyes unfocused from alcohol. "After, I stayed and had a few drinks by myself and I remembered that you lived in the neighborhood. My best friend is away for the weekend. I think that shithead fucked her too."

I gave her a cup of coffee. She seemed on the verge of tears.

"Thank you, Tomás, you're... you're a doll."

"Do you want sugar, milk?"

"Nothing, thanks."

She lifted the mug with two trembling hands. She took a sip. The rain was still pounding the windowpanes in a steady bombardment.

"Do you want to take a shower?"

"I want us to make love," she said with a mischievous smile.

"First you have to take a shower."

I helped her up and led her to the bathroom, trying unsuccessfully not to think of Inés. I helped her undress. First her top, then her pants, which were plastered to her skin. I had to sit her down on top of the toilet so I could yank them off. For some reason, I had the impression that her tattoo was in a different place. Now she was in just her underwear, also soaked.

"I think I might..." she said.

She managed to fall to her knees on the tiles and get the lid to the toilet open before vomiting. Most of it went in the bowl. I left the bathroom and closed the door. I could hear her violent retching even from the kitchen and despite the rain. I poured myself a cup of coffee. I heard the shower come on. I washed up the dishes and went into the bedroom. Fernanda had slid into the bed, her hair

wrapped in a towel. She lay on her side, in the fetal position. She was snoring softly. A string of saliva dribbled
from her half-open mouth, leaving a small blotch on the
sheet. I turned off the lamp. I stretched out alongside her,
on top of the bedspread. I leaned over to kiss her shoulder and to take in her scent. I went back to the kitchen.
I poured the rest of the coffee down the drain. Then I
crossed the threshold into the living room.

SIX

WE descend laboriously down the lee side of the ridge, battered ceaselessly by the wind. The gale beats at our clothing as if we were in a free fall, instead of picking our way cautiously, testing the consistency of packed snow and strips of ice beneath the clouds of snow swirling around our legs. Ramiro shouts something that I can't make out. He points to the top of the ridge, some five meters above our heads, and we continue to descend. In the flat, meager light, the crests of sharp rock are the only indication of the arête. The bare spikes of rock jut out into the blizzard like a branch piercing the surface of a torrential flood: the snow forms horizontal sheets and tentacles that extend out above us, giving us an idea, against the dark storm clouds hovering higher up, of the wind pattern. Aside from that, I can't make out a thing except Ramiro's silhouette moving a few meters below me, and I try to step where he's stepped. It's only in relation to him that I can tell where the slope tilts.

Ramiro stops. He appears to be trying to get his bearings in the middle of the blinding whiteout. The wind changes direction and a white gust whips viciously up from the depths of the gorge. Ramiro squats down, hunched against the stab of cold. I do the same, turning my back to him. The gust passes, followed by a moment of relative calm. We stay like that for a few minutes, catching our breath. The snow accumulates around us. I look up at the stretch we've just descended and see that, beyond ten or fifteen feet out, the storm has erased our tracks. I'm about to speak, but Ramiro appears to have read my mind and nods. We'll leave a flag further down, where it's narrower, he shouts. Okay, I shout. Ramiro closes his eyes and remains in place for a long moment. At last he stands up and we start moving down the slope, which has become more precipitous. I would have preferred not to rest. I feel weak and a little dizzy, I'm thirsty, blood pulses in my temples. My numb feet send pain signals that seem to be coming from somewhere beyond my legs, as though I'm touching sensitive spots in the snow each time I bury my crampons in the scarp.

We're cutting across the slope on a diagonal, which forces us into the wind in certain stretches. With its incessant whistling, I can't hear the hollow thud of the crampons, or the clinking of metal gear or my own breathing. Though we're thigh-deep in the snow, I see Ramiro making footholds in the deepest sections, which I use to trace his trajectory. The snow stuck to our clothing freezes, forming an armor that cracks at the joints with each stride. The coil of rope I'm carrying over one shoulder is now a solid hoop. We peer out over what appears to be the edge of a cliff. The edge begins to collapse beneath our weight, but Ramiro doesn't react. He sees that I've stopped a few feet above him and he gives me a thumb's up. Don't worry. We're right on track. Then he stretches out his arms and drops down the slope.

We come to a place where the undulating crest of the ridge doubles back on itself, creating a kind of bowl, at the base of which the terrain flattens out, forming a narrow shelf before plummeting over a precipice. This is the place Ramiro has been looking for. A wave of energy seems to come over him. He signals for me to wait at the base and I see him climb skillfully up to the top of the bowl, burying the toes of his crampons in thin crusts of dirty ice adhered to the rock, clinging to cracks and outcroppings invisible to me from below. He makes it to a swath of snow and stabs the handle of his ice axe just beneath the arête. The snow is hard and he struggles to place the axe. A shroud of fog or powdered snow rises up between us and, from one moment to the next, I lose sight of him. I'm overcome with panic. I'm about to scream, but the veil recedes and he's there in front of me, less than a hundred feet straight ahead. For the first time in a long while I think of Osvaldo and I'm flooded by a wave of shame and remorse. Osvaldo is alone higher up, in who knows what condition, searching blindly for us in the storm, provided he still has the strength to walk. Ramiro manages to set the ice axe. Now he takes something out of his backpack. A dark-colored article of clothing. A fleece or a long-sleeved t-shirt. He ties it to the ice axe to make a flag that flaps madly in the wind. He gives me another thumb's up and starts to descend, skirting around the top of the hollow bowl. The force of the wind tips the ice axe and the t-shirt tears apart. Only a small piece remains stuck to the handle. Ramiro continues to descend, not realizing what's happened until he's halfway down. I signal for him to turn around and look up. He makes it back to the ice axe, our signal for Osvaldo. He couldn't possibly reach this spot, even in the middle of the night, without coming across that small serrated cross or our tent at the base of the bowl. Ramiro sets the ice axe again, in the hard-packed snow a few feet higher up, and leaves it there, with the shred of fabric waving furiously in the wind. He descends to where I'm waiting. He's exhausted. I ask if he wants to rest and he shakes his head.

We dig out a flat area in the most sheltered spot on the shelf. I hold the tent down with my hands and feet while Ramiro works to set it up. We pound in the stakes and Ramiro runs a rope in a zigzag over the top to further secure it against the wind. We crawl inside. I take the lantern out of my backpack. I take my mittens off so I can light it. But I can't do it. My hands are shaking, as is the rest of my body. My head throbs like a second heart. Ramiro tells me to take off my parka and snow pants and get into my sleeping bag in my clothes. I do so, groping about in the dark. Ramiro lights the lantern. I see him rummage around in his backpack. Then he unzips the tent and reaches an arm out to fill the receptacle on the portable stove with snow. He lights the stove. Do you want coffee or soup? Coffee, I answer. He holds out a piece of chocolate. No, thanks. Eat it, huevón, he says. Small drops of blood collect in the cracks of his pale, chapped lips. I obey. I have to chew the frozen chocolate with my molars. I ask Ramiro if we should stay awake in shifts to wait for my brother and he tells me it's not worth it. We have to try to recuperate our strength for tomorrow. Most likely, Osvaldo decided to make the descent. If that's the case, he'll turn up here in a couple of hours. Three, at the most. It's also possible he found a sheltered spot on the rock wall and decided to spend the night up top. The storm's bound to let up tomorrow, and we'll go up and look for him. I shrug. I lie back. I close my eyes and am asleep in seconds.

I wake up just before dawn. I prop up on one elbow and know immediately that Osvaldo is not in the tent. I can make out the bulky shape of Ramiro's sleeping bag and the measured rhythm of his breathing. The storm is still raging. The wind howls, shaking the tent as though we were sailing it through violent ocean swells. A muted light filters through the nylon dome with a phosphorescent glow. The snow assaults the walls of the tent in an incessant drumbeat that makes me think of an attack by living beings, insects, and piles up around our heads nearly halfway up the tent. I linger for a long while, studying the tracks of condensation on the tent fabric, slowly emerging from the deep trance of sleep. Encased in the double cocoon of my sleeping bag and the tent, I think again of Osvaldo, seeing his smiling face during one stretch of our ascent the previous morning. For the first time, I'm aware that he could be dying or dead.

I need to go to the bathroom. I lie there another twenty minutes so as not to wake Ramiro. He jolts awake at my first slight movement. He looks at me for a moment and lies back down, turning his back to me. I'm going out to piss, I say. He doesn't answer. I pull on my snow pants, boots, helmet and parka. I debate whether to strap on my crampons and decide against it. I go out. I have to lean over, lowering my center of gravity like a rugby player bracing against a tackle so the wind doesn't knock me over. The vertical snow stabs the few exposed centimeters of my face like needles. I adjust my balaclava, goggles and mittens. Visibility is near zero. The tent appears to be resting, half-buried, in a white universe without features or dimensions. There's no separation between the snow and the sky. I can't see the sharp ridge of the mountain or the small stone bowl that we chose as our point of reference or Ramiro's ice axe or the plunging abyss a few meters behind me. I'm afraid that, in stepping even a few feet away from the tent, it too will disappear into the whiteness and I won't be able to find it again. It takes an enormous effort to move forward over the horizontal terrain without my crampons. I move the bare minimum distance away, tracing what I believe is a route parallel to the cliff edge, never taking my eyes off the tent, which shrinks to a vague orange blur through a curtain of white powder. I kneel in the snow, my back to the wind, and urinate. I retrace my steps. The color of the tent regains its brightness. I've almost made it back when I slip on a patch of ice beneath the white powder. Instinctively, I rear upwards, stretching my arms out to catch my balance, and the wind hits me full in the back, lifting me off the ground as if I'd just jumped on a trampoline, pushing me toward the cliff. I close my eyes. To my surprise, I don't continue sailing into the void, but instead fall on something solid, winding up buried in three feet of snow. I get up carefully. I clear my goggles and try to make out the edge of the cliff. I imagine I could touch it by just stretching out my hands. But I'm not sure of my orientation. I can't see the tent. Snow has filtered through the top of my parka and the neck and back of my t-shirt are soaked. I move straight into the wind, nearly dragging myself, feeling along the terrain with my mittens. The tent materializes before me. I fall inside, panting, without shaking off the snow covering my feet and head.

We wait for Osvaldo. I ask Ramiro if we should try to look for him and he tells me it would be impossible. We'd only manage to make things worse. His only hope is to come across the tent in the middle of the snowstorm. And soon. We both know — and there's no need for Ramiro to say it out loud — that his chances of survival grow smaller with each passing minute. And there's nothing for us to do but wait. The storm shows no sign of letting up. Through the constant wail of wind and hammering snow against the still-exposed parts of the tent, we can clearly hear the muffled rumble of avalanches in the gorge. Avalanches are not a concern in this area or at the base of the rock wall where Osvaldo must be, though there could be ice slides, and the crumbling snow will surely make our descent from here difficult. We organize the tent. We try to dry the puddles of water from the snow I tracked in after my fall. We roll up our sleeping bags. Ramiro comments, with no apparent emotion, that we have enough fuel and food (coffee with sugar, soup, cereal, raisins and chocolate) for three or four days, more if we don't find Osvaldo. Ramiro methodically organizes and takes inventory of the climbing gear: bolts, pitons, nuts, carabiners, belay devices, rappelling hooks, helmets, harnesses, hammers, shovels and ropes. He does this with a maniacal meticulousness. When he finishes, his face suddenly contorts in a wail. He covers his face with his hands and gets himself under control so as not to burst out sobbing. Without looking at me, he picks up the portable stove's receptacle and unzips the tent to fill it with snow. He melts it over the stove. We drink coffee. We wait.

At regular intervals, Ramiro turns on his cellphone to check the time and then turns it off again to save the battery. There's no signal up here. Long stretches of silence elapse. Ramiro keeps me apprised of the time. We do not mention Osvaldo. At one point I remind him that, on the first day of our ascent, we'd crossed paths with a team of mule-drivers, and surely they'd alerted someone. When the weather improves, I say, they'll launch a rescue operation immediately. Ramiro nods and we fall silent again. He sits motionless, his forearms on his knees, his head tilted forward so as not to touch the roof of the tent, his gaze fixed on a spot on the back wall, outside of which the snow has accumulated, forming a protective hollow. Everything in his manner demands that I respect that ominous silence, which only heightens my temptation to talk incessantly, to assuage my anxiety with a torrent of words. I'm aware that we're sitting as far apart as the dimensions of the tent allow. Continuous waves of animosity flow between us. I tell myself that it's a result of our confinement and circumstances, and I try hard not to take it personally. But the truth is that, as must also be happening for him, as the hours pass, his company is becoming unbearable. The slightest provocation and I'd be on him with my ice axe or pocketknife. I find his tacit condescension about my inexperience as a climber particularly irritating.

It was Osvaldo's idea for me to come with them on this training expedition and it was obvious from the start that Ramiro was annoyed by my presence, just another burden to haul up the mountain. But it's also true that this climb didn't involve the least bit of technical difficulty, except for the vertical faces sheathed in ice at the top of this section, which I wasn't going to even attempt to climb. Further, my lack of skill is relative and only in relation to my brother's. Though it's an irrefutable truth that everything I know about mountaineering I've absorbed indirectly through Osvaldo, it's no less true that I've spent more hours on the mountain than many supposed enthusiasts. Mountaineering has been Osvaldo's great obsession for the past ten years, the central driving force in his life. He dedicates the least possible amount of time and effort to work, and even to his marriage, to be able to take off for the mountains whenever the opportunity arises. In contrast, I've kept a safe distance. I've allowed myself to be drawn in by its gravitational force, but always retained, I tell myself, a degree of control. Osvaldo confessed that one day, in the middle of a particularly difficult climb, he had a revelation. He understood that mountain climbing was a type of training, that he was developing and refining faculties for a different purpose, for something else, though he didn't know for what. Ramiro and Osvaldo met in Concepción, in their first year studying biology, and bonded over their compulsive passion for the mountains. They were inseparable at the university. Now they rarely see one another, except when they go on climbs, which they have less and less time for, especially since the birth of Jonás, my nephew. Once, Osvaldo told me that Ramiro had gotten angry with him over it, saying they didn't spend time together like in the old days, that they only got together to go climbing. Osvaldo shared with me that, after several weeks in the mountains with Ramiro — whom he loved like a second brother — the last thing that would have occurred to him was to spend more time with him. And that was even without his wife Gabi's recriminations. Deep down, he told me, aside from the mountaineering, they no longer had very much in common. More and more, Osvaldo had chosen to climb solo.

Even so, I wasn't surprised by the news that Osvaldo had decided after all to join Ramiro — a hardier, more seasoned climber than he was — on his most ambitious climb to date: Cerro Torre, one of Patagonia's majestic granite cathedrals, among the world's most difficult mountains to climb. The idea, explained Osvaldo, was to follow the most beautiful and classic route, established by Jim Bridwell in 1979, the upper half of which coincided with the route taken on Cesare Maestri's first ascent, in 1970, in which he'd used a compressor to more quickly drill bolts into the rock. They planned to camp on the glacier — practically at the base of the gigantic stone spire — for five weeks, from the middle of December until the end of January, where they would wait for a window of good weather during which to attempt the ascent. They would try to make it to the summit, crowned by an ice cap, and descend again within a week, more than twice as long as the record Bridwell and Steve Brewer had set.

This excursion, at the beginning of April, was to be the first in a series of training climbs. The plan had been to climb in one day to the base of the escarpment, some three hundred meters above the place where we were now waiting, and to set up camp there so Ramiro and Osvaldo could do their practice ascents on the rock, with and without ice. According to Ramiro, the ice there more or less reproduced the conditions on the lower section of Cerro Torre, where Bridwell had gone off-route along an ice fissure and where, in 1959, the Austrian Toni Egger had plummeted into the void during his first attempted ascent, plunging into the snow covering the glacier, where he was found sixteen years later.

We arrived Friday, after dark, at the site at the base of the rock wall, from which a constant rain of rocks and ice shards was falling. We couldn't find a spot sheltered from the wind. Ramiro mentioned this place, a relatively protected bowl where we should set up our tent in case the weather got worse. The weather report predicted unstable conditions: wind and some snow. Osvaldo and Ramiro agreed that this matched the conditions they could expect to encounter on Cerro Torre on the mildest days (with ninety mile an hour gusts at the summit) and they decided to assume the "calculated risk." I was going to stay at basecamp the entire time — the ascent up the rock wall exceeded my capabilities — and my presence there would improve the security of our camp. We got equipment ready in case we had to descend in the snow. Ramiro said he'd studied an alternate route down in case of bad weather. But nothing had prepared us for the storm that, suddenly and with uncommon fury, descended upon us.

Yesterday, as dawn broke, at Ramiro's insistence, the first thing we did was break camp. Osvaldo suggested they do a few short climbs and return here by mid-afternoon to set up a second, more sheltered camp. There was a strong wind, but the sky looked clear, except for a few high, scattered clouds. We had breakfast. Osvaldo was the first to ascend. Ramiro and I sat on a flat rock and watched him climb nimbly up the vertical wall of the escarpment, following an established route which, according to Ramiro, didn't present much in the way of technical difficulty. About a hundred feet up, he stopped to rest beneath an overhang formed by a jutting section of rock. We saw him squat down and pull gently on the rope to test its resistance and then attack the overhang, using miniscule hand and footholds. When he pulled himself up over the splintered rim, we lost sight of him. He reappeared fifteen minutes later, much higher up, shifting over to the right in order to avoid a spur. He moved carefully. He came to a dark colored seam, turned and waved to us. He motioned for Ramiro to follow him. Ramiro shook his head. Osvaldo started the ascent of the final pitch, climbing diagonally along that darker seam. Within a few minutes, he'd reached the target: a thin cornice on the near-vertical face. After hooking into his protection, he sat on the shelf, his feet dangling over the edge into thin air. He signaled again for Ramiro to ascend. Ramiro, in turn, gestured for Osvaldo to descend first. With a gesture of irritation, he stood up, patted me on the back in farewell and started up the wall. Twenty minutes later, he was sitting next to Osvaldo on the shelf. They stayed up there a long time, gazing at the panorama unfolding before them.

They started moving again, continuing to ascend, much to my surprise. Osvaldo waved at me and I waved back. I saw them climb up to a small obelisk of brown rock and continue toward its summit, cutting across the escarpment to the south. Ramiro was leading. The wall must have undulated, as I lost sight of them in certain sections. From below, it looked as if they had merged with the rock, only to reassume, momentarily, their human shape. Until they stopped reappearing altogether.

The wind started to blow harder. To warm myself up, I did a few short descents and ascents along a north-facing ravine. But I spent most of the time watching the mountain. As the hours passed and still no sign of them, I began to feel anxious. The cold was deepening, but I didn't want to leave my observation post. Big clouds gathered around the summit of the mountains and within the space of a few minutes covered the entire sky. Details on the escarpment disappeared, transforming it into a single, gray, monolithic mass. A new layer of clouds, dark and turbulent, hurtled against the rock face, covering it almost completely. It started to snow. A dense curtain of horizontal flakes imposed itself between my observation post and the rock. I couldn't think of anything better to do than stay put, my gaze fixed on the last spot on their route that I could still see, where hangers and carabiners clinked against the rock.

Finally, past four in the afternoon, I glimpsed what I had been waiting for hours to see: the end of a rope dangling down from the dense mass of fog. In a few minutes, Ramiro's floating silhouette issued out of the clouds. He landed with a dry thump on the snow and stood motionless for a moment, his back to me. He unclipped from the rappel rope. I waited for him to yank on the rope or to step away, but he didn't do anything. I understood that he was alone. He turned around to look at me. His face was contorted. He said a few disjointed sentences. I took him by the shoulders to question him. Apparently, at a certain point, Osvaldo had suggested doing a few short solo climbs. Ramiro had said they should go down since the wind was blowing too hard, but Osvaldo was determined to do one more route, the last one. Osvaldo headed up a wall without an established route. They'd been apart for about fifteen minutes when the weather turned. A cloud of fog surrounded them and it started to hail. Ramiro expected Osvaldo to return any minute so they could begin the descent — in these conditions, much more dangerous than the ascent had been — but he didn't return. He waited ten more minutes and then climbed up the wall. The ascent was very difficult; the rock had become slippery, visibility was nil, and, he said, it felt every minute like the wind was going to rip him from the wall. At a certain point, the anchors stopped. Based on what he'd been able to see from the bottom, Ramiro had the impression that, over to the right, across a concave area that, because of its architecture and poor rock quality, would have been arduous even under normal conditions, there was a series of cracks and crevasses where one could take shelter. It was possible that Osvaldo had headed there to wait out the hailstorm. Or that he'd continued climbing without anchors. Or taken an unpredictable route. He explained to me — or at least this was how I chose to interpret it — that, if Osvaldo had fallen, he would have come down very near the place he'd set up to wait for him. Ramiro told me that he stayed there, clinging to the rock, being battered by the storm, for a long time, maybe half an hour, not knowing what to do, unable to bring himself to abandon Osvaldo, until his arms started shaking from cold and fatigue.

By the time Ramiro arrived at the base of the escarpment, I was numb with cold. Ramiro fell to his knees, exhausted, determined to wait there for Osvaldo to return. The end of the rappel rope twisted in the wind like a serpent. For a long while, that twisting movement made me think that Osvaldo had hooked on to the rope and we'd soon see him emerge from the clouds, just as, to an inexpert eye, the drag of current in a river against a fishing line might look like the agonizing tugs of a fish. I told Ramiro that I was freezing and asked him if we could go down to the place he'd chosen to set up camp, but he refused. We'll wait here, he ruled. He closed his eyes and remained still, kneeling in the snow, for more than an hour. I jumped up and down on that platform exposed to the wind and snow, careful not to get too close to the edge, where a constant, fine rain of stones pelted down from the overhang, forming a sort of protective fence, like a ring of asteroids. I strapped on my crampons and climbed up and down the ravine several times, opening and closing my hands inside my mittens. The cold boring into my bones prevented me from thinking clearly about Osvaldo, kept me from any concern other than the necessity of getting warm, drinking a cup of coffee. The snow began to accumulate on Ramiro's back, shoulders and helmet. He remained as motionless as a statue. He had fallen asleep. I approached him. I raised a hand to touch his shoulder. Just before contact, he opened his eyes and looked at me, unsurprised. We have to wait, he said, he could come down any minute. We waited until the light began to fade and the formless, depthless white began to turn to an equally uniform gray. Ramiro stood, put on his crampons and walked over to the rope. He yanked on it a few times to be sure it was firmly attached. He remained there for a moment, staring at the point where the thin violet line was devoured by the clouds, and he seemed to be fighting the temptation to climb back up the rock. At last, he released the rope and we began our descent.

Ramiro turns on his cellphone. He notes the time

without the least hint of emotion. He turns the phone off. Four o'clock, he tells me, not looking up. I realize with total clarity something that, immersed in my own anxiety, I hadn't registered before: Ramiro is in shock, paralyzed, defenseless. I lie on my side in my sleeping bag and curl up my legs, trying to impose the greatest possible distance between me and his personal space. I think, with a stab of anguish that I try hard to keep at bay, that Osvaldo has been missing for over twenty-four hours.

I stand up. I unzip the tent to refill the basin of the cook stove. The snow has accumulated on this side halfway up the zipper. I have to use my shovel to see outside. Visibility has not improved at all. The tent seems to be floating in the center of a maelstrom, a primordial chaos, a confusion of molecules in frenetic turmoil. I return to my spot inside the tent and become aware, for the first time, of the stench emanating from our sleeping bags and clothes. Within a few minutes, I've grown used to it again. It's melded back into the warmth, and I no longer notice it. The confinement makes me think of a childhood game. I remember that Osvaldo and I used to climb up onto a bed or an armchair, which we'd designated as a spaceship or a boat, and it was us against the unknown, against everything outside of that boundary. We had countless adventures, launched endless attacks — in which he, as the older brother, always played the role of the hero — combatting cannibals or rescuing princesses or unearthing treasures, but always, the best part was being enclosed inside the ship, the constant and familiar in the midst of the unknown and uncharted, that niche of belonging.

We eat dried fruit, chocolate and granola bars. I make coffee with sugar. I comment that coffee isn't the best thing for hydration and Ramiro doesn't answer. I'm overwhelmed by a sense of loathing and I have to restrain myself from insulting him. I want to scream at him: React, huevón, we have to help Osvaldo and make it out of this alive. Instead, I tell him to lie down for a while and to try to get some sleep. To my surprise, he listens to me. He closes his eyes and falls into a deep sleep. Even in the strange orange dusk that reigns inside this nylon capsule, his face looks very pale. His helplessness makes me feel doubly at the mercy of our circumstances, as if the encircling barrier between us and the storm were closing in on us. I hear, over the howl of the wind, the distant rumble of an avalanche. I have the impression that the ground beneath the snow, the entire mountain, shakes a little. I melt more snow and let it cool. I set about carefully pushing away the snow that's accumulating outside the tent, warping the fabric and threatening to tear it. The storm shows no sign of letting up.

Ramiro sleeps for more than an hour. When he wakes up he looks a little bit replenished. He goes out to urinate and returns after a few minutes. He tells me, as he's unstrapping his crampons, that visibility is still terrible. I suggest that we climb, roped together, to the base of the escarpment and he says that, in these conditions, it wouldn't be feasible. We drink the water and Ramiro melts more snow. He comments, abstractedly, that we need to start rationing fuel. When he finishes, he stretches out on his back in his sleeping bag. With one finger, he traces runnels of moisture in the film of condensation that covers the tent fabric. I get ready to go out to pee, strapping on my crampons. I put on my parka and helmet. I go out. The storm hasn't let up at all. I grab onto the rope reinforcing the tent so I don't lose my balance. The rope has become as stiff as a steel cable. With its convulsive movements, the half-buried tent makes me think of a living organ, a beating heart in the middle of a white tapestry. I don't have to pee, but I needed to get out of that confinement for a few minutes. In an almost physical way, the wind clears my head, sweeping away my anxiety and fear and even my antipathy toward Ramiro, leaving my mind momentarily empty. A small certainty lodges itself in the center of my consciousness. A subtle, yet clear and irrefutable signal. Osvaldo is alive. I even think I see him for a moment: lodged in a cleft in the rock, badly injured, using every shred of willpower in order not to fall asleep. This state of clarity passes. Thoughts clutter my mind again, coming one after another, disordered and contradictory, fighting for dominance. But the certainty remains. I'm about to go back inside the tent, from which I've not moved a single step, so I can tell Ramiro. I pause. What will I say to him? That I've just had a vision, a hunch?

While one part of me — the place where that certainty resides? — observes me with indifference or disapproval, I move away from the tent and head toward the base of the bowl, navigating the gusting wind. After a few unsteady steps, I look back and can no longer see the tent, and I feel like a person who's just jumped ship in the middle of the ocean. I'm not sure about my decision and I struggle to stick with it. Why had I been given that knowledge if not to do something about it? I have to find Osvaldo. I'm moving blindly, impelled by a sense of duty that's gradually becoming untethered from its own content. I calculate that I've walked thirty or forty feet and I still haven't come to the base of the bowl. I tell myself that I'll know it by a change in the strength or sound of the wind. It's possible that I calculated the orientation of the tent incorrectly and that I'm now walking parallel to the edge of the cliff somewhere off to my left. A wave of vertigo washes through me. I correct course. With each step, my legs sink in the snow up to my thighs, but I don't lose my footing. I struggle, not against the physical obstacles, but against the unsteadiness of my conviction. One part of me knows that this is not a good idea. Ramiro said it: climbing up to the escarpment — is that what I've set out to do, or am I just searching blindly for my brother? — is not feasible. I don't care that this excursion doesn't make sense. What matters is that I adjust it or align it to my vision and, especially, to the certainty that came over me a short time ago and that remains inside me like a guiding light.

I make it to the base of the bowl, near its steepest side, and a severe slope rises before me. I can still go back, I tell myself. This is the border beyond which it will become improbable that I could find the tent again. I think that I should have brought rescue equipment. I have no ropes and no food, or even my ice axe, but I can still help him get down. It was also a mistake not to have told Ramiro of my intentions — Ramiro must be wondering where I am by now — but if I'd told him, he wouldn't have let me leave. I stay here for a minute, catching my breath after a strenuous horizontal traverse of no more than a hundred and fifty feet. The wind and snow batter me in furious, painful blasts. I can't abandon Osvaldo, I decide. With my second step, my crampon hits something hard buried in the snow and I almost fall. I grope around. It's Ramiro's ice axe. It must have been dislodged by the wind from its place at the top of the bowl and fallen down here. Is it possible that Osvaldo could have descended, skirting the slope, without seeing the tent? I don't think so. In my vision (or imagination) I thought I saw him lodged in a fissure. If he had made it to the base of the escarpment, he would surely have found us. I start walking.

I advance up that first slope, nearly dragging myself,

opening a furrow with my head and shoulders through more than three feet of powder. My crampons slip on the rock of the bowl and, every two or three steps, I slide downhill, undoing my progress. This exasperating task takes me at least half an hour. When I finally make it to the top, the wind batters me with redoubled violence. The snow whipping along is so dense that I catch nothing but mere glimpses of light gray within what looks like a torrent of white foam. I keep moving, leaning into the wind like a drunk against a friend, trying to bear most of my weight on my fully outstretched left leg. Although I can't see it, I'm sure I'm moving along the protected flank, just beneath the ridge, retracing the route I'd descended with Ramiro yesterday. Having oriented myself in the blinding storm gives me a strange feeling of exultation or euphoria. Here, the snow is more substantial and I progress, albeit slowly, at a regular, sure pace. With each step, the distance between me and Osvaldo shrinks by half a meter. The clarity of purpose I hadn't been able to summon a few minutes before now coalesces into a physical tenacity, into the concrete effort of climbing the mountain. This step, this breath.

The light begins to fade and I'm able to glean a vague idea, amid the volleys of snow, of the general contours of the terrain. At one point, in a fleeting window of visibility, I make out a serrated fin of rock marking the edge of the ridge, somewhat higher up than I had calculated. I lose sight of it. I correct course. As I approach the summit, I enter a turbulent zone in which the wind seems to be blowing in all directions at the same time, but turns out to be less intense. The wind whistles a single, piercing note as it whips over the edge of the ridge. For a few minutes, as the light fades, I have the impression that what light remains is emanating from the snow itself. Then, all at once, it's dark. Everything around me is tinged an opaque, uniform gray. I keep climbing. Suddenly, circling under a rock jutting out from the side of the mountain, my left boot fails to find purchase and I fall. I slide downward into a ravine. My back hits something hard, a rocky outcrop, which stops my slide. I realize I'm no longer holding Ramiro's ice axe. I do my best to shake out the snow that's gotten past my waistband and into the hood of my parka. I climb, following the furrow made by my body, so as not to lose my bearings. I find the ice axe. I ascend back up to the rock. I climb around to the left and continue skirting the arête.

I come to a slope ridged with intermittent bands of ice. The ice is extremely hard in these sections and my crampons barely nick their surface. In the sections between the ice, I sink to my waist in snow. When I do finally make it to the other edge of the slope, I fall to my knees, exhausted. With every breath, I can feel the entire internal structure of my lungs, as though each bronchiole were filling with a burning liquid. I tell myself that I should stand up and keep moving, but my legs won't obey. I'm too tired. In the few minutes I've been crouched down here — two, three at the most? — the cold has permeated me. I can feel it advancing from my feet and hands, which have gone numb. I'm covered in a shroud of snow. I have to muster every last shred of willpower to get up. With both hands braced on the ice axe, I push myself to my feet. I become aware that the terrain has almost leveled off. Maybe I've already made it to the base of the escarpment. I advance, shaking violently with cold, trying to rid myself of it, toward where I ought to find the rock wall and the rappel rope Osvaldo can use to descend. But I don't come to the wall. The slope here pitches downward, and a little to the left. I cut over to the right, but the slope sinks away here too. I have no other choice than to keep moving, as I did below, near the tent, directly into the wind. After twenty paces, the slope begins to ascend once again. I understand that I've come back to the ridge, that I need to keep climbing. I pause to catch my breath. I stand there, my mittened hands braced on my knees. I let out what I recognize as a sob, not of desperation or fear, but of fatigue. My body's giving out. And I can't shake the cold. I feel it gaining ground, centimeter by centimeter, moving up my legs and arms, seizing my back. I grit my teeth and keep climbing.

Every step is utter agony. I can't keep going. At any moment my strength will give out, I think, unalarmed, one of my cramping legs will refuse to take the next step. But I continue up the mountain. An irresistible urge to sleep comes over me. I could dig a small niche in the snow and lie down for a little while. Just a few minutes would be enough to regain my energy, I tell myself, and waves of pleasure wash through me at the mere prospect of rest. But I know that I wouldn't wake up again. During one stretch, I close my eyes (visibility is so bad that it hardly makes any difference) and I see Osvaldo. He's in a bathing suit, standing on a rock at the edge of a swimming pool. He's ten years old. His hands are on his waist. I watch him from the water. He smiles, backlit by the sun. Then he plunges in. I open my eyes. We'll be together again, I tell myself. Once again, I sense his presence higher up on the mountain, like a signal, and I note, moved, that the certainty that brought me this far is still with me. He's not dead, I think, he's not dead. My stiff mouth tries to say it out loud. He's not dead. But there's not much time. I have to find Osvaldo and guide him back to the tent. Before it's too late, before the storm closes in on him like reality does for all dead people. Suddenly, surprisingly, I'm climbing more easily. Not with renewed energy, but with a sensation of lightness, as though my body had found a way of avoiding its own misery — the cramps, the stabbing pain in my lungs, the numb absence of my feet and hands, the dead weight of cold anchored to my shoulders, the nausea, the sleepiness — and is moving, in part, through another dimension. Images of Osvaldo pass before me, one after another. Also the photo of a newborn baby. Our older brother, Simón, who died at two weeks old from a respiratory infection. They'd taken him to the same hospital where he'd been born and he never came out again. I also remember how our mother avoided talking about him or would put an end to the subject, declaring that, if it hadn't been for his death, I never would have come into the world. I remember reading somewhere that many people are conceived as twins and that, in the majority of cases, only one of the fetuses ends up being viable and the other one is reabsorbed, transformed into a sort of internal twin. I don't know if this is true. Simón would be my internal twin, dead so that I could live. I struggle to remember my mother's young face, but what materializes before me is the image of Gabi, in Valdivia, on the day of her marriage to Osvaldo. And then the weekend when I paid them a surprise visit and they got into a shouting match about, as usual, a climbing trip. And later, Gabi's silhouette in the darkness, leaning over the sofa where I was sleeping and how, still half-asleep, it took me a few seconds to realize that she was naked.

I keep going. The slope grows steeper but it no longer has much to do with me. In the images floating before me, I begin to notice slight incongruities and I understand that I'm nodding off for brief moments as I climb. I move in and out of sleep like a swimmer keeping himself afloat by means of his own forward momentum. And these brief immersions give me the strength to keep going just a little bit further. In one of these fragmentary, fleeting and disjointed dreams, I experience the illusion of being or having been someone else. I'm sitting in the dark, in an armchair in an unfamiliar room, facing a window pelted by rain. I'm holding a bottle of beer. A cat glides lazily across the parquet floor. I wake up. I think of Osvaldo again and his presence higher up the mountain merges with the memory of Simón. I have the impression that he's walking somewhere off to my right, very close by, on the other side of a wall that makes him invisible and that this wall is eroding, losing solidity, until it's reduced to a thin membrane which, in turn, disintegrates into the sheets of snow driven on the wind.

SEVEN

I FOUND myself barefoot on the parquet floor of the dark living room, gazing at the ribbons of rain running across the windowpanes, refracting light from the streetlamps across the walls and ceiling. I noted that I wasn't facing the window directly, but rather observing the street in the direction of Lastarria from an oblique angle. A wild idea assailed me: had I just come out of the wall behind me? I backed up a few paces and pressed the palms of my hands against the wall, next to the sofa. Its surface was solid. There was no trace of the sneakers I'd been wearing when I entered the living room. An empty bottle of beer sat next to the armchair. The same one that Aurelio had glimpsed? The crushing exhaustion and deadly cold that had been closing in on me a moment before had abruptly disappeared, but the memory remained as a sort of tingling, an involuntary tension in my muscles. I returned to the window. The rain had let up a bit. To the north, I noticed a gap in the clouds, and through it, the remnants of sunset. Had I gone backwards in time? I found the bedroom empty, the bed made, the bathroom immaculate. The smooth surface of the bedspread held the shape of an outstretched body, certainly mine, and an open book: a travelogue through India. I understood that a day of absence had elapsed, that it was already Sunday evening. I turned on the bathroom light and rummaged about in the metal trashcan in search of a used condom. Instead, I found a crumpled up piece of paper, a note from Fernanda:

Dear Tomás:
Sorry about last night! Thanks for everything. Here's my
cell number. Give me a call sometime.
F.

I smoothed out the paper and left it on the bedside table. Why had I gone straight for the trash can? Was I really looking for a condom or had I gone instinctively to recover the note — a note I had tossed in there myself and about which I remembered nothing? Or did I have a subterranean memory, a subterfuge perpetrated by my consciousness in order to navigate the lapses?

In contrast to my previous return, taking possession of myself was less traumatic and distressing this time around. I processed it with my body, astonished by and grateful for the horizontalness of the floor, the consistent hardness of the wood, the hospitable temperature, the capsule of protection and domesticity the apartment provided. At the same time, I was engulfed by a feeling of overwhelming sadness. I was certain that Aurelio had just died or was dying at that very moment and that Osvaldo had already frozen to death. I knew it the way you know things in dreams. That was one difference from the previous vision. Another was the way I had transmuted into Aurelio instantaneously and completely, with no notion of myself whatsoever, until the very end. What's more, the majority of that doubling had occurred in real time.

I came across Lola in the hallway, her back arched in a stretch and her tail raised in the shape of a question mark. I greeted her fondly, but she headed for the kitchen, ostentatiously ignoring me, irritated that my trips up and down the hallway had disturbed her sleep. On my computer, I confirmed that nearly twenty hours had passed. And Fernanda? Had she awoken early, cleaned the bathroom, put on her still-wet clothes and tiptoed out? Had I called her during the day? I looked through my cellphone but there was no record of any calls. I could have used the landline. Spotlighted in the extensive and hysterical news coverage of the violent storm that had descended on the country that weekend, already causing two deaths and hundreds of injuries, was the news of three young climbers who'd gone missing in the mountains north of Chillán. Their families were alarmed. The climbers had crossed paths with a team of mule-drivers on Friday, so their approximate location was known, but a search operation could not be launched until conditions improved. The storm was expected to let up within the next twelve hours. I looked up their names: brothers Osvaldo and Aurelio Silva. And Ramiro Inostroza. For some reason, as I read the names, I burst into tears. I sobbed uncontrollably. After the episode with Inés, I took refuge in the obsessive certainty that the experience had been given to me for a reason: to intervene in order to save her. But now there was nothing left to do. Her nephews' fate was already sealed.

The sobbing fit and the fact that I'd felt the living room wall in search of a place where I might pass through and return to the mountain and the storm were the first indications that that transition — despite the blessed absence of a panic attack and vomiting — was no less traumatic than the previous one had been. The apartment, which had at first closed around me in a warm, protective embrace, was suddenly squeezing me too tightly. Every room and hallway was a few centimeters too small. And I was finding Lola's company grating. If it hadn't been for the rain, I would have put her out in the courtyard. I locked her in the kitchen instead, but her indignant meowing forced me to open the door. I pulled on a windbreaker and went out for a walk. The traffic on José Miguel de la Barra y Merced was slow, the sidewalks empty. The rain and fresh air revived me. Something of the sensation of being Aurelio remained with me and, once again, I was surprised that, just as it had been when I was Inés, it wasn't all that different from the mundane, everyday consciousness of my own self. That intimate commingling was most distinct in the first minutes following the rupture, when I found myself freed of my own circumstances but not yet subsumed in someone else's. For some reason, I associated it with different modalities of myself, with the various roles I'd been forced, like everyone else, to perform: Tomás the good student, conciliatory, anxious in the face of failure or success; Tomás the pitcher of ad campaigns, arrogant, ironic, secret improviser; the efficient boss, paternalistic, workaholic, controlling, seducer; the obsessive-compulsive, greedy for food, sex, gadgets; the friend; the husband; the lover; the whiner; the miser; the dreamer; the observer; the owner of Lola. The current self was no more different from Aurelio than he was from the Tomás attending a rock concert or paying a bill. As I reconstructed them in my memory and imagination, I found the junctures between those gear changes painful, jarring. But as I recalled them, I was also recovering a degree of self-possession. And, instead of undermining me, they lent a greater density to Aurelio's experience. Despite how faint the difference of being someone else felt, it was also a form of freedom, I thought; a gift.

Once again, I was overcome with the certainty that

these episodes had been given to me (or inflicted upon me) for a reason. The repetition was an insistence. I had to be able to decipher the signs beyond the obvious connection between Inés and her nephews, to learn a lesson that could then, I was certain, be translated into decisive action. It was possible that the transposition of identities acted like a kind of disguise that allowed me to observe certain events from perspectives inaccessible to my regular self, or that it was a test or a preparation for something, that I must complete a task that could only be accomplished from unexpected angles. Whatever it was, I needed to find a logic, a pattern. The differences between the two episodes (one gradual and the other sudden, one situated in the future and the other in the present) suggested that there *was* one. It was possible that, over time, I would be able to direct the phenomenon in the same way one can learn to steer the course of a dream. Perhaps, just as I had inhabited the skins of Inés and Aurelio, other men and women had been my "guests," or were doing so at that very moment, I thought, without my knowing it, maybe even subtly altering my decisions. I imagined a web, a system of exchanges or superimpositions of consciousnesses — which, in my fantasy, took the form of a tree's root system, with a central core splitting into countless branches — a subterranean labyrinth I'd been allowed to glimpse, perhaps by accident, through a sort of back channel. Maybe it was possible to trace or uncover a map, a design. My modest portion of that map was drawn, I was sure, by the communicating vessels of Inés, Osvaldo and Aurelio, causal junctions that had not yet been revealed to me but through which I would be able to eventually figure out the rules of the game.

When I returned to the apartment, shortly before midnight, I was seized by a foolish desire to talk to someone, to confess. I called Manuel. He answered, shouting into the phone from a jazz club in Bellavista.

"Dude, come down here!" he yelled.

The music was deafening; he must have been right next to a speaker. I thought I recognized a piece by Thelonious Monk.

"Who are you with?"

"With Trini?"

"Who's Trini?" I asked. She must be the woman from the night before, the friend of his date.

"What do you mean, who's Trini?" he shouted over the guttural strains of a saxophone. "It's my friend Tomás. He's asking who Trini is."

"Hi," shouted a female voice, "I'm Trini."

She sounded at least as drunk as Manuel, maybe more.

"Nice to meet you."

"What's your name?"

"Tomás."

"Tomás. We'll wait for you."

"Are you two alone?"

"Yeah, but come anyway."

"Ok. Bye."

I hung up. I went to the bedroom to look for Fernanda's note. I dialed the number. A male voice answered.

"Hello?"

"Sorry," I said. "Wrong number."

"Who do you want to talk to?"

"No, wrong number."

"Tomás Ugarte?" said the guy.

"Yes."

"Fuck you. If you call this number again I'll kill you."

I froze. I tried to think of something to say, but he hung up. I went back to my desk and, in a notebook, the same one from which Fernanda had ripped a page in order to write her note, I wrote down the date, time and a brief description of my call to Manuel (and Trini) and my conversation with…Nicolás? From now on I was going to keep a diary; or better, a logbook of brief entries. There was no guarantee that I would remember those events in the future or even the act itself of writing them down in the notebook. But I had to preserve, through that logbook, at least some minimum of temporal continuity.

I couldn't sleep that night. Lola demanded that I open the kitchen window and, despite the rain, she disappeared into the night, unable to tolerate my agitation. I decided to write a detailed account of both episodes. First the Aurelio episode, as it was fresh in my mind, and then the Inés episode. I composed a few sentences. I erased them. I found myself irritated by the brightness of the screen, the pulsating cursor. My mind would not fall into sync with the rhythm of writing. The content seemed so banal: the mere consignation of the impossible. I took a bath, tempting fate. I made myself some scrambled eggs, thinking of Inés. There were only two beers left in the refrigerator. I went out to buy more at the liquor store. It was already closed, so I had to go to another one, farther away. When I returned, I scribbled "liquor store" in my logbook. At three in the morning, I got into bed. Lying face down, I let myself fall into sleep as though dropping off the edge of a cliff, but I started awake after a fraction of a second with a shudder of vertigo. I was awake, implacably lucid. I went to the kitchen, opened a fresh beer and stood at the threshold to the living room. I tried to recall the instant just before the blackout, but I couldn't pinpoint anything out of the ordinary. Literally, in the blink of an eye, I was Aurelio. As I paced about the parquet floor, just as during my long walk in the rain, I was struck every now and then by a feeling of imminence — a slight shift in the electrical charge in the air surrounding my body, a thin, inaudible crackling — and I flinched as though anticipating a physical blow. But nothing happened. At the same time, I feared I was suffering infinitesimal lapses of memory, just beneath the level of consciousness. I suspected that the constant flow of my perceptions and ideas was nothing more than an illusion. I had to resist the maniacal impulse to write everything down, to account for every minute. I wrote down the word "insomnia" and closed the notebook.

I finally fell asleep at dawn, by which time the rain had stopped and big holes were opening up in the mass of clouds. I slept for half an hour. I was awoken by the silent presence of Lola, who had come to demand her breakfast and was waiting motionless, like a statue, at the foot of the bed. Mid-morning, Fernanda called.

"Tomás, I'm sorry about last night. And about Saturday. How embarrassing!"

"Don't worry about it."

"Thanks for taking care of me. That was so nice of you. I mean it."

I could hear techno music playing in the background.

"Where are you?"

"At the gym," she said. "Nico monitors my cellphone."

"I'd like to see you."

"I can't, Tomás."

Fernanda sighed. I refrained from asking her for details about the night she'd slept in my apartment. She was the privileged witness to what had doubtlessly been a perfectly banal scene and wouldn't shed any light whatsoever on the mystery of the doublings. She'd surely found me snoring on the sofa and had left discreetly. That was all.

"I'm back together with Nico," she announced, her voice at once proud and hesitant.

"Oh, come on."

"He promised he'd never do it again."

"Do what? Hit you or cheat on you?"

"Neither," she replied, pretending not to have noticed my sarcasm.

"Good for you."

"Do you hate me?"

"No, not at all. Are you happy?"

"Very. I think we're really gonna make it work this time."

I remembered Nico's threat from the night before. Someone should rescue Fernanda from that loser, but I wasn't the right person for the job and it wasn't the right time either. It would be Nico himself and the passage of time that would do it. Fernanda was about to embark on a long and arduous journey.

"Good for you," I said again from somewhere far away.

"Tomás, I have to go," she said nervously. "Thanks again."

"You're welcome."

Lola didn't come back at all that day. Or the next. I was afraid that something had happened to her. Or that she had abandoned me. This idea brought with it a feeling of guilty relief similar to the way I'd felt when Inés had fled or, more precisely, when I thought she might flee before it had actually happened. But no, I told myself, Lola hadn't left me. Not yet. She was just demonstrating her independence. I'm young, I'm beautiful, I'm fast, I can hunt, I can adopt another house and another owner, I can take care of myself. I left the window open, propping it ajar with a flowerpot. Lola didn't touch her food or water. The apartment was becoming progressively unbearable, the walls closed in on me, expelling me as though from a contracting bodily cavity. It was due in part, I thought, to the fact that all of the episodes had begun there. Maybe the map, the contours of which I had intuited out in the rain, was a grid of sensitive points, access thresholds, one of which was located, at that time, in the apartment on Rosal Street. What I knew for certain was that I felt calmer, more lucid outside in the fresh air, wandering around the neighborhood, lounging on benches in the park, people watching, or standing near bus stops, pretending to be waiting for the bus. I would only return to the apartment at dawn, to doze for a few hours on top of the bed, write a few terse sentences in my diary and wait, no longer holding out hope for Lola to return. Her disappearance affected me more than I was willing to admit to myself and led me to consider to what extent that responsibility, as minimal as it may have been, was a scaffold that had kept me whole and functional. That's what work had been and what a daughter would have been, had I given into Paula's incessant pressure. Without even the minimal anchor of my morning rituals for the cat, I was beginning to drift.

One night, very late, as I passed a small cluster of people standing outside the Catedral Bar, a guy bumped into me. I saw, out of the corner of my eye, another guy moving in to take my wallet, then decide against it when he realized that I was less drunk than he'd assumed. After that, I started leaving my cellphone and wallet on the bedside table, taking only a bit of cash, the key to the apartment and my ID along with me on my meanderings. Over the course of my zigzagging rambles I began to feel gently sucked in by a gravitational force, imperceptible to everyone else. I sensed that the episodes were gaining ground inside me, integrating themselves like drops of mercury. The intervals of memory felt like flaws or ruptures in the continuity of things, slight fissures that were always there, imperceptible, until they began to expand.

I was aware that I was moving across a grid — which did not correspond to the layout of the city — made up of paths that grew ever narrower, leaving inevitably widening dead spaces between them. I would end up balancing, if I was lucky, upon a spider's web of thin lines, tight wires that would, in turn, disintegrate, occasioning the definitive fall, the ultimate collapse. This was everyone's fate, but only I was constantly, minutely, intolerably aware of it. In contrast to this, everything around me seemed devoid of density. I felt like an intruder. I told myself every second that I could easily not be there, that every step could cast me into the void and that when I fell, the city would close up around me, leaving no trace or scar. Sometimes I sensed that real time was that future of invisibility, of absence, and that the present was nothing more than its memory, a faint shadow.

One night I drifted downtown, crossed Alameda and continued south along San Diego and Arturo Prat. I walked past the ATM, which had been repaired and now gleamed aseptically, a box of immaculate light, free of the signs of deterioration that consumed the rest of the bank. I decided not to return to the apartment. This imbued me with a strange feeling of freedom, conscious that I was letting go of one of my final footholds, that from then on it was going to be more and more difficult for me to return. I went into a café and ordered a hot dog and a draft beer. I was only able to finish half of the hot dog. I went into the bathroom. I peed. I wet my hair, studying my image in the cloudy mirror. I'd lost weight, I thought. Suddenly, for a few seconds, I didn't know who was observing whom. I raised my hand to touch one of my cheeks and I didn't know if it was my left or my right. I had the impression that the mirror was vibrating slightly, that the surface enclosing the reflection advanced and retreated like a lens coming into focus, that the room was spinning around itself in an irregular rhythm, an unspecified number of times, such that I lost my bearings. In which direction was the street? Which way had I come in? I closed my eyes. I leaned over the dirty sink and washed my face, feeling the water spill across my chest, staining my shirt. I felt for the door. I glanced sidelong into the mirror one last time, anticipating the other's gaze, suspicious of a smile that wasn't mine. I left the café. The cold air revived me, although my heart still beat in alarm. I sat down to rest at a bus stop. It was about a twenty-minute walk to the apartment, but there was no going back. It was late. A police car passed by with its headlights off. Further down the block, on the other side of the street, the lights of a strip club flashed, framing the intermittent outline of a neon pin-up girl. I started walking. The bouncer at the strip club called out to me from across the street, but I ignored him. I came to the Plaza Almagro and turned west, moving along the edge of the construction zone. The shadows under the trees created vast dark regions inside which you could make out the silhouettes of couples or small groups. I came to the winos' cluster of benches. Five or six bodies lay stretched out on mattresses or on the grass, wrapped in blankets and jackets and ratty down quilts against the autumn cold. The parking lot was almost empty and the booth, deserted. Following a vague memory, I crept into the space between the privet hedge and the fence encircling the vacant lot. I came to a small, natural niche inside the hedge, where the old woman had stashed plastic bags of clothing and an old, dirt-encrusted sleeping pad in among the branches. I spread it out on the ground and lay down. It smelled exactly like Inés. A vile stench, worse than animal, predominated by shit and two or three layers of rancid urine. After a few minutes I got used to it, or else resigned myself to it. Lying on my side, in the fetal position, I closed my eyes. More than an homage to Inés or a penance for the damage I'd done, I felt that this was a way of settling a debt with her; that cavity was a vanishing point, an imperfect approximation of the place to which she tried to return and to which she perhaps had returned.

The cold woke me long before dawn. I left everything as I'd found it and left the plaza, which was deserted. I was shaking. Even walking quickly, it took me a long time to warm up. My steps led me instinctively toward the apartment, tracing the route Inés had taken. I came to the arcade with the print shop, but the gate was locked. I pushed against it, testing the strength of the lock. A caretaker appeared around the bend of the arcade. I waved at him and walked away. I turned the corner and went back to the ATM. This was not the final goodbye, I promised Inés. I'd bring her flowers tomorrow. And I'd sleep in her spot. Why not? I went back to my neighborhood, but I resisted the temptation to go home. It seemed too easy. Comforts were a trap. For how long? What was I trying to prove with this? To whom? When the shops opened, I bought a notepad and a pencil and recorded the events of the past twenty-four hours. That day I cut across Bellavista and walked along the river until I came to Pedro de Valdivia Norte, to our old building. I felt ashamed that I hadn't thought of Paula that entire time. I called Alejandra from a pay phone. I left a message on the machine, sensing that my ex-mother-in-law was listening to me, and I was surprised that my voice didn't sound any different.

That night, I decided to go back to Inés' spot, but by the time I got to the Parque Forestal, I found that I was exhausted. I sat down on the grass with my back against a tree, seeking shelter from the frigid wind that whipped the first dry leaves from the trees. It was six in the evening and the temperature had dropped abruptly. I was wearing only a t-shirt and a button-down and my throat had started to hurt from the chill of the previous night. I would have to go back. I decided to strike up a conversation with the vagrants who lived in the park. Maybe one of them could offer me a clue. I imagined a guild of telepathic mendicants, secret masters of the world who condescended to appear just the opposite. I didn't come away with anything useful. Despite my disheveled appearance, I didn't blend in with them. Not yet. They recognized me as an imposter, an intruder. To me they seemed like casualties from an unnamed war or some vast process that neither they nor I could glimpse in its entirety. I initiated a conversation with an old man with long, gray hair and a white beard. I walked with him to a shop on Merced and, by his gait, I understood that he was younger than I had thought. He insisted that I buy him wine and, when I refused, he shouted insults at me. I was just a few steps away from my building, but I headed for the park again. My legs hurt. I stretched out on the grass and fell asleep. I was awoken by a hand rummaging in my pants pocket. Five teenagers stood around me. One of them had extracted a thin wad of bills. I sat up abruptly.

"Hey, man, take it easy," one of them said.

My sudden movement had alarmed them.

"You got good reflexes for being wasted."

"He's not wasted, huevón."

"I said take it easy," the first one who'd spoken put in. "You know what this is?"

He was holding an object in his hand, wrapped in a cloth like a bandage. I said nothing.

"A piece. So don't try any shit."

The one who had robbed me walked away to count the bills in the light of a streetlamp.

"Hey, this dude's loaded," he shouted.

"How much is there?" the one with the gun wanted to know.

"More than a hundred."

"Where'd you get the cash, huevón?"

"It's mine," I said.

I moved to stand up but the guy pointed the gun at me with both hands, very close to my face. I sat back down on the grass and raised my hands.

"Anything else?" asked the one who appeared to be the leader.

The other one ran up to me and went through my pants pockets. I let him. He didn't find the key.

"His ID," he announced, angling it into the light in order to make it out. "Tomás Ignacio Ugarte Jensen. "This fucker's a señorito."

"What are you doing here?" asked the leader. I noticed that the person standing next to him, the only one who hadn't spoken, was a girl.

"Resting."

"Don't you know there are thieves around here?"

The rest of them burst out laughing. They all seemed eager to impress him, but were careful not to overstep in any way. None of them seemed older than fifteen.

"And rapists," insisted the boss.

"Yeah, huevón," added another. "They catch you hanging around here they'll fuck you up the ass."

"Squirrel, hold this for me," said the boss. He handed the gun to one of his companions, who raised it with trembling hands. "If this asshole moves, shoot him in the face."

I closed my eyes. I was surprised by a warm liquid wetting my things, stomach and one shoulder. The boss was pissing on me.

"Don't you fucking move," he warned.

I noticed that the other guy, the one holding the pistol, was no longer aiming at my face and seemed more relaxed. I told myself that it wasn't likely he'd shoot me. I wasn't even sure it was a gun.

"Anyone else need to go to the bathroom?" asked the leader.

No one spoke. The guy yanked the gun out of his companion's hands and adjusted its wrappings. He began to walk away and the others followed suit.

"You got off easy…Tomás Ignacio," he said, turning his back to me.

The thief tossed my ID and it landed in the grass at my feet.

On the way back along José Miguel de la Barra, I saw Bobadilla, one of the copywriters from the agency, coming toward me. Just as he recognized me, I turned and walked off in the direction of Catedral Street.

"Hey, boss!" he shouted behind me, but I pretended not to hear. When I'd turned the corner, I took off running as fast as my aching legs would carry me.

On the parquet floor, behind the door, two notes awaited me: one from Manuel, another from the housekeeper. Lola greeted me with a meow and rubbed against my ankles. Moved to tears, I took off my shoes and got into the shower fully clothed.

When I got out of the shower I felt feverish. I gave the cat food and water. I threw the contents of the refrigerator and the wet clothes into the trash. I made myself pasta with tomato sauce. There were seven messages on the answering machine. The first five were from

Manuel: two from the restaurant where we'd agreed to meet, three over the following days from his office. They followed a contiguous arc, beginning with impatience, passing through concern, and on to alarm. He'd come to the apartment building a few days before, spoken with the super and left a terse note under my door. Where are you, buddy? Call me, Manuel. The sixth message was from my lawyer, reminding me that the determination hearing was scheduled for Thursday of the following week. My flight was on Friday. I had nine days left before my trip, three days until my move. After the final beep, I was surprised to hear Alejandra's voice:

"Tomás. Are you there? It's Ale. I got your message. Call me if you hear from Paula. I'm really worried. Thank you. Bye."

I dialed the number. It was only when I heard her groggy voice that I realized it was one in the morning.

"Hello, Paula?"

"Alejandra, I'm sorry to call you so late."

"It's okay," she said with some difficulty. "Have you heard anything?"

"What happened?"

My ex-mother-in-law was silent for a moment.

"Tomás, it's one in the morning," she declared, more awake now and indignant.

"I'm sorry. I didn't realize it was so late."

She sighed.

"Paula arrived early Monday morning from Spain. She stayed in the apartment resting and sleeping. She looked terrible, I won't mince words. Yesterday after-noon she left in the car. She said she was going out with Bárbara. I haven't heard from her since," she said in a frightened voice. "Her cellphone is off. Bárbara didn't see her yesterday. She didn't even know she'd come back.

Since you called, I thought maybe she was with you."

"No, I haven't seen her."

"Do you have any idea where she might be?"

I remembered the trip north, the job.

"No," I said. "But if I were you, I wouldn't worry."

"You wouldn't?"

"I think Paula needs some time alone to process everything with Mariana."

"You think?"

"The death of your only sister, a sister you're only just getting to know, is no small thing."

Alejandra appeared to be digesting this idea. This whole exchange obeyed a dynamic established long before: me trying to erect a protective barrier between Alejandra and her daughter, safeguarding Paula's privacy, giving her room to breathe.

"How was the funeral?" I asked.

"She didn't tell me much," replied Alejandra, distracted. "Just that the mother and a few friends were there."

Another silence.

"Let me know if you hear from her, okay?"

"You too," I said.

"Okay."

"Don't worry about Paula. She's a grown woman and knows how to handle herself."

I can take care of myself, Inés had said.

"But why would she have changed plans like that, without telling anyone?"

"It gives you an idea of how much this has impacted her."

"Good night, Tomás. Thanks for calling."

I hung up.

The next day, my fever was higher and my throat hurt. I should have come back and gotten a jacket, I thought.

The kid from the night before was right: I'd gotten off easy. I wasn't built for life on the streets. One grows accustomed to everything (probably those episodes would come to seem normal; I'd come to accept them as a chronic and tolerable condition, a minor ill in comparison to other, more radical forms of mental or physical disintegration, and not as what they really were: transit points toward something unknown), but it would take a long time for me to assimilate with the vagrants in the park. And it wasn't a goal worth pursuing. There were other, less laborious or contrived methods of self-destruction. It wasn't my fate to follow in Inés' footsteps. In the apartment, despite the latent risk of another absence, I felt safe. I remembered the climbers. I combed through the daily papers from the past two weeks and reconstructed the search carried out by the police and the Andean Rescue Corps; the photos distributed among the villages in the region; the discovery of Ramiro, unconscious in the tent, buried beneath six feet of snow, whose life they had saved despite acute hypothermia and dehydration; the failure to find (after a certain point they began to be referred to as "the bodies of") Aurelio and Osvaldo, who would probably surface with the spring thaw. I studied the photos carefully, surprised and relieved by the absence of any resemblance between me and Osvaldo.

I called Manuel's agency. The receptionist put me on hold and then my friend's voice came on, erupting in a cry of joy. I told him that I'd been sick, that I still was, but we agreed to meet for lunch at the Japanese restaurant. I spent the rest of the morning transcribing the tremulous notations from the notepad to the logbook, unwinding the skein of temporal continuity. Lola capped off our reunion by offering me a decapitated bird.

On my way to the restaurant, I went into a barbershop

and got a haircut. My feverish eyes in the mirror reminded me of the episode two days before, in San Diego. Now
I had no doubt which was the real barber and which his
reflection, but I felt afloat inside the fever, which rocked
the barber chair in gentle waves. Manuel arrived at the
restaurant uncharacteristically on time. He made an effort
to hide his concern or dismay at the sight of me. His sarcasm from two months before with respect to my midlife
crisis had vanished. His somewhat affected cheerfulness
communicated that this was a serious matter. We settled
down on a tatami mat. Manuel ordered a veritable ban-
quet. Also an Asahi and the best sake on the menu.

"Sushi is the new junk food," he declared with a wide
smile after the waiter had left.

I apologized for my disappearance the week before,
but I didn't offer many details.

"How's Trini?"

It took him a fraction of a second to recognize the name.

"Oh, Trini," he said without enthusiasm. "It didn't
pan out."

The waiter brought Manuel's Asahi and my mineral
water. Manuel downed the beer nearly in one gulp.

"You look thinner, dude," he said anxiously. "The time
off has been good for you. When are you planning to go
back to work? I know of at least two agencies that would
be interested in talking to you today."

"I'm going on a trip. I leave next Friday."

"You did mention that the day of the divorce hearing,"
Manuel allowed.

The sake arrived. He poured two cups.

"Salud."

He tossed his back. He poured himself another.

"I'm flying to Paris," I said. "The idea is to go by train
from there to Spain: Barcelona, Madrid, Granada."

"Will you see Paula in Madrid?"

"No. From Spain, I'll cross over to Morocco. From there, I'll probably take a flight to Cairo, although I'd like to do part of the trip overland. Then I'm thinking I'll go from Tunisia to Sicily, travel north through Italy and end up back in Paris. I have a plane ticket from London to Bombay in two months."

"Bombay!"

"I don't know how long I'll stay in India. Probably not longer than a year. I also want to go to Nepal and Tibet, if I can."

"It seems like you have it all super planned out."

"As far as you can plan these things."

The sushi arrived. An outlandish amount. I forced myself to swallow a few pieces. Manuel ordered more sake and attacked the tray of sushi, concentrating his full attention on the food. That encounter (which, so far, had been more of a misencounter) served as a reference point, a measure of the length of the journey I'd been on during the nearly two months since we'd last been together in that place, on the night before my birthday. I still didn't know in which direction I'd drifted, but it was clear that it was away from Manuel, among other things. I wondered what the ingredients were that made it possible for my friendship with Sebastián to withstand distance and lapses in communication, ingredients that were clearly lacking in my relationship with Manuel. I now realized just how much our connection had been associated with a certain lifestyle and, above all, with a velocity that I'd disengaged from. We would remain friends only if, at the end of my trip, I went back into advertising. It was ironic that what bound us was our insistent declared hatred of advertising, embodied in the clients, the sum of the mediocrity and idiocy of the entire system; a contempt which, furthermore, was utterly unoriginal, shared as it was by all the creatives. Few in that subculture (in which the words creative, creation, creativity were earnestly used and abused) were advertisers by calling; the contingent was weakly divided into two segments: frustrated filmmakers, writers and artists on one side, and those just passing through on their way to real careers as filmmakers, writers and artists on the other. That resentment — which fed the flow of "creative" energy — was a secondary effect of the guilt that permeated everything and kept the machinery oiled and functioning: the guilt of being an advertiser, the guilt of not being or having what advertisers admonish you to be or to have.

"I guess you haven't heard anything about Paula," I commented, in part to shift the conversation away from myself.

"When was she leaving again?"

"She already went and came back."

Manuel looked at me in surprise, holding a sea urchin roll aloft.

"No shit."

He swallowed the sea urchin and poured himself more sake.

"You know what?" he said. "Ever since you told me Paula's story, I've heard of two other cases of people our age suddenly discovering brothers or sisters. Just the other day, in fact, I ran into an ex-girlfriend's brother at the dentist's office, and he told me their old man had just sprung it on them that they have a brother who's twenty years younger than them. Their father invited him and my ex to lunch and they knew something was up because he was guzzling pisco sours to gather his courage. The kid's mother was an intern in the office where he worked back in the eighties. She had to demand a DNA test to prove paternity. Weird, right?"

"It's everywhere," I said.

"A strange coincidence."

It wasn't really that strange after all, I thought. Anything was possible. That I was, at that very moment, on the brink of hell, that the tatami mat and the table and the strips of gleaming fish were nothing more to me than a thin membrane that threatened to tear apart at any moment, that everything around me could vanish in the blink of an eye and exist only in the memories of the person sitting across from me.

"It might be," I said instead, "like selective brand bias. When you buy a car or a pair of sneakers, it suddenly seems like everyone else you see has the same brand. You become attuned to that frequency."

"Do you want some more sake?" offered Manuel.

I shook my head. He finished the bottle and signaled to the waiter for a third.

"Maybe," he added pensively, "but I think it happens much more often than you might believe. Really, it's a demographic phenomenon: the secret children of the hippie generation, the free love generation."

"I don't think that would make Paula feel any better."

"Do you remember my parents' house on Los Dominicos?" asked Manuel, suddenly drunk. "When my dad built it, in the late sixties, he thought it was the most original, badass thing he'd ever done in his entire life. A fifteen-hundred square foot parcel with fruit trees and a view of Manquehue Hill. It didn't matter that it was a small house. My grandfather was pulling his hair out. Why would you want to be so far away from downtown? That was my old man's great founding gesture, the wager that paid off. That's why, when he had to sell the house after thirty years, he almost couldn't bear to do it. And I believed the story until it occurred to me that going from Providencia to the foothills simply reproduced what had happened in the United States ten or fifteen years earlier: the migration to the suburbs. I said that to him once, when he was already really sick. He told me to go to hell, to put it mildly.

The new bottle of sake arrived. He drank a glass.

"Now that I think about it," he added, "another of the cases I've heard of is really similar to Paula's. After her dad died, a friend's cousin discovered that she had a half-sister. The girl lived in Canada. They connected and it was super emotional. She came to Chile and they went to visit her in Vancouver. And a little while later, the sister was diagnosed with cancer and died within a few months."

Manuel's words came to me warped by a subtle echo, through the fog of the fever which, in some way, reflected or compensated for his drunkenness.

"Paula's dad did the same thing, right?" he persisted.

"Yes," I said. "He made sure he kept the seas parted."

"Do you remember how he used to smoke weed at the table after dinner? He didn't give a fuck."

"Of course I do."

After that we were silent for a while. Manuel finished the sake and asked for the check. He insisted on paying. We hugged goodbye at the door. We agreed to get together sometime before my trip.

I hailed a taxi. I asked the driver to drop me off at a pharmacy on Merced. I waited in line, trying to keep the slight trembling in my legs in check.

"Good afternoon, sir," the clerk smiled at me.

"Hello. I need a — "

EIGHT

I **PAY** for my thirty minutes of Internet. I go out to the street. My hands feel sticky from touching the mouse and keyboard. No message from Cristián Almagro. I had to resist the impulse to reach out to him again. I can't write to him every day. I called his cell yesterday, but he didn't answer. He seems to have vanished into thin air. It's already been a week since I sent him the latest version of the outline. A mere formality. I have lots of creative leeway as long as the story takes place at the station. But he could at least condescend to show some sign of life.

It's early, but I cross Francia Avenue and head for the hot dog shop. I order an Italiano and a mineral water. I eat it standing at the counter. The paper napkins smear the avocado and mayonnaise without absorbing it. The owner of the shop smiles at me. Her daughter has her back to me. After ten days, they treat me as though they've known me my whole life. I had too much beer last night. A bad idea, not only for my workday today, but also because the vibe in the bar was a little threatening. I don't think it had anything to do with me. It's best not to go alone to that kind of dive, but I was already too drunk to care. I suppose I was lucky. I should call Cata. I decide to put it off until after work. I buy a bar of chocolate for dessert and more water to dilute the alcohol still coursing through my veins. I head back to the guesthouse.

My surprise is due not to finding myself suddenly in Valparaíso in Matías' skin, but rather to the different quality of this episode, which I've recognized immediately. In my first transposition (I'm not sure what to call them exactly: displacements? incarnations?) I suddenly found myself in Inés' body, but still in full possession of my own consciousness and memory, which then gradually disappeared as she gained ground. In the case of Aurelio, the exchange was immediate and complete; I had no notion of having been someone else until the final seconds, when sleep was overcoming him, and I returned to myself in the living room on Rosal Street. Now, however, I can see what Matías sees, hear his thoughts, feel the sensations he experiences — the heat of the sun and the hangover and the aftertaste of the hot dog he's just gobbled down — but I'm no more than a witness. I've not merged into him, nor he into me. The seas do not touch. (At the same time, I'm surprised all over again that this intimate communion with another person, this transentience, is so akin to the dialogue going on between the different components or variants of myself, that the certainty of being someone else doesn't differ significantly from the certainty of being, or of having been, myself. I'm still not sure if I've become aware of Matías' actions and circumstances — and Inés and Aurelio's — on a subliminal level, or if they are, in fact, memories, walled off during episodes of amnesia, that I later integrate in a hallucinatory way. Do we all feel like ourselves in the same way, even animals, my cat Lola, cattle at the slaughterhouse?) I don't know Valparaíso well, but I think I remember that there's a defunct funicular on the hill just behind Matías. I urge him to turn around, I whisper it in his ear, so to speak, but he ignores me. I try more modest gestures. Matías, scratch your left cheek, touch the cellphone in the back pocket of your jeans. It's no use. If I were granted some measure of control over his actions, I'd have to warn him of the danger. Hadn't both of my previous experiences ended in violent deaths? I'm afraid that, at any minute, one of the ancient balconies on the avenue's townhouses will break free and come down on his head or that a truck's brakes will go out just when he's looking the other way or that he'll be felled by a heart attack. There's no way for me to warn him. And my motives are not entirely selfless. Perhaps I ought to have drawn some sort of conclusion from my previous experiences and now, in payment for my ineptitude, I won't escape Matías' death alive. It's also possible that, as with Inés, the episode could shift, evolve, that I might be able to communicate something to him through dreams or that I'll melt bit by bit into him. There's nothing to do but wait.

The house smells of fried garlic. Doña Lucrecia appears in the dark hallway. She checks that it's me. She nods. Who else would it be? As far as I know, I'm the only guest. Backlit, I can't see her expression, but I smile half-heartedly. How did you sleep? Very well, thank you. How's the work going? It's going. Would you like something to eat? No, thank you. I walk by her. Through the open door, I glimpse the frayed velvet bedspread, a framed reproduction of a Virgin with a childlike face and the television, on which the morning shows are just ending. I come to the stairs. I'm always the one who ends our brief conversations, with the feeling that I'm tearing through a scrim of guilt and anxiety. The previous afternoon, breaking with the routine established on the very first day, she knocked on my door simply to ask how I was, if I needed anything. She moved as though to enter my room, but I intercepted her on the threshold and all but closed the door in her face. I climb the two uneven flights of stairs too quickly. By the time I make it to the second floor my pulse is throbbing in my temples and a wave of nausea clutches my stomach. I study the photographs arranged around the window frame: the theater, the station with a tank car in front of it, a few shacks that appear to be sinking into the desert. I open the computer. I reread the beginning of the scene I wrote yesterday. Not bad. Why hasn't that bastard Almagro written me? With this one, which won't take me more than half an hour to finish, I'll have four scenes, all from the second act. What I want is to really dive into the crux of the story, start at the beginning. But I need his go-ahead for that. I suppose I could just dive in anyway, though I'd have to make revisions later. And what if they don't like the story? Better to wait. At least for a few more days. This work's getting my juices flowing, in any case.

I hadn't seen Almagro in ten years, since I left the School of Economics to switch into Journalism. He wrote to tell me he had a business proposition. We got together for coffee. I arrived a bit late and I didn't recognize him. I walked right by that bald, stout, round-faced man, already beginning to get angry that he'd stood me up. Throughout our entire conversation, I struggled to associate him with the Cristián from back at the university, with whom the only thing this large man had in common was — in an unsettling way — his voice. He slid his card across the table. Above his name and title (Project Manager) it read: Castor Philanthropies. He told me he represented a non-profit organization established by an individual who wished to remain strictly anonymous. All he could say was that he was Chilean, more or less our age, living in New York and a luminary in the hedge fund world. For personal reasons, he had decided to focus his foundation on three areas of specialization: research

on certain hereditary childhood diseases, ecological con-
servation in the north of Chile, and promotion of the
arts, especially audiovisual projects. This would be the
first film he'd financed. A feature film. He'd been in contact with a producer. Cristián mentioned his name, but I
didn't recognize it. They still hadn't decided on a director.
They wanted me to write the screenplay. I asked why
they'd thought of me. Cristián said it had been his idea.
He used to read my film reviews and had seen my name
as junior screenwriter on a couple of series. He remembered our time at the university and knew he could trust
me, he said. I had absolute freedom to propose a story,
with one condition: the plot must take place in the desert
in the north of Chile and use, as its principal location, an
abandoned train station northwest of Taltal, where there
still stood a theater built by a Welsh railroad magnate, a
minority shareholder of John T. North's, who had died
before seeing it completed. The reasons behind this extravagant requirement were, once again, personal and
private. Cristián had heard it said, he added in a confiden-
tial tone, that the young Chilean millionaire had toured
the north a few years back with his girlfriend at the time
and that the experience had changed the course of his
life. That's all he knew. Cristián proceeded to offer me
an exorbitant sum. I told him, with a mixture of suspicion and greed, that that amount was well above the local
going rate. The now-corpulent Almagro smiled and said
that was usually the case with foundations: not subject to
the rules of competition, they either paid way too much
or way too little. I accepted. Almagro opened a checkbook and paid me an advance of half the agreed-upon
fee. By way of a receipt, he asked me to sign a brief letter written in English, on which appeared, as on the card
and check, the Castor Philanthropies logo. I signed with

a trembling hand. Not so much because the amount was multiple times more than everything I had ever earned in my thirty years of life, but because I'd just been hired to write a screenplay for a full-length feature. My first film!

Cata found it ridiculously corny that I wanted to hole up in a guesthouse in Valparaíso to write. You've seen too many movies, she told me. I explained to her once again that, at least for me, the task of writing encumbers a place. Frustration builds up in an almost physical way. That's why, in our house, I have to move every few days from my desk to the bedroom and then from there to the dining room, to the living room and, weather permitting, to the back yard. Though I do the bulk of my work in the small room adjoining our bedroom that serves as an office and from which I'll be evicted when children arrive, those small relocations are always beneficial. They allow the air to move. They offer me a fresh perspective. Valparaíso is the equivalent but on a larger scale, commensurate with the importance of my task. We'd agreed that I would visit her on the weekends. Or every other weekend, depending on the work. Cata resigned herself to this eccentricity, proud of (and relieved by) my triumph, my lucky break. I'd have to be crazy to think it had been purely a result of my merits as a screenwriter. In any case, I've no doubt that it was the right decision. The work has been going well. With the sole exception of Doña Lucrecia — whose intrusiveness would surely diminish if there were any other guests but which, if it gets worse, will force me to move to a different guesthouse — the lack of distractions, the simplicity of the room and even my nighttime rambles through Valparaíso, all facilitate my concentration on the writing. In just a few days, I finished what I think is the final draft of the outline. All I need is the green light from Almagro and I'll be off and running. If he doesn't take too long getting back to me, I should be able to finish a first draft before the deadline. That is, within the timeframe I'd set for myself. They hadn't given me a date. I reread the beginning of the scene. Here we go.

.

Another surprise, aside from my role as witness to Matías: sometimes I wander away from him. The writing process, for example. For a while, I found it fascinating, both what I could glean of the story he's piecing together as well as the process itself, the combination of planning and improvisation, the way he incorporates dialogue overheard on the street and fragments of conversations with Catalina, with Almagro (ought I to read something into the coincidence between his name and Inés' plaza? Doesn't it mean "Maghrebi?"), and even with Doña Lucrecia. But after a half hour, I started to get bored. I've never considered writing as a profession. At least in comparison with Matías, who's overcome with a euphoric enthusiasm for what he considers the-opportunity-of-a-lifetime, I suffer from a serious attention deficit. Okay, my friend, good work; but how about we turn on the TV or take another walk? What if Almagro's written to you? We could see if we can hack into a neighbor's Wi-Fi so we could do without the cybercafé. After a while, this resistance bore fruit. Or was it just a natural oscillation, comings and goings inside my own hallucination? I separated myself from him. Or, more precisely, I absented myself, as though I had fallen asleep. When I returned (from where?), Matías was lying on the bed, smoking, staring up at the peeling ceiling ornamentation, mentally retracing the succession of events and dialogues from the first act. I immediately recovered his memories from the past two hours and the sense of elapsed time. I decided to check out again; maybe that was the way to get back to being Tomás. But I couldn't do it. I don't know what degree of control I had over that first retreat. I don't know if it will happen again. Resigned, I returned to Matías, grateful for the temporary relief the interruption had provided. It isn't that being him is particularly arduous. I know very well that it could be worse.

I can't stop myself from going back to the cybercafé. It's getting dark outside. The screens seem to emit a single stroboscopic vibration in the dim light of the café, like the windows of a train hurtling at top speed through a tunnel. I sit in the same place as I did this morning. All I have is one message from Cata, acknowledging receipt of my message about my visit to Santiago. Nothing from Almagro. Try to stay cool, don't let on that you're anxious, I think. Wait at least another week before you write to him. You can still write two or three more scenes before you get his approval. I draft a long, recriminatory email. I cut it down to one line, in which I request, once and for all, his go-ahead. I send it. I receive an automatic reply, in English. It says that he is away from his email (it does not indicate until when) and that he will be in touch soon.

I leave the café. I head for a place that sells chicken and fries. The owner, whose apron sports the same grease stains as yesterday, sees me coming and greets me with a wave of an enormous knife. I wave back from the sidewalk but don't go in. I keep walking. I've only been in Valparaíso for ten days and I already feel like a prisoner of habit. I've fallen into a small network of streets, people and places. My new routine has been conducive for work, but when it comes to my free time I'm starting to feel burned out. Maybe it wouldn't be a bad idea to move guesthouses. Maybe one up in the hills. But what if, for some reason, I find I can't write in my new location? That's the whole reason you're here, huevón, away from your wife and your friends and the comforts of home: to focus on your screenplay. I cross Victoria Plaza, one of the borders of my range of action. I keep walking, heading toward the port. The heat of a windless afternoon still radiates from the cobblestones. I realize I've gone out without any cigarettes. I buy a pack in a corner store. I veer off the main street to get away from the traffic. On the narrow side streets I can see staircases climbing torturously up the hillside, forming narrow canyons between wooden walls and sheets of corrugated metal, beneath hanging balconies, eaves, porches and knots of electrical wires. I'd like to climb up there and wander around the architectural chaos (what was that hillside called?) until I get lost. But it's not possible. Valparaíso is a labyrinth slanting to the sea in which, oddly, one can never get lost. The layout of the streets forces me back to the main avenue. I go into a bar and buy a beer and a sandwich. I don't realize how thirsty I am until the bartender sets the beer down in front of me. I drink it straight down. I order another before the sandwich arrives. And a third. By the time I leave it's already night outside. I'm tired. Instead of heading in the direction of Aníbal Pinto Plaza, I retrace my steps back to the guesthouse. I consider heading to the station and catching a bus to Santiago that very night. Not waiting until tomorrow. But it's already late. I take out the keys to the guesthouse. I weigh them in my hand. I go into a bar.

.

Monday morning. Cata drops me off on Apoquindo Avenue. Before going to Valparaíso, I decide to drop by Almagro's office. I head for the address on his card, listed beneath the New York address. I know that Almagro spends most of his time in the States, that this office is nothing more than a landing pad on visits to Santiago.

A new building. Nineteenth floor. The same logo on the door: Castor Philanthropies. No one answers the bell. I go down to the reception desk. The security guards have no information about the employees of that particular office. Their attitude suggests that, if they had such information, they wouldn't necessarily share it with me. As far as they know, there's no one around. I go out to the street. I walk toward the metro, heading for the bus terminal.

Stepping out onto the street, Matías lights a cigarette. He walks for a while, head down, lost in thought, brooding over Almagro and his inexplicable disappearance. Just a few weeks ago this project was of the utmost urgency, he thinks, and now Cristián appears to have forgotten all about it. That's what happens with every job, I'd like to tell him, no one pays any attention to you for weeks or months and then, all of a sudden, they want it done yesterday. Be thankful for your freedom and quit complaining. Matías turns his head to get a look at an attractive young woman as she passes by. She has blonde dreadlocks and rings on every finger like brass knuckles and a tattoo of a sun around her belly button. For a moment, Matías studies his own reflection in the glass front of a building. Looking back toward the entrance to the metro station, sweeping his eyes along the sidewalk, he finds himself face to face with me, Tomás Ugarte. We pass one another with complete indifference. I will him to turn around, to look carefully at that guy in a dark shirt and suit, but he doesn't do it. I saw myself disappear out of the corner of his eye, with that strange sense of half-recognition we feel seeing ourselves on video, an angle different from the two-dimensional image we see in mirrors. If we've just passed each other and I'm accompanying Matías — his guest or his prisoner — who is the other man? What is he thinking about? Where will his

memories end up? Possibly I've just had the privilege of
seeing myself during one of my blackouts, during which
everything functions normally except that, at some point,
my memory will erase a complete sequence of recent rec-
ollections, leaving me with the impression of having leapt
through time and space. Or is it that, during these dreams
or visions, I am in fact transported into another body and
my own body goes on functioning like an automaton,
blindly going about its routines? Now that I think about
it, it seems to me that I put on that suit and gray shirt last
month. Yes, the account executive at the bank had called
me in to discuss what turned out to be some minor issue and, at the last minute, as I headed out, I'd opted for
the suit. Matías walks down the steps to the metro. I try
to concentrate on that block, that staircase, but nothing
has survived in my memory, not even the blonde woman
with the dreadlocks who was walking a few steps ahead
of me. I try to visualize Matías' face, but only manage
to see him in the guesthouse's bathroom mirror, shaving.
This means that the episodes can also take me to the past.
It's possible that there's a sequence: Inés's journey was
premonitory, while Aurelio's, as far as I know, seems to
have taken place in real time. I'm going backwards. Why?
What threads do I need to connect? Maybe there is no
lesson to be learned (or if there is, could my own impulse
to seek it out be driving it away?), no pattern. Matías
steps into a mostly-empty metro car. We're on our way
to board a bus that he took a month ago to Valparaíso. I
hope it didn't crash.

.

I write. Yesterday, when I got back from Santiago, I
felt a little tired and decided to take the afternoon off.
I played the tourist. I visited the Plaza Sotomayor, the
port, the Artillería funicular, the Iglesia de la Matriz, the

El Peral funicular, the Paseo Yugoslavo and most of Cerro Alegre. A college friend studied architecture here and had lived in a huge old house with seven or eight housemates. I used to come on the weekends and spend the night in a sleeping bag in the loft, whose only window looked out on the entire curve of the bay. They threw a wild New Year's Eve party in that house every year that started with everyone perched on the roof like vultures to watch the fireworks, more or less aware that a fall would land us on the cobblestones fifty feet below. I remembered one party in particular at which, before midnight, we drank an entire bottle of mescal, worm included, with Gabriel, one of the housemates. Gabriel lay down for a minute to rest on his bed — a mattress thrown down on the hard-wood floor — and he fell asleep. Then I made out with a woman in the darkness of the dance floor who turned out to be his girlfriend. The only dark spot in my memory of the house — which I wasn't, in fact, able to find — was the kitchen. A narrow, poorly ventilated space where dirty dishes piled up in geological layers and the stench of rotten food had been absorbed into the walls. I wandered for a while around Cerro Alegre, a bit run-down ten years ago but filled now with designer shops, boutiques, tea rooms and bed & breakfasts, their corrugated metal walls painted in bright colors. A stage set for tourists. And I, of course, was one of them.

In an extraordinary coincidence, I ran into Gabriel in Cerro Concepción. My stunned assertion that I had just been thinking about him sounded fake. We had coffee. Gabriel hadn't changed at all: the straight, black hair pulled back in a ponytail, the goatee, the melancholy ex-pression that was once an affectation but now seemed to have settled as a permanent feature. He's a professor in the School of Architecture. I told him about my screenplay and he seemed interested. I don't really know why, but I became quite garrulous. I told him the plot in great detail, something that — out of superstition — I hadn't even shared with Cata. It's a road movie, I said. Four characters travel — separately and for different reasons — to the desert and they cross paths at different points along the way, converging on an old train station. A thirty-five-year-old woman, a music professor, separated from her husband, whose son has just died of a strange illness. A twenty-eight-year-old publicist (inspired by Cata, which I don't mention), in the midst of a professional, emotional and existential crisis. A twenty-three-year-old guy from Concepción, recently graduated from architecture school, who's just quit a rock band headed up by his brother because he had an affair with that brother's wife. An older man, in his seventies, moved by mysterious motivations. The movie, I said, pieces together these parallel stories that will all intersect in the north. Until deep into the second act, the audience doesn't suspect that it has to do with the strange influence an abandoned house, an old theater, is exerting on the characters. The house has some unsettling characteristics: it's only possible to see the back of the house at close range. If you move even a short distance away, the house — because of refracting light and the fact that all four sides are nearly identical — seems to rotate to face you. Although it's weather-beaten by sun and wind, it's curiously intact, down to the last windowpane. From one day to the next, the empty rooms appear to undergo slight changes in size, to gain or to lose ground. The house is situated in the exact center of an uninhabited circle, one hundred and thirty-three kilometers in diameter. The townspeople — mostly miners — who live along the perimeter, ignore the house's existence... At this point I broke off. Gabriel appeared to have lost interest. It sounds like a horror movie, he said. But it isn't, I insisted, not at all. It's a classic road movie, with a gothic feel. The house's influence can be benevolent, depending on the person and the set of circumstances. It acts as a catalyst, I said. I'd been improvising most of the details on the fly as I spoke. I'd felt a sudden inspiration connected to my memories of the big house in Cerro Alegre, and I was running with it. So what happens then, how does it end?, he wanted to know. I don't know yet, I said. I left it open-ended in the outline, the plot summary I sent to the producers. All I know is that one of the characters (the young guy) will take over the life-long project of the other man (the old guy). I still need to fine-tune a few details. Aside from that, I said, all I need to do is write it down.

With memories of that party — and Gabriel's ex-girl-friend — fresh in my mind, I bought a bottle of tequila on my way back to the guesthouse. They didn't have any mescal. Now the bottle sits on the table, next to the computer, within easy reach. I write. Instead of using the glass left upside-down in front of the bathroom mirror, every so often I take a pull straight from the bottle. Not so much that it affects the writing, but enough to situate me at a certain angle in relation to this room, to the window looking out over the back patio of the next building over, to the photos, the table and the computer. This morning I woke up early, not having touched the tequila the night before. I carried out the ritual of checking my email in the cybercafé. Nothing from Almagro. In this way a secret ultimatum was fulfilled. I left the café to go write. The first act. The first scene. The little boy's death.

.

Torrential rain and huge swells out to sea. "April showers bring May flowers," Doña Lucrecia intones. I write and write. I've been working furiously for two weeks.

I've established a new routine, which my hostess has respected without question. In any case, she had a new guest to focus her attention on. A thin man with a mustache whom I ran into one day on the staircase. He stayed three or four days, in town for business. I wake up early. I go out for breakfast at the spot on the corner, where I also buy a sandwich for lunch. I wait for the cybercafé to open. I check my email. (I have resisted the temptation to write to Almagro.) I return to the guesthouse. I make coffee in the kitchen. I fill the thermos. I shut myself up in my room. I work all morning and most of the afternoon. Around six I go out for a walk to clear my head. I eat something for dinner. I'm back at the guesthouse by ten at the latest. I dedicate half an hour to preparing what I'll write the next day. Then I do it all over again. I write without stopping. I haven't even interrupted the routine in order to visit Cata. Last night we talked for a long time over the phone. Things are tough at the agency. She can't stand her boss, the creative director. Unquestionably brilliant at publicity but stunted when it comes to interpersonal relationships. An abrasive woman, given to throwing tantrums. I told her that if things didn't change, she should quit in a week. That cheered her up. I miss you, she said. Gabriel called to invite me to dinner, but I put him off. I'm superstitiously afraid that any change at all in my routine could affect the work.

I write and I write and I write. The story changes a bit as I go, but for the most part follows the sketch I'd laid out during my fortuitous encounter with Gabriel. Certain stretches unfold at such break-neck pace that I can barely keep up, seeming to obey an impulse and momentum independent from me. I'm so deeply immersed that everything else — Cata, Almagro, Doña Lucrecia, Valparaíso, the rain, the guesthouse, this room, the desk, even the idea of the task itself — fades, vanishes. At certain moments I have the impression that the world I'm delving into is more real than the one that surrounds me when I come out of my work trance.

.

I finished the screenplay yesterday. I typed the word "CREDITS" just after two in the afternoon. I called Cata to tell her that I'd be coming back to Santiago this evening. She's still reeling from the death of her ex-boyfriend, Osvaldo, who went missing in a storm in the southern mountains last week. I sent an email to Almagro. I received the same automatic reply. It's been six weeks since I last heard from him. Doña Lucrecia invited me to lunch by way of a send-off. She's making a cazuela. I paid her this week with a bank transfer from Cata. She's going to loan me cash for the bus fare.

Last night I decided to celebrate over a few beers at the neighborhood bar, the same dive I'd gone to weeks before. The place was empty. I went up to the bar and ordered a beer from a bartender who looked about eighteen and who didn't remember me from my previous visit. In truth, I didn't remember much from my previous visit. It might even have been a different place. A heavyset woman wearing a miniskirt was perched on the stool next to mine and suggested I buy her a drink. Maybe some other time, I said. I downed the beer and headed for the door. The bartender intercepted me. He informed me that, since I had been drinking with the lady, I would have to pay for her drinks as well. The tab was exorbitant, obviously meant to compensate for a slow night. I tried to shove my way past him, but two more guys stepped in to restrain me. I threatened to call the cops. Then I realized that one of them was a cop. I had no choice but to pay. They let me leave, hurling threats and insults. I went into the bar next door. I guzzled two beers under the harsh fluorescent light, trying to calm my frustration. I went out to the street. Someone hugged me and patted me affectionately on the back. How's it going, man, what's up? How's it going? I said. We walked a few feet like this, his arm still around my shoulders. Then he walked away from me. I saw that it was the bartender. He was holding my wallet. He removed the bills, an expression of disappointment on his face. He dropped the wallet to the ground. Hey… I started to say, but another guy shoved me hard into an alleyway. He punched me in the stomach. He started shouting that I'd puked on his sneakers and that they were going to kill me. Suddenly, all four of them (I think there were four of them) disappeared running down the alleyway. I staggered toward the main street and peeked out. I saw a police van stopped outside the bar with its lights flashing. I walked over to the cops. I tried to explain that I'd just been assaulted. I recognized the cop who'd shaken me down in the bar. I couldn't find the wallet. They loaded me into the back of the van and took me down to the station to file a report.

I finish closing up the suitcases, including the bag holding my computer and the script. Doña Lucrecia knocks on the door. Lunch is ready.

·

For long stretches of time, days and even entire weeks, I disengage completely from Matías. I sink into a darkness from which I fear I'll never emerge. When it happens, I have no sense of the passage of time, but Matías' profuse, incessant interior voice — despite the fact that he's a rather quiet guy — keeps me up to date on what happened during those blank segments. Sometimes, coming back from that black zone, I have the fleeting, ineffable sensation of having in some way drawn close to Tomás.

Possibly he senses, in dreams, a disembodied version of himself accompanying him in the darkness, whom he confuses or merges, in his unconscious state, with the stealthy presence of the cat. What is Tomás up to? What am I up to? Am I still worrying about Paula's breakdown? This has been, far and away, the longest episode. It's already been a month. Should I see this, coupled with the passage from the future (Inés) to the past, as a progression? Is the length of this episode a herald of other, even longer episodes, leading to the final one? Of course, the duration doesn't correspond with the ruptures in Tomás' life. This might last a year, only to discover upon my return — if there is a return — that in my other life, my real life, no more than a few days or hours or minutes have passed. As time passes, though I don't become one with Matías, I don't confuse his memories for my own, I'm attuning my ear in order to hear him. Aside from his principal voice — torrential, clear, even resonant — I think I can make out other voices in the spaces in between. I wonder if I'll eventually be able to communicate with them, to shape their behavior. Those voices remain mostly silent, but I know they are there, waiting, modulating the main line, interceding, manifesting themselves by means of tiny pauses and inflexions (at times also in writing), in glimmers of irony that are not at all like Matías. For example, from the very start, Matías has been secretly unsettled by the suspicion that there's something off about Almagro, something that taints the purity of his proposal. It isn't embodied as a concrete fear, but rather as a continual, low-level anxiety, interwoven with a degree of guilt over the excessively generous advance. Matías knows that, with certain types of work, payment tends to happen asynchronously; that is, it isn't (it shouldn't be?) concurrent with the work it's meant to compensate.

Thus, in some fields, the relevant figures — who reap the fruits of what they could no longer sow — only appear to be relevant. To receive such an exaggerated sum at his age, in the current stage of his career, is a sort of inverse asynchronicity, one that will surely bring consequences. Something deep down tells him (and it's not me) that the only payment he should have accepted is the satisfaction of the task itself and that even this could have been consumed with moderation; a portion of it postponed. I wonder if a drop of my own resentment has filtered into his sense of unease, interpreted as a part of himself that harbors doubts, that lacks solid footing and conviction. I tell myself that my rancor towards him is due to this deprivation of freedom, to my being his prisoner, but the truth is it's comprised at least in part of envy: sometimes I see in him a younger version of myself, one who still has plenty of options and who's been offered, without deserving it, an opportunity that I never had.

Another strange feature of this long episode, perhaps a by-product of its discontinuous, intermittent nature: I experience it with varying degrees of intensity. Sometimes, when I take up my role as witness to Matías, his voice and the sensations coursing through him come to me tempered, as though through a veil. It has happened that, in the darkness that surrounds me during my absences, I sense his nearness in a certain direction — let's say, up, for example — and when I turn in that direction, I discover that I've lost him and I keep searching blindly for him, until I dissolve once again into the blackness that is also comprised in part of Matías' (and Tomás') oblivion. Or I can get only so close to him: his awareness of himself, his state of mind and his physical sensations form a sort of blotch of colors and smells and temperatures that I perceive with tremendous clarity, down to their last details, but from a distance, like miniatures in a crystal ball. I strain to get closer, but he stays the same size, even shrinking slightly. My eagerness seems to drive him away, like a swimmer whose strokes create waves that propel a floating object away. But most often I have the feeling that all of Matías' facets are muffled, especially his interior voice, in which I recognize a metallic reverberation, an echo. I'm not certain, but I've begun to fear that these oscillations obey a downward trend, a progressive weakening. I don't know if, as my contact with Matías fades away, I will too, and I'll no longer come out on the other side. If this is the beginning of the end.

Since returning to Santiago I've sent five emails to Almagro. Some only a single line, others that stretch into interminable, more or less disconnected paragraphs, in which merge diatribe, reproach, manipulation, threat, insult and the most ludicrous conjectures about the reasons for his disappearance. In response to each email, an automatic reply in English. The same one I've been receiving for almost a month now. Almagro is out of the office, but will be in touch as soon as possible. As soon as possible. What does that even mean after three weeks? That he's had an accident? That he's been abducted and the patrons of Castor Philanthropies haven't decided to pay the ransom? The only thing I know for sure is that, whatever the reason for the collapse of our correspondence, my persistence and abrupt changes in tone are not going to make any difference. The only thing I haven't done is send him the screenplay. It's the last bargaining chip I have left, I think.

I tried to remember the name of the producer Almagro mentioned. It started with an S. Santibáñez, Sandoval, Santoro? I searched the web and found a Santoro on the lists of film and television producers. I called the produc-

tion company where he was a partner. A hostile receptionist informed me that Mr. Santoro was away on a trip.
She didn't know when he'd be back. For two days I tried
to get in touch with Rodrigo Velasco, the other partner,
but no luck. Yesterday I went in person to the production
company and settled down in the reception area to wait
all afternoon, if necessary. If at first the receptionist had
been unfriendly, she now radiated an unmitigated disgust.
After three hours of waiting, Velasco appeared in the reception area to speak with me. He did not invite me into
his office. He was a nervous type, who kept moving his
hands in and out of his pockets. I explained the situation.
The project in the north sounded familiar, but he didn't
have any further information about it. In their company,
Santoro was the producer and he was the director. As far
as he knew, Santoro had never mentioned the possibility that he, Velasco, might direct the film. In any case, at
such an early stage (according to what I'd told him), the
project would be in Santoro's hands, and he was away on
an extended trip across Asia. I asked for Santoro's email
address. He hesitated for a moment and exchanged looks
with the receptionist. With a look of disdain, she slid a
card toward me.

As I walked away something strange happened.
Suddenly, and with total certainty, I knew I was being
watched. I turned around. The street was empty, but the
knowledge that someone was watching me remained.
Covertly, I scrutinized the parked cars, peered through
the windows of the houses. I patted my clothing in search
of a microphone. What if it was all a perverse joke, a set
up? There was no lack of suspicious evidence, beginning
with Almagro's disappearance. The job was too good to
be true. A dream opportunity that completely reversed
my accumulated failures, that aligned, with pinpoint

accuracy, with my fantasies of redemption. How had I not suspected it before? I imagined that every one of my movements over the last few weeks had been recorded in some way. Maybe the anonymous financier was a collector of small, private humiliations. Perhaps he got some strange satisfaction out of manipulating certain people like marionettes, leading them into dead ends. But why had he chosen me? It didn't make sense. Unless I was the sole victim, and his anonymity concealed some link to me. Who would want to take revenge on me? Why? The patron might not even exist. Or Castor Philanthropies, for that matter. Maybe it was all some machination of Almagro's. Had I done something to him at school? Had I embarrassed him in public? Excluded him from a party? I don't remember. It seems unlikely. And what if Cata were involved? Impossible. I thought of Cata and her reservoir of enthusiasm for my future splendor as a screenwriter, which had been drying up, bit by bit, as my bright promise remains unrealized, as I move into my thirties still an up-and-comer. I started walking. I headed for the metro, taking a winding, erratic path, trying hard to shake not just my invisible pursuers, but also the certainty that someone was watching me every step of the way.

When I got home, just as I was about to write to Santoro, Cata told me that Velasco had just called and had left his cell number. I called him. He told me that he'd just spoken with his partner. As it turned out, Cristián Almagro had been in touch with the production company as a representative of a philanthropic entity with a proposal to make a feature-length film located in the Atacama Desert. As if we need another one of those, Velasco added with a little laugh. But it certainly wasn't anything concrete. They hadn't signed any agreements and, according to Santoro, they hadn't heard anything from Almagro for at least a month and a half. He said that Almagro had held meetings with a screenwriter and a photographer, asking the latter to scout and document the architecture of the area where they were planning to film. He had also traveled north to see the location, a train station called Santa Ignacia. As far as Velasco knew, they hadn't chosen a director yet, although Santoro, obviously, had pitched it to him. I asked him if he knew who the photographer was. He did not. He added that he and his partner were very interested in reading the screenplay. I reminded him that my contract was with Almagro. He recommended — with a touch of condescension — that I relax, that I keep in mind that, in this business, only one in ten projects ever sees the light of day.

This is what Cata had been telling me over and over, with growing impatience, ever since my return from Valparaíso: forget about the entire thing until Almagro resurfaces. You have no idea what's going on with him. I'm sure he has more urgent things to deal with than this project, other priorities you know nothing about. You don't need to take it so personally. And anyway, there's nothing you can do about it. What about the rest of the money we agreed on?, I'd asked her that morning over breakfast, my voice harsh. Be happy with what they already paid you, she suggested with the sort of equanimity reserved for other people's problems. Stop investing your time in a project that, as far as we know, will never pan out.

She's right. There's nothing to do but wait. That's what I told her. You're completely right, I said, it's over, we won't speak of it again. Cata told me there was going to be a vigil the following Friday in Temuco in honor of her ex and his younger brother, both of whom had disappeared in the mountains a few weeks before and who were presumed dead. Osvaldo's parents had invited her.

She's leaving tomorrow, by plane. She already told the agency that she was going to take a few days off. It occurred to me then that I might travel too, but in the opposite direction. Visit the location. I don't know why I didn't do it before writing the screenplay. I think I mentioned it during my meeting with Almagro and he'd dismissed it as unnecessary. It's possible that the locals had heard something or might have more information than me about the project. First thing tomorrow, as soon as I get my replacement driver's license, I'm heading north.

.

During this period, aside from pestering Almagro and the partners at the production company, I'd been consumed with the process of recovering my identity: securing a credit report — as well as the police report from Valparaíso — cancelling and renewing my debit, credit, department store and ID cards. Also, on the advice of a lawyer friend, I registered the screenplay with the Intellectual Property Office. The document I'd signed for Almagro didn't mention anything about this aspect of the deal; my signature had simply acknowledged receipt of a sum of money as means of an advance for writing a screenplay. I got up early this morning. I hope this trip brings you some closure, Cata said, smiling, her eyes still closed. Me too. I'm going to miss you, she said. She kissed me. We ended up making love. I got to the Civil Registry to pick up my ID card before they were even open. I went down to the Municipal office to renew my driver's license. I was on the road before noon.

I've just passed a police cruiser, half hidden in the shade of a willow tree. I glimpsed one of the cops pointing a radar gun towards the south. A hill. I think I was going a couple miles over the speed limit, but I expect they'll let it slide. It's not a great idea to have sex before a long trip. By the time I got to Til-Til, an oppressive torpor had come over me. Even through my sunglasses the glare is blinding. It mingles with my drowsiness and the cigarette smoke to form a sort of singular viscous miasma. I drive straight down the highway, keeping an eye on the tremulous needle of the speedometer. It remains perfectly vertical, at exactly the speed limit. I make slight adjustments of the steering wheel, imagining that I'm also calibrating what's happening outside the car. The course of the highway. The equilibrium of the world. To my right, the snaking branches of the Aconcagua River. I have to stop at the next gas station to buy an energy drink. Or two.

All of this comes to me from a distance of several meters. Or that's how it seems. The elongated view, which corresponds more or less with the shape of the windshield, appears outlined in black. It's like being submerged in a bathtub whose bottom is a vast dark space, which could also be a well, the only source of light the oval surface of the tub's mouth. It gives me an easy, expansive feeling, as though I could drift off to the side and lose track of myself entirely. I'm suspended, staring upwards, my gaze fixed on the scene unfolding simultaneously — without any apparent contradiction — on the horizontal plane of the oncoming lane. With no trace of fear or anxiety, I foresee an accident coming.

NINE

I WOKE with a start. For a moment, I didn't have the slightest idea where I was. During the seconds it took me to recognize my bedroom on Rosal Street, the room seemed to change shape, my body shifting its orientation. The sweat soaking my temples and chest had cooled my fever. The digits on the alarm clock read 3:00 a.m. A wave of relief washed over me, turning into something like a sob of joy; it had all been a dream: Matías, Aurelio, Inés, the episodes of amnesia. A multi-layered, labyrinthine dream. But the details were not fading, not reducing to a mere glimpse, to foreshortened narratives or vague emotional chords; they remained all too intact. On the other hand, I remembered nothing about what had happened the previous afternoon at the pharmacy, from the moment I'd gone in to buy, if memory served, a box of ibuprofen. In the Matías dream, in the intervals of darkness or when his senses became attenuated, I'd had the impression that I'd drawn near to this room, to this bed, of wavering in a sort of limbo. Now, lying on my back atop the tangled mass of sheets, unlike the other "returns," I felt no radical split between the two states or personalities: between being Matías and being me. Along the trajectory separating us (a distance measured by what parameters?), I thought I sensed a continuum; though I was at the far end of a spectrum, the disparity with Matías — and with my

(200)

other avatars or incarnations — seemed a mere difference of degree.

I began to fall back into the dream. What if this was no more than a brief visit, if I couldn't come back again? I forced myself to open my eyes. I sat up on the edge of the bed. I turned on the lamp. My notebook lay next to the clock, on top of the India travelogue. I opened it. I confirmed that my lapse had begun the previous afternoon unless, for some reason, I hadn't kept up with my notebook entries and more time had passed. I went to my desk in the living room. Lola was asleep in the armchair. I confirmed by the computer that it was three-fifteen on Saturday morning. The lapse had lasted for thirty-six hours. The longest episode, though insignificant in comparison to the month I had lived, on-and-off, in Matías' skin. I looked through my appointment book for the day I had met with the executive on Apoquindo Avenue. I had passed Matías on the sidewalk three days before the second Inés episode. The brief notation in the appointment book sparked no new memories of that morning beyond the meeting with the executive, an approximate idea of the number of people in the lobby of the bank, the light falling on the birch trees through the window of his cubicle.

I opened the notebook and reread the first three lines from the morning of the previous day, which I remembered perfectly well having written standing up, leaning against my desk, before heading out to the barbershop and my lunch with Manuel:

Thursday 13:
Breakfast Lola
Called Manuel — agreed to have lunch
Lola — bird

After that, in the same small, neat handwriting, but in its looser form, meant only for me to decipher, the list, incredibly, went on. A series of banal items, reasonable but fantastical, because I did not remember having written them down and, after the pharmacy, I hadn't the slightest notion what they referred to. Adding to the sense of unreality, of slight vertigo, was the fact that, after my return from the pharmacy, I had used a different colored pen — black instead of blue — from the preceding section. The handwriting was the same (perhaps slightly more meticulous; surely I had been calmer than in the morning, on my way out the door) and this made it more unsettling, intensifying my suspicion that it had been written by an alter ego, a double:

Barbershop
Japanese Manuel — sake — talked about Paula, other
    siblings
Pharmacy — ibuprofen
Bed, nap — slightly better
Called movers, two attempts — possibly change to Tuesday
Bed — with Lola
Dinner: chicken soup
Call from Alejandra — nothing about Paula

The list suggested a more or less plausible chain of events, a series of dots economically connected by an imaginary line. When I'd gotten home from the pharmacy I'd taken a nap, after which I felt better. I thought I understood that I had postponed the movers until Tuesday (otherwise they'd be here in a few hours and I still had a lot to do to be ready for them, including buying cardboard boxes and packing my books, movies and clothes); it would be a simple matter to call in the morning to confirm some small detail, the time, for example, and to surreptitiously get the rest of the missing information out of them.

The list from the following day held only a few minor surprises or enigmas:

Friday 14:
Valparaíso dream
Breakfast Lola
Fever 101 - bed
Called landlady — delayed move
Called lawyer
Nap
Fever down
Manuel
New to-do list: move, security deposit, storage unit, trip, etc.
Dinner: soup
Watched TV
Call from Alejandra — I didn't answer

What did "Valparaíso dream" mean? When I'd woken up that morning, did I have the impression that I'd dreamed of Valparaíso? Did it mean that a part of me had interpreted as a dream that which another part of me experienced as a transposition? Did it correspond to one of the pauses during the vision, to one of the blank spaces in which I was separated from Matías? Was the dream a sort of bordering territory or conductive material between the two states? It appeared that I had spoken with the landlady to inform her that I'd postponed my move until next Tuesday; this suggested that the moving company had, indeed, agreed to the change in schedule. From now on, I told myself, I was going to have to include more details in the diary, since it really served as an aide-memoire; that is, it presupposed a memory of the events it recorded. The entry "barbershop" made perfect sense; "Valparaíso dream" or "Called lawyer" did not. I must have called the lawyer in response to his message from two days before about the divorce determination. What had we discussed? It must not have been anything crucial or I would have been sure to include it in the diary. The same trick would work with him as with the moving company: call him about some trivial matter, leave gaps in the dialogue so as to obtain the most possible information without revealing my amnesia. Had Manuel called or stopped by?

I decided I needed to stay awake. I started surfing the web at random. I was surprised to find myself nodding off over the keyboard. I went back to the bedroom carrying the notebook. Before lying down I wrote:

Saturday 15:
3 a.m. — I wake up — Valparaíso dream

TEN

I **OPEN** my eyes. It's ten in the morning. I leave my motel room without putting on my sneakers. I walk over the already searing-hot sand toward the sea. I let the warm waves roll over my feet. I try to remember a dream and I can't. I feel it pass through my memory as through a sieve. I think a little boy's voice was whispering something to me. An insistent message, a warning. My back aches a bit from the drive and the too-soft bed. I walk down the beach. Yesterday afternoon, at a certain point on the highway north of La Serena, I crossed a threshold and began floating in drowsiness, the sensation just like being slightly drunk. I could have kept going, arrived at my destination after midnight. I had to force myself to stop at this motel. I slept for over ten hours straight. I go back to my room. I shower and shave, pack my things. I stop at a gas station to fill the tank of the Golf and to clean the windshield. I drink two espressos and head north.

.

Just before noon, about eighty kilometers north of Taltal, I glimpse a dirt road heading into the desert. Though there's no sign or any other point of reference, I leave the highway and head down that dirt track. In a few minutes I crest a hill and lose sight of the highway altogether. The road splits into two, and both ways look identical. I take the one on the left. In ten minutes I've come to the Pan-

American Highway again. I turn down a smaller track that leads deeper into the desert. The turn-offs multiply. Soon I'm lost. At that hour, the vertical light erases all details of the terrain. The landscape is reduced to a mere outline, as though it were covered in a fine layer of snow. I strain to make out if there are rocks or potholes along the deep, narrow track. To my right, I see a row of wooden posts. The railroad tracks. I turn down a road that converges with the tracks and then down another running parallel to them. Two men approach on foot, walking on the railroad ties. One of them shoulders a shovel. I ask them where Santa Ignacia is. The one with the shovel says I have to head away from the tracks about three or four kilometers to the north and continue on between two hills, of which I can glimpse only a flattened peak floating like an island above a shimmering mirage. Don't I follow the tracks? I ask. They shake their heads. The tracks leading to the station were removed… Thirty years ago, the other one interrupts. I thank them. I start driving. I cross the tracks. I drive with my gaze fixed on the two hills. They appear to be settling down into their bases as I approach. I find a small road that snakes through the ravine dividing the hills, between the ruins of two saltpeter mines, one on either side of the road.

.

I arrive at the station. It looks abandoned. The road gives out onto a flat dirt yard in front of a long, single-story structure that looks like a depot, from the front of which extends a wooden porch with a corrugated metal roof which, in another time, must have served as the platform. Above the battered eaves is a sun-bleached sign on which the words SANTA IGNACIA are scarcely visible. Facing the main building is a line of five or six half-ruined wooden cabins. I park the car in the shade of a scrawny carob tree. I call out. No answer. A skinny, dusty dog peers around the side of the depot. It approaches me, wagging its tail. I hold out my hand for him to sniff, but he backs up, frightened, his tail between his legs. I walk around back, where the structure casts a thin strip of shade. The ground is littered with broken bottles, plastic containers, leftover sections of pipe, rusty cans, tires, springs and the remains of a trampoline. There is also a dead dog. I walk over to the carcass, the other dog following me at a cautious distance. It's nothing but bones, with remnants of sun-cured skin on its head and paws. Next to him, I see a square, concrete lid, secured with a padlock, weeds sprouting up around it. The mouth of a well. In the distance, on the slope of one of the hills, I make out the vaguely architectural shapes of one of the old mines. The sheet metal door of the depot hangs open. Inside, I see machinery that looks new. I circle the structure and climb up to the porch, which has several broken boards and creaks with each step. Through the holes in the zinc roof, the framework of the eaves is latticed against the pale, dazzling sky. I climb down from the porch and, under the blazing sun, cross the dirt yard, heading for the cabins. I call out again but there's no response. The cabins look abandoned. Most are missing windows or doors or parts of their roofs. Inside, crude messages scrawled in charcoal. In the third cabin I find a pair of cages built from wood scraps and chicken wire. In the largest of the two, a sleeping puma. It's motionless, except for the faint rhythm of breath through its ribcage. In the other cage huddles a family of rabbits. The largest ones (the progenitors?) gnaw industriously on a few limp pieces of lettuce, their eyes locked on their neighboring captive.

I see you've met Aarón. An old man appears in the cabin door. Forgive me, but you arrived during siesta. We

shake hands. Néstor González. Matías, I say. I don't really sleep much, not even at night, but at this time of day
it's better to stay inside, the old man adds. I'd guess he's
around seventy-five. He's wearing a faded T-shirt and
pants that are too heavy for this heat — which he has to
constantly hike up with one hand or the other — dusty
boots and a wide-brimmed straw hat. He looks Amerin-
dian. Deep furrows mark his skin. He's happy to see me
here. I imagine that any visitor to this place is somewhat
mystifying and also a kind of blessing. Is the puma yours?
No, of course not, the old man says with a yellowed, gap-
toothed smile, a nephew from the south brought him, for
a movie. Really? Yes, indeed. The heat here is really hard
on the poor thing. I hose down the cage every other day
to clean it and to cool him down a little. Just imagine
how he must feel in that fur coat. Do you live here alone?
The old man smiles again. I'm the only one still here. The
puma lifts its head to look at us and then closes its eyes
again. That subtle gesture appears to irradiate the rabbits who, still chewing and never taking their eyes off the
puma, tense their muscles and flatten their ears. That's
why I'm here too, I announce after a pause, because of
the movie. The old man looks surprised. Really? I'm the
screenwriter, I declare, unable to conceal a note of pride
in my voice. What's that? Néstor wants to know. I'm the
one who writes the movie. The old man is still confused.
The one who decides what's going to happen, I add, in
the story... in the movie. Oh, says Néstor.

We leave the cabin and walk across the dirt yard toward the station. The heat compresses everything like a
giant rolling pin. The dog, who had kept well away from
the puma, now joins the old man. This is Alacrán, he announces. We climb onto the platform. We enter Néstor's
office. The old man leaves his boots at the door. I hesi-

tate a moment, but he gestures me inside. The room is large and dark. In the corner, on the floor, lies a stained mattress and a tangle of sheets, where he'd been resting when I arrived. I wonder how, at his age, he manages to lie down and get back up. An ancient Sony television sits on an overturned plastic crate. On the wall hang old railroad maps, faded centerfolds and rosters from the Colo-Colo soccer club. The old man sets his hat on the table. He wears his abundant, white hair combed back. He opens a small refrigerator, takes out a large bottle of Fanta and pours two glasses. He sits down behind his desk — a sheet of plywood resting on sawhorses — and motions for me to sit across from him, on a bench splattered with dried paint. Salud, he says, here's to the movie. We clink glasses and drink.

Two months earlier a pale, pudgy man in a button-down shirt and baseball cap had appeared in a huge SUV. The old man can't remember his name, but I recognize him from the description. Cristián Almagro? The old man slaps his hand on the table, excited. That's right! Cristián Almagro! Almagro had announced that he'd come as a representative of someone else (Néstor didn't quite catch who or particularly care) who was going to film a movie here and had sent him to check out the location. He was most interested in the theater, says the old man, pointing to the north with his thumb. Ah, yes, the theater, I say. He was only here one day, the old man continues, but he found time during his stay to hire several locals, beginning with the matter of the puma. He explained to us that the puma wasn't going to appear a whole lot in the movie but that it was a "crucial element." I was the one he hired to find it and he paid me up front. He said it was just half what he'd pay me total. My nephew Eleuterio, who works at El Litio, the lithium works in the salt flat, was the one who found him. He bought him from some friends of his, hunters from the south, from Ovalle, and he brought him through back roads in a cage, drugged, in a closed pick-up truck. You'll understand that a thing like that's illegal. Of course, I say. I ask myself why Almagro never mentioned a puma. It would have been easy for me to find a place for it in the plot. The old man also informs me that Almagro hired several laborers from the surrounding area to take care of renovating the house, seamstresses to help with wardrobe, a pair of guides and some twenty-five extras. He took photos with a small digital camera. He paid out huge sums of money in exchange for their signatures on receipts. The old man gets up from his chair. He digs through some cardboard boxes. He removes a piece of paper and holds it out to me. I recognize the logo. It's in English. I ask him if he understands what it says. He says that his nephew assured him that he wasn't selling his soul to the devil and he lets out a laugh. Almagro did all of this with startling speed and then picked up and left and they hadn't heard anything from him since. You haven't had any more news about the movie? I ask. The old man shakes his head and takes a sip of Fanta. Not until yesterday, he says.

He explains that yesterday he'd had a visit from a photographer named Paula. She arrived in a small, white car, more or less at the same time of day I'd arrived. She said she'd come to take photos of the locations and the surrounding areas. She didn't talk much. The old man tried to ask her about the next phases of production, but she didn't seem to know very many details. And neither does the old man, I think. I've come here to gather information, but he seems equally determined to get information out of me. Using a large, modern camera, the woman took photos of this office, of the inside of the depot and of the puma. She said she needed to wait a few hours for the light to fade so she could photograph the exteriors. She asked about the theater. Néstor offered to go with her, but she made it clear that she preferred to go alone. She needed to concentrate on her work, she explained. The old man saw her leave, heading down the dirt road. His nephew called last night from El Litio to ask who was camping near the house. A white Suzuki. The foreman at the sodium sulfate mine had passed by in his pickup, headed toward the road to La Escondida, and he'd mentioned it. Do you know her, this Paula? No, I don't know her personally, but I knew she was going to be here, I lie. Néstor takes in this information. She's very serious, he comments, but nice. He adds that he assumes she'll come back today, when the light is good for her photos. The old man wants to know more about the movie, action plans, timeframes. I hedge. He confesses that he'd started to worry about the delay, the lack of news.

Paula. Of course. I should have guessed. I'm overcome by a wave of tenderness, the sweet anticipation of coming across an old friend in this improbable place, this seclusion. What will it be like to see her, literally, through other eyes, without being recognized? At the end of the other visions I only cared about one thing: establishing the relationship between my guests (Inés and Aurelio) and me, tracing the map of threads that had carried me toward them, under the assumption that there had to be a reason for these transpositions that I needed to decipher like a sort of encoded message. In Inés' case, of course, my own eagerness to resolve the enigma created and accentuated that link, contributing, I know, to the outcome. Is there, then, a progression, not only through time but also through space, a trajectory leading to Paula, to a homecoming? Or is her presence here an anomaly, a mere coincidence? Maybe the crux of these episodes lies in their arbitrariness (which is what I did not understand in Inés's case until it was already too late), in their disconnection with me, in the obligation to become the others.

Néstor tells me there's another mattress at the back of the machine shed, in case I'd like to lie down for a while until the worst of the heat passes. I'd prefer to go to the theater, I say. If you want, I'll go with you, he offers with a smile. We climb into the Golf. Despite the shade from the carob tree, the steering wheel burns my hands. Néstor rests his hat in his lap. He gestures vaguely to the north. We cross the dirt yard and head down a sandy track. The tires skid going around the first curve. The side of the rear fender hits the berm. The old man says nothing. Alacrán follows us for a stretch, trotting along to the side of the track so as to avoid the worst of the dust. After a while he gives up and I lose sight of him. The house appears in the middle of the desert three or four kilometers from the station. There's no trace of the photographer. As we approach, I'm already thinking about the changes I'll have to make to the screenplay to account for the discrepancies between reality and the photos Almagro gave me. I stop outside the front of the house, which is covered in scaffolding. Tattered sections of plastic sheeting wave in the breeze. The house is bigger than I had imagined. It looks half built. The façade — with its false columns, second floor balcony, ticket office window, is in a sorry state and tilts ominously forward in such a way that the scaffolding at the base stands a few meters from the entrance and they've had to shore it up with metal bars. The rest is nothing but a skeleton of new beams through which you can see the open landscape. In the interior, I can make out a small amphitheater with wooden seats, an orchestra pit and the place where the stage should have been. Behind the house are two huge stacks of boards covered with canvas tarps, bags of cement, a shack built of corrugated metal sheeting, sawhorses, an old suitcase and a pair of plastic drums.

Néstor explains that the house was in a terrible state of disrepair when Almagro arrived, that the damage was irreparable. The old man put him in touch with a miner and ex-carpenter named Jacinto. Almagro made him head of construction. He paid him an impressive sum to restore the exterior. He said that in the movie, the house should look "old but well-preserved." In fact, three or four days after Almagro left, when Jacinto — who, with the advent of this new job, had set aside his duties in the sulfate mine, and used the money to fix up his own house and get a better pickup truck — was still getting a crew together for the job, a main support had given way and taken out most of the old roof. So, they're going to rebuild it? I ask. That's the idea. They spent nearly a month disassembling the house, reducing it down to its basic frame, which was still sound, separating what could be reused from what could not. The workers divvied up and carried off the most damaged pieces of lumber, so what they stripped away from the house never accumulated anywhere. It was like an army of termites was devouring it, says the old man. Meanwhile, Jacinto tried repeatedly to get in touch with Almagro to inform him that they were going to need to do a much more extensive reconstruction job than they had originally estimated. But he couldn't reach him. After three weeks of intense work (Néstor tells me that he liked to come here and sit in a chair in the shade of an awning to watch the proceedings), from one day to the next, Jacinto decided to stop work. He said that's what the construction business was like. Sometimes the people paying the bills had second thoughts or dropped a project halfway through, who knows why? You had to know when to hit the brakes before you started losing money. He paid his crew and they went their separate ways, awaiting another visit or a message from Almagro. They left the house just as you see it here, says Néstor.

So, the façade and the beams are original, I comment. The old man nods. It's all original. It's an amazing house, he adds, it's survived everything: earthquakes, break-ins, fires. Fires? Yes, two of them. The last one was in 1966. I remember because the World Cup was in England that year. In those days, the train station was still in use. The theater caught fire one night and the flames lit up the whole sky. When we arrived, the flames had engulfed the house. The owner at the time lived in Iquique and came to see the house a few days later. All that was left were a few beams, like blackened stumps, and the theater seats that disintegrated at the slightest touch. So the whole house burned down, I say. The whole thing. So, it's not the original house. It's the same house, Néstor responds. The owner brought the plans and they rebuilt it on top of the ashes, identical, down to the last detail. It even looked a little weathered, lived-in. But it's not the same house, I insist. Of course it is, he replies, looking at me in puzzlement. It's not the same wood, but it's the same house. Four or five years ago some ministry officials came to see it, he adds. They said it was part of the process to turn it into a national monument, but then after that, nothing happened. And who owns it now? I ask. A young guy, like you, says Néstor. I think he lives in the United States, in New York. You don't say. In fact, it was Mr. Almagro who showed me the title. It was in the same name as the company on the receipt. Castor Philanthropies?, I ask, astonished. Something like that. And how do you know the owner is young? Because I remember him perfectly. He's Chilean, but with a gringo-sounding name. What's his name? I don't really remember. He came around a few years back. Robert or something like that. He's very tall and has red hair. He had his girlfriend with him, a really pretty gal, blonde. They seemed very happy together. They went all over the desert, visiting the old nitrate mines. They had come from San Pedro, I think. They asked my permission to stay in the house. I told them I didn't have authorization for that, but not to worry, no one would bother them. In the middle of the night, the girl, who apparently was a sleepwalker, got up and walked out across the pampa. From what we learned later, she walked along the road to the north and then veered off to the east. The guy came to the station around seven in the morning in his Jeep, very upset, shouting that he couldn't find his girlfriend. We called the police. We spread the word with the locals and went out to search the pampa along the dirt tracks, driving in big circles, calculating that she couldn't have gone more than twenty kilometers during the night. But we didn't find her anywhere. At that point, the police began to suspect that she'd been kidnapped or that she'd gone off with someone. But the young man insisted that it was the sleepwalking. We didn't see her footprints along the road but it's possible that we'd erased them with all our comings and goings. Late in the afternoon, it occurred to us to go back to the house and look more carefully for her tracks. The sun was setting when someone saw the marks where she'd gone off the road. That didn't help much, since she could have gone in any direction from there, but it was something. It was around that time the helicopter arrived. The cops landed over there, he says, indicating a vague spot in the desert, and we told them about the tracks and they headed straight toward the mountains, but they didn't find her because it was already too dark. They found her early the next morning, curled up in some rocks. She'd walked more than fifty kilometers during the night and the next day. Was she dead?, I ask. No, but she died on the flight to Antofagasta.

And Paula? There's no sign of her. To miss each other by so little would be a mockery of fate. Another one. I see the Suzuki's tracks. Where would she have pitched the tent? The foreman said that someone was camping near the house, right? Matías doesn't seem particularly eager to run into her. Why would he be? Now he's walking around the perimeter of the house while the old man talks on his cellphone, observing it carefully from every angle, feeling that some passages in the screenplay no longer hold up. He asks Néstor if he can spend the night in the station, and he says of course. He wants to know how long he plans to stay. Matías says he doesn't know, maybe a few days. Privately, he decides to leave the next morning. There's not much more he can do here. His inquiries should focus now on Robert (or whatever his name is), in New York. But he's not going to keep pushing it. He owes that to Catalina. Jacinto's attitude — know when to throw in the towel — is a good example to follow, he thinks. He isn't interested in delving deeper into Robert's tragedy. Though if Almagro had communicated those details, he would have included them in the screenplay. It's a plausible story, but too close to home. Robert, it seems, needs to tell it, but in an indirect, partial way, through others and projected onto this house. Could he be the same guy I'd run into last year in New York coming out of the funeral home? At this point, I no longer believe it could be a coincidence. The vision grows dark for a moment and I see them in the car, presumably returning to Santa Ignacia; then, in the station. Néstor opens the lid to the rabbits' cage and grabs one by the ears. It doesn't resist. He drops it into the puma's cage through a trapdoor. The young, black rabbit leaps away and crashes into the wire mesh of the cage. He sits motionless in the furthest corner, stunned. The puma doesn't move a muscle, doesn't pay it the least bit of attention. The old man leaves the cabin, followed by Matías. The intermittences and fluctuations of this episode are increasing. There are periods when the vision gains and loses in intensity, rhythmically, flickering like of an old movie. I suspect it could be more than one episode, since sometimes, in the darkness, I have the sensation of finding myself once again in an intermediate zone between Matías and Tomás, that is, of my body, which I sense stretched out in the darkness, writhing in a restless dream. I ask myself if, through a force of will, I could return to him and sometimes I think I do draw a little bit closer. But it's possible that this degree of control is illusory. Except for that one occasion, at three in the morning on Saturday, I haven't gone as far as to recover myself.

We hear a vehicle coming. Néstor appears in the door to his office and waves. He comes out and I follow him. It's Eleuterio, my nephew, says the old man. Eleuterio turns off the engine of his pickup. He climbs up to the wooden floor of the platform. He shakes my hand and asks me immediately, in a jovially anxious tone, what I think of the puma. I explain that I'm the screenwriter, not a producer, that I don't have anything to do with that. He looks at me in total incomprehension. His smile, in which a gold crown gleams, freezes on his face. He's a short, wiry man. He's wearing a faded orange cap, a Cobreloa T-shirt, pants cut off at knee-length and a pair of dusty sandals. He's come here to talk about the animal and he seems disconcerted. An uncomfortable pause. A woman riding shotgun and two men in the bed of the pickup stare at me. I comment that the puma, in any case, is incredible and is going to be great in the movie. Eleuterio's smile swells. We head for the cabin. The black rabbit is in the same place, in a state of alert, its body plastered against the mesh. The puma dozes, indifferent. Eleuterio explains that he likes to hunt at night. He tells me in great detail about the odyssey of finding and bringing the puma here. I try to seem interested. The men from the pickup appear in the doorway. Eleuterio introduces me. They're going to be extras. One of them takes a wrinkled piece of paper from his shirt pocket and holds it out to me. It's a receipt from Castor Philanthropies. I smile and, without knowing why, give him a thumbs up. Another vehicle arrives. We file out of the cabin and see that it's Paula, the photographer. She must be about thirty-eight. She's wearing a green tank top and long pants of some lightweight material. She's holding a camera. We form a semi-circle around her. Néstor introduces us and she looks each of us in the eye, one by one, for a fraction of a second, without much interest. She points her lens at us from the level of her navel. She clicks the shutter without the others appearing to notice. She tells Néstor that she's going to take some photos. She turns around and gets to work, not waiting for the old man's reply.

How amazing to find her here, occupied with something that goes beyond, or is at least distanced from the nucleus of her grief. The sorrow is visible, of course. I'd give anything to be able to commandeer Matías for a few minutes, control him like an automaton, and go up to her, tell her who I am and embrace her. She looks tan, healthy, but the pain in her eyes is overwhelming. It's good that she decided to take this job. It doesn't matter that the project doesn't look particularly promising.

Even if the movie doesn't get made, even if all of this is nothing more than a whim of a traumatized megalomaniac, the fact that Paula is here with her camera justifies it all, fills me with gratitude. I know her method and her eye so well that I can visualize the photos she's taking as they'll look in the future, displayed on her computer screen. Matías diverts his attention from her. Eleuterio wants to know when the rest of the production crew is arriving. Matías confesses that he doesn't know the schedule. They should ask the photographer, he suggests. She has no idea, interrupts Néstor. Everyone looks at Paula, who has walked off to the far end of the platform and is shooting up into the eaves of the depot. She'd explained to him, the old man adds, that she'd meant to come three weeks ago but was delayed: she'd had to travel out of the country. One of the men wants to know about the construction. What are they planning to do about the house? I imagine they'll want to continue with the renovations, Matías says uncomfortably. What you need to do, he adds, is get in contact with them. That's the problem, says Eleuterio, there's no way to locate them. I know. The small circle stands there in silence. Matías examines Paula out of the corner of his eye. For some reason, she's photographing the line-up of the Suzuki, Eleuterio's pickup and the steel-colored Golf. He finds her attractive. If she were ten years younger, he thinks, and if Cata didn't exist… Yeah, huevón, in your fucking dreams. In addition to intriguing him, Paula's also rubbed him the wrong way. Her indifference makes him uneasy, though he assumes that her grim, slightly arrogant attitude is an instinctual defense against the huddle of five men in this remote place. This isn't true, but he doesn't know it. He thinks she's the same type of woman as Cata (with which I also disagree, according to the little I've seen of his wife), that, despite the lack of physical resemblance and the age difference, they have a similar vibe. I wouldn't be surprised if the production got underway soon and quickly, he announces to the men, and you have to be ready, because that's how this business is: it moves at a snail's pace for an eternity and then, suddenly, everything becomes extremely urgent. The men don't look too convinced. Eleuterio tells Néstor that they'll come back the next day. Paula joins Matías and Néstor. She tells the old man that, the night before, she heard some people pass by on the road, singing. They sounded drunk. Néstor nods but doesn't say anything. Is it okay with you if I pitch my tent here?, she asks. Of course, says Néstor.

.

I sit on the edge of the platform as the sun sets, smoking. Néstor invited us for dinner. I accepted; Paula did not. The scent of fried onions emanating from the open door of the office mingles with the acrid odor of the puma carried on the breeze. Paula parked the Suzuki at the far north end of the cabins. She's already pitched her tent. I see her heat water on a camp stove and eat fruit out of a tin. Holding a mug of soup and with her camera slung around her neck, she crosses the dusty yard and sits next to me on the platform. I don't know what's more dangerous: the drunks or the puma, she says with a half smile. I offer her a cigarette. She shakes her head. Paula sets the mug down on a plank. She aims her camera, without shooting, sweeping the desolate landscape. I tell her that she seems familiar, that she reminds me of someone but I don't know who. She gives me a mocking look, acknowledging the cliché, but I insist. I interrogate her about her friends and acquaintances, trying to untangle the degrees of separation and, in fact, these turn out to be few. One of my best friends worked for a while at the ad agency where her ex-husband was creative director. The younger sister of a friend of Paula's knows one of Cata's cousins. It's likely that there are other connections, but they're not worth exploring. People always say I look like other people, Paula says without enthusiasm, I think it's my nose, standard issue. She snaps a photo, aiming at an apparently arbitrary spot out on the plain. It must happen to everyone, she adds, I suppose there's only a limited number of types of people. We sit for a while in silence. I tell her that this visit has been useful for me. I'm going to have to make quite a few changes to the screenplay. She asks me about the plot. I summarize it in broad strokes. And the woman?, she asks. What woman? Roberts' girlfriend. I thought the movie was about her. I confess that, until today, I'd never heard her mentioned. Almagro just said that...Roberts? Yes, she puts in, Juan Pablo Roberts... that Roberts visited this place with her and he wanted to include the theater in the story, but in a tangential way. Paula shrugs. How strange, she says.

The sun drops behind the ridge. In the clear evening sky I can make out the silent, distant trail of an airplane. Paula drinks a sip of her soup. I ask her how long she plans to stay in the area. She says she doesn't know. For her, the work part is easier: they paid her to take preliminary photos. Once she sends them off she won't have anything more to do with the project. The puma lets out an alarming growl. I remember the black rabbit. Silence falls again. The only sound is Néstor stirring a pot or skillet in the kitchen. What will they do with the puma after the movie?, asks Paula. I don't know, I say. What must he think of all this?, she goes on. I shrug. I would give anything to be able to explain to him what a movie is and that he's going to be a part of a story and that people far away from here will see him, says Paula. If you really think about it, it makes your head spin. She waits for me to say something, but I remain silent. I don't really know what she means. I can't help but wonder why Almagro didn't mention the puma (or the story of the sleepwalker). I must figure out how to add it to the screenplay so it won't seem forced or, worse, symbolic. It's like he sees the world in two dimensions while we see it in three, she says. Sometimes things happen...things that make you feel like this, like there are more levels than you can... Her voice breaks. She seems about to start crying, but she goes on: it makes you wonder if there's another reality against which ours is as secondary as a movie, if we're a sort of piece or a figure in... She breaks off. She looks at me, her eyes filled with tears, waiting for a sign of understanding. I can't think what else to do but touch her. I lift my hand to her shoulder, but she stands up. She swipes the back of her hand across her eyes. Forget it, she says angrily, looking away. She grabs the mug and walks off toward her campsite. I stay where I am. I light another cigarette, but I have to put it out after two or three drags because the old man calls me in to dinner.

.

I sleep badly. The mattress on the concrete floor of the depot is soft and lumpy. I toss and turn and end up so tangled in my sleeping bag it's like I'm in a straightjacket. The pillow I made using my rolled-up jeans scrapes my sunburned face. Starlight filters through the cracks in the ceiling. I listen to the creaking of the wood as it contracts and the stealthy movements of rats along the rafters. In dreams, I make love to Paula. I know it's her, though I can't see precise details. We're in the motel in Caldera. Afterward, I go to the bathroom and look at myself in the mirror. Curiously, I'm not me, but rather her ex-husband,

Tomás Ugarte, the advertising executive. Just as dawn breaks, exhaustion finally overcomes me. I sleep.

I wake up after ten. If it hadn't been for the sound of voices and hammering I could have slept all morning. I walk out barefoot onto the platform. Néstor, who's brought out his desk chair, offers me coffee. I accept. I take his place in the chair, still groggy. I notice that Paula's Suzuki is gone, but the small yellow tent is still there. Two pickup trucks are parked outside the cabins. I recognize one of them as Eleuterio's. Through a window without glass or shutters, I see a woman sweeping. Two men are repairing the door to another of the structures. Néstor hands me a cup of coffee. He insists that I stay seated. What do you think?, he asks proudly. I don't know how to answer. A third pickup heads towards us from the north, moving at top speed. It parks parallel to the platform. The driver is a man of about forty-five, wearing a shabby pair of overalls and a St. Louis Cardinals baseball cap. He mounts the wooden platform in one leap. Néstor introduces him: it's Jacinto, head of construction. He wants to know right off the bat where the project stands, if the restoration work is starting up again, what the timeframe is for completion. The old man explains to him that I'm the screenwriter and don't have much to do with the production side of things. Jacinto takes this information in solemnly. I offer him a cigarette. We smoke. I explain to him that I need to familiarize myself with the place in order to refine certain aspects of the story. And the girl?, he asks, pointing north. She's not directly involved with production either; she's a photographer. Jacinto nods slowly. He asks me about my level of contact with the producers. I indicate that it's sporadic and unpredictable. Would you be so kind as to ask them about the renovation project? More than a request, it's an order. A pause.

And, please, tell them we need more money. Okay, I say. Jacinto climbs down to the dirt yard. I'm going over to look at the house for a bit and then I'm heading back to Toconao, he tells Néstor. You know where to find me. He gets in his truck. He drives away.

A group of three men and five women, who'd been observing us from a cautious distance, approach the platform. Néstor introduces them one by one. Nice to meet you, I say. I smile at them, wishing I'd put on my shoes. The old man explains that two of the women are seamstresses. The other three arrived this morning from a sodium sulfate mine. Ah, I say, though this doesn't mean anything to me. They're going to be extras, along with the two men, both of whom are miners. One of the seamstresses and one of the men timidly hand me pieces of paper, to confirm what Néstor has said. I squat down and spread out the documents, knowing already that they're receipts from Castor Philanthropies. The figures are generous. I return the papers. I hand the wrong ones back and they have to exchange them. Silence. I have to say something, but I can't think what. Welcome! I exclaim half-heartedly and I smile. For the second time since I arrived here I give a thumbs up. They remain impassive, looking up at me from below as if at an actor or a politician at the front of a stage. I'm seized by the irrational fear that they're going to grab me by the ankles. I fight down the impulse to take a step back. I keep smiling. Okay, let's leave the gentleman alone now, Néstor says suddenly, and gestures them away with an emphatic wave of the hands, as if shooing children or birds. They walk away, disappointed, across the dirt yard.

I light another cigarette. Eleuterio appears around the side of the puma's cabin. He waves to me. I wave back. Néstor brings the paint-splattered bench out of the office. We sit and drink more coffee. A small, beat-up truck appears out of the south. Twenty or so people are crammed into the truck bed. Néstor walks over to the far end of the platform. Holding onto a beam for support, he lowers himself carefully down to the ground. As they climb down from the truck, the old man hugs the men, kisses the women, ruffles the children's hair. Some of them greet me from afar. I do the same. The old man climbs back onto the platform and sits down next to me. Are they all here because of the movie?, I ask. Of course. And what will they do? Most of them are or would like to be extras, says the old man, they'll play themselves. But usually this place is deserted, I say. Doesn't matter. After a pause he adds, smiling: this is how it used to be, in the good old days.

.

People continue to arrive throughout the day. There's no sign of Paula. Matías is finding it hard to believe that all of this excitement could be due to the mere fact that his arrival coincided with hers. He wants only one thing: to leave. But he doesn't dare. He feels vaguely guilty that his presence here appears to reaffirm Almagro's promises. He owes them something that he can't manage to identify. As the locals continue to arrive, a ritual establishes itself. Each new group sends a single representative to greet him. Matías, worn out from lack of sleep, remains seated on the raised platform like an indolent, condescending monarch. He receives the envoys with an increasingly stereotypical attitude, as though they were all already acting. And perhaps they are. At times he fears that they've been tricked on a level different from his own deception, that they're unwittingly acting out some elaborate joke. They all appear to be busy doing something — they wait in line to see the puma, repair the cabins, carry water from the well, check the fluid in their vehicles, crowd together in the thin strips of shade under the eaves to drink from bottles of juice — and to Matías this activity seems forced, self-conscious, as if they were waiting for him to suddenly leap up from his chair and shout: That's it! Exactly! Now do it again for the camera! The town appears to have come back to life. But it's an artificial, anomalous rebirth, thinks Matías. He can feel at all times, even when they pretend not to be paying any attention to him, the pressure of their need. He's afraid that, from one minute to the next, the general mood might change and the multitude could set upon him to demand their due.

Mid-afternoon he decides to leave. It's the hottest time of day and the activity has dwindled. He tries to surreptitiously carry some of his things out to the Golf. He leaves the sleeping bag where it was, in an untidy heap on the mattress, so as not to arouse suspicion. When he starts the engine, Néstor comes out of the office. He waits for the old man. Néstor asks him where he's going and he says to take a spin around the area. He's studied a map and found the paved road that goes to La Escondida. His plan is to head north and to converge, if possible, with the railway line. Once he's found the road, all he'll have to do is head west until he intersects the Pan-American Highway. He knows he's too tired for a long trip, that he could easily fall asleep at the wheel, but he needs to get away from this place. He already has everything he needs. If you want, I'll go with you, says the old man. No, thank you, Néstor, I prefer to go alone, I have to think about some specific issues with the screenplay. But the old man has already opened the door and is climbing laboriously into the passenger seat. If he took off right now he'd leave the old man sprawled on the ground and they would all come after him. Let's go take a look at the nitrate mines, says Néstor. Why not?

.

Midnight. Once again, I can't sleep. A few hours ago, sitting around after dinner with the old man, my eyes kept closing. But as soon as I lay down on this wretched mattress, my mind started working at full throttle. Could the old man be drugging me? No. I don't think so. Though he does know that I want to leave. It's been decided. Tomorrow morning, at first light. That's why I need to sleep a little now. But I'm so exhausted that I can't fall asleep. I hear noises outside, muted voices. What if they're stealing a battery cable from the Golf or deflating a couple of tires so as to keep me prisoner? I could get up and go look. But it's not worth it. Try to sleep, huevón. Tomorrow you'll be on your way.

The depot's sliding door opens a crack. Someone enters and closes it behind them. They've come to kill me, of course. Or to settle the score with a beating. Who's there?, I ask in alarm. Shhhh!, scolds Paula. It's me, she adds in a whisper. She comes toward me, feeling for the shapes of the machines in the darkness, and stops by the mattress. She takes something off, drops it to the floor. Where are you?, she asks, and kneels down. I raise one hand and realize that she's naked. We kiss. Paula, I say, I can't. She doesn't answer. We struggle for a moment, me trying to stay sitting up and she trying to push me down on my back. I fall sideways across the mattress and hit the back of my neck against the baseboard. Are you okay?, she asks. I adjust my position. I can't, I repeat, with wavering conviction. Paula leans down to kiss me again. She moves very slowly, which ought to give me time to react, to move her off of me. But I let her keep going.

We hear a growl from the puma and a muffled commotion. Aarón has chosen this moment to attack today's rabbit. Silence falls once again. How can you sleep on this shitty mattress?, murmurs Paula. We lie shoulder to shoulder in the dark. The sweat on my chest and thighs begins to cool. Hey…I start to say, but she interrupts me: shhhh. She puts a finger to my lips. No, really…I insist. Shhhh, she says again. I'm leaving tomorrow, I manage to say, first thing in the morning.

.

Paula sleeps in the fetal position, her face to the wall, snoring slowly. I can't sleep. I haven't slept at all the entire night. The first light of dawn filters through the gaps in the depot's walls. If I fall asleep, I'll have to stay another day. The warmth of Paula's body tempts me to abandon myself to sleep, but that's one more reason for me to leave. Once can be forgiven (or I can forgive myself for it; Cata won't know about it), but to stay here with her would be something very different. I kiss her shoulder. I get dressed. I go out to the platform. The town is asleep. I'd give anything for a cup of coffee. I walk to the end of the platform, trying to make the old boards creak as little as possible under my weight. I get in the car. I close the door with a quiet click. It's the moment of truth. I turn the key. The motor starts up. I start driving. At the end of the yard, as I'm turning onto the dirt road, I see Néstor come out to the platform, shirtless. He waves both arms in my direction. I accelerate, kicking up a great cloud of dust that erases him from my sight.

I make it to the house. Everything's the same, except for a corrugated metal lean-to under which three or four men are sleeping. I pass right by, heading north. The dirt tracks branch off again and again. I try to choose the main routes. When in doubt, I go left, trying to meet up with the railroad line. I'm driving faster than I should in this terrain, allowing the rear of the car to skid around curves and accelerating over rutted sections. I imagine a phalanx of pickup trucks filled with spurned, angry extras screeching wildly after me in hot pursuit. My eyes keep closing on me, but I keep going, lathered by fear. I tell myself that Paula and I have little in common. I'm sure she never would have chosen me as a lover, but I was in the right place at the right time. She resigned herself to me. Unless that was also planned, part of Almagro's warped script. If they filmed it, I'm at his mercy. I can kiss my marriage goodbye. Then is blackmail — and not humiliation — his goal? After an hour I see a lone figure walking along the side of the road holding a sledgehammer. I stop to ask directions to La Escondida. Are you the screenwriter?, he asks me. That's right, I reply, alarmed. Are you going to the mine? Yes, to the mine, I lie. He uses the head of the sledgehammer to point at a minor-looking dirt track. I follow it. The terrain grows more solid beneath my tires. It takes me another hour to make it to the paved road. I almost don't recognize it, as it's mostly covered in sand, reducing it to a thin, winding strip. I stop for a moment, flooded with relief and joy. I need to fill the tank. I should sleep for a while, but I need to put a lot more distance between me and Santa Ignacia. It's the only way I'm going to feel safe.

ELEVEN

I WOKE up at eight on Saturday morning, at the exact moment Matías was turning west on the road to La Escondida, headed for the Pan-American Highway and Santiago. Lola had leaped onto the nightstand and was lazily arching her back, demanding her rights, in her oblique way. I gave her food and water. My breakfast consisted of a triple whiskey on the rocks. The sensation of Matías touching Paula persisted in my memory with the immediacy and precision of a physical pain. Only with the second whiskey did I manage to achieve a little distance from it. I remembered reading somewhere that one of the elements at work in jealousy was the anxiety, encoded in our biological inheritance, that the children we raise as our own are not actually ours. As I was pouring my third whiskey, I was struck by the parallel with Aurelio's memory: the weekend he'd stayed at Osvaldo's house, when his sister-in-law came into his room at night and approached the sofa. I also thought that these visions were something like curses: they ended in the deaths of their protagonists. Just as, in the case of Inés, I'd needed to do everything in my power to avoid her death, now I was driven by a symmetrically opposite obligation. I made the unavoidable decision to murder Matías.

I walked unsteadily to a nearby gun shop. I had stopped once outside the narrow shop window, crowded with hunting rifles, fishing poles, fish hooks, knives, camp stoves, lanterns, tents, sleeping bags, flare guns... and, while I hadn't been drawn to any object in particular, I'd felt I was peering into an unexplored, exotic world. I went in and walked over to a glass case inside of which a dozen or so pistols and revolvers lay in rows.

"Are you looking for something in particular?" the shop's owner, a large man with a receding hairline and faded tattoos on his forearms, wanted to know.

"A revolver."

"What do you want it for?"

"To kill someone."

The man looked at me in silence. I smiled, indicating that it was just a joke, but he didn't return the smile. I stood for a while staring at the guns, which filled me with equal parts revulsion and fascination, possessed of a latent will of their own concealed beneath their feigned hibernation.

"Can I get one today?

"I'm sorry, sir," said the owner. "You'd need to leave a deposit and then bring me, as soon as you have them, a special-purposes criminal background check, a police-issued certificate of residence, a psychiatric evaluation and the questionnaire pertaining to Law 17,798 that you fill out at Garrison Command on the safety and handling of firearms."

"Psychiatric evaluation?"

"Yes, sir."

"Forget it," I said.

With an emphatic gesture, I turned on my heel. I miscalculated and my right shoulder slammed into the doorframe. I lost my balance and fell flat on my face on the sidewalk.

"Hey, sorry."

I used a parked car to pull myself up. I started walking home. My exhilarated determination of a few minutes earlier was beginning to peter out, replaced by an agonizing heaviness. It felt like I was moving through a swamp, that my sneakers were sinking into the concrete of the sidewalks and streets. I was worried about Paula. Something was wrong. Not just that she'd gone north without telling Alejandra or any of her close friends, but also her appearance, her demeanor. I hadn't seen her since the divorce hearing, before she'd gotten the news about Mariana's death; I was struck by the visible toll that blow had left on her. Especially in her eyes. It scared me to think about her eyes. In the midst of my struggle against my own anticipated disintegration, I hadn't, until that moment, considered the possibility that Paula might collapse. She was, without a doubt, the stronger of the two of us. She had been the constant surrounded by a proliferating multitude of variables.

Back in the apartment, I finished off the last of the whisky. I kicked myself for not having bought more. I stretched out on the sofa. I closed my eyes for an instant. I woke up at four in the afternoon, with the feeling that someone was drilling a hole through the center of my forehead using a dull object. I went into the bathroom, but I couldn't find the ibuprofen that I must have bought at the pharmacy two days before. I checked the bus schedules on the Internet. I had two options: head for Taltal and, from there, hire a taxi to take me to Santa Ignacia, which I calculated would take an hour and a half or two hours; or take a bus to Antofagasta and get the driver to let me off on the highway more or less at the same latitude as the station, and then figure it out from there. I chose the second option. I took a shower. I packed a small backpack. I had two days. I needed to be in Taltal or Antofagasta by Monday afternoon to catch a bus to make it back to Santiago in time for my move. More than likely though, I'd need to postpone it again. Sleeping off my hangover, I'd just wasted a valuable day that I should have spent getting ready for the move and for my trip, and I was about to squander at least two more. But there was no doubt in my mind that it was the right thing to do. I had to go look for Paula.

At the San Borja bus terminal, I bought some aspirin and devoured a churrasco and a beer. I hadn't eaten all day. The beer had a more beneficial effect than the medicine, skewing slightly the level of my hangover. I settled into my seat in the middle of the bus, leaned my head against the window, and fell asleep before we'd even left the station, lulled by the idling engine. I woke up several times during the night, the last time going up a long hill south of Copiapó, where the bus stopped for a few minutes and then started off again very slowly, avoiding a pair of police cars with their lights flashing and a truck whose trailer, judging by the deep gouges in the pavement, had gone off the roadway and the berm, threatening to plummet over the edge of a deep gorge. Through my window, I saw the battered cab of the truck and the small car that had crashed into it head-on, now reduced to a mass of twisted metal. I was scarcely surprised to recognize, from the intact fragments of the car's body, the steel-gray color of the Golf.

I fell back asleep. When I woke up, the bus was descending toward the lights of Chañaral in the first glow of dawn. I opened my notebook and succinctly noted the main events that had occurred since the previous afternoon, including Matías' accident. I thought of Lola. I imagined her returning to the apartment and finding an alarming number of bowls filled with food and water covering the entire kitchen floor. I pleaded silently with her to be patient, to wait for me at least a few days, to not take my absence as definitive. I was surprised to find that the certainty about my decision to go after Paula, which I'd made the previous afternoon while still under the influence of the whisky, was still with me. It was my duty. My motives were inconsistent, they wouldn't stand up to an objective assessment. I recognized, however, a thin, internal, common thread that wove through not just the past two months, but also recent years, a tenuous line of continuity that I couldn't put into words or link to a specific frame of mind, but which was there nevertheless and was with me now, aligned with the bus's progress down the highway. I was once again regaining my own stability by taking care — or at least intending to take care — of another person, by means of a deceptive altruism. I remembered something that Sebastián said to me the evening when he'd quoted the English poet, that all fathers knew that their sons' difficult phases heralded the crossing of a developmental threshold: growth was a discontinuous and traumatic process. I was consoled by the hope that the chaos of the past few months would culminate in a different level of integration, in a new phase of existence that would probably be revealed to me during my travels. India seemed like the appropriate place for those kinds of epiphanies. The logic of the episodes, however, remained opaque. I glimpsed a pattern that moved from the future to the past and took me from Inés to Paula, but that was all. Perhaps you could say the same of me that Catalina had said in recrimination to Matías: I'd seen too many movies in which the supernatural, while enigmatic at first, always ended up following a secret pattern which the hero or heroine, after overcoming numerous obstacles, would elucidate to the benefit of themselves and everyone around them. The only thing I was sure of was my duty to Paula, and I clung to it.

Just past the turn-off to Taltal, I took advantage of the assistant's being occupied at the back of the bus to make my way up to the front. Resting my hand on the sign prohibiting passengers from talking to the driver, I told him that I needed to get off near the Santa Ignacia station, that it was an emergency. The driver shook his head. His mirrored sunglasses created the illusion that the highway was splitting in two, parting as we passed.

"Not possible," he said in a jovial tone that told me it would, eventually, be possible. "It's against regulations and it'll be recorded on the GPS."

"It's really an emergency."

"You're going to walk there?"

"I'm getting picked up," I lied.

The man drove on in silence.

"Do you know anything about that accident," I asked, "back in Copiapó?"

He nodded. I sat down in the attendant's seat.

"The guy took the curve too wide. He didn't brake at all, so he must have fallen asleep."

"What time did it happen?"

"Around five p.m.," said the driver. "Another bus driver had seen him further north. He was swerving." He imitated the motion with his hand. "He had to blare his horn at him so the guy wouldn't sideswipe him as he was trying to pass."

He waited a moment before adding:

"The truck driver saw him coming a ways off. He tried to avoid him but he didn't have much room to maneuver. He's pretty banged up. They took him to Copiapó. His passenger was uninjured."

"And the guy driving the car?"

"Killed instantly. Luckily, he was alone."

"What kind of car was it?"

"A Golf, I think."

The attendant, in shirtsleeves and cap, inserted himself between us, giving me a reproachful look.

"Excuse me, sir."

"I'm sorry."

"Passengers are not allowed to talk to the driver."

I nodded. I went back to my seat. After a half hour, the bus suddenly braked and stopped in front of a dilapidated bus stop in the middle of the desert. I gathered my things and got off, thanking the driver effusively. When the bus started off again and disappeared around a curve, leaving me alone in that open expanse, my euphoria vanished quite suddenly.

The previous afternoon, at the San Borja terminal, I'd had the good sense to buy a bottle of water. I pulled a baseball cap out of my backpack and put it on, along with a pair of sunglasses. The bus stop was a metal shed sheltering three brick walls, the plaster marred by a dense crosshatch of scratches made with metal objects. At this hour, a long shadow knifed diagonally, like a monolith, across the empty highway. My cellphone rang. Alejandra. I didn't answer. I called Paula. Her phone was still off or was out of range. Fifty feet from the bus stop, a dirt track led east into the desert, climbing up over a hill. How far away was the station? I wasn't sure. Some twenty or thirty kilometers, I calculated, too far to go on foot across the desert. I was hungry. I hadn't eaten anything since the sandwich at the bus terminal. I waited almost an hour until a local bus headed for Antofagasta pulled in at the bus stop. I explained the situation to the driver, asking if he knew the number of a taxi service or for the information line in Taltal. He shrugged, mumbled something unintelligible and drove slowly away.

I took a sip of water and started walking down the dirt track. By the time I got to the top of the hill, a little less than a kilometer from the highway, I was short of breath and my shirt was drenched in sweat. I kept walking, heading downhill. A minute later, a rickety pickup truck crested the hill and came to a stop alongside me before I'd even thought to stick out my thumb. Riding in the passenger seat was an ancient blind man wearing an old pair of horn-rimmed glasses with black electrical tape covering the lenses. He gave me a toothless smile. The driver, although also old, must have been his son.

"Where are you headed?" he wanted to know.

"To Santa Ignacia."

"Are you with the movie?"

The old man's question caught me by surprise. I hesitated.

"Yes, I'm...the creative director."

"If you don't mind," said the driver, "you can ride in the back."

"Thanks."

I scrambled into the truck bed, piled with burlap sacks, shovels, rolls of wire and a toolbox, as well as two panting black dogs who watched indifferently as I climbed in and sat down on one of the sacks. When the truck started up again, they took up posts on either side of the cabin, sticking their heads out to enjoy the breeze.

In the still slanting morning sun, I thought I recognized the general shape of the terrain, though I was certain Matías had taken a different, less direct route. As we approached Santa Ignacia, I was overcome by the strange anxiety that it wouldn't match up with my vision. What would happen if some of the details I'd seen through Matías' eyes — poor, doomed Matías — didn't correspond to the reality of what I would find there? Would that divergence, if it occurred, indicate a superimposition of slightly dislocated planes of reality, an inexact correspondence? Was it possible that my own presence would slowly alter things, opening a path to new possibilities, just as had happened with my disastrous intervention in Inés' fate?

That irrational apprehension was ripped away as soon as we made our rattling approach to the station. Everything matched up, down to the smallest detail. The depot with the half-destroyed roof covering the platform, the dirt yard, the cabins: everything was where it was supposed to be. This — having seen this place through another's eyes — made it no less alarming than its opposite and it confirmed what had happened between Paula and the dead man. I did notice that there weren't as many vehicles and people around as there had been the previous few days. Had Matías' desertion provoked a general sense of disillusionment? I also noted the absence of the Suzuki. I jumped down from the truck bed just as Néstor came out of his office and laboriously descended the stairs at the far end of the porch on his way to greet me. He was wearing the same wide-brimmed hat and the too-large pants and the dusty boots. We shook hands enthusiastically.

"Tomás," I introduced myself, "the creative director. I'm looking for a photographer named Paula. She was supposed to come pick me up at the Pan-American Highway. It seems she doesn't have any cell service out here."

"She spent the night over there," the old man indicated the place I'd seen her pitch her tent. "She left a few hours ago. I think she was going to the house."

"The theater?"

The old man nodded.

"Where is it?" I asked, though I knew perfectly well.

The old man pointed to the dirt track heading north.

"Well, Don Néstor, I'll see you later then."

I started walking, but the old man seized my arm.

"Someone can take you, if you'd like."

"Don't worry, I'll just walk."

I resisted the impulse to yank my arm out of his surprisingly firm grasp. I realized that I hadn't asked how far away the theater was.

"Is it very far?"

"A few kilometers."

The old man released me. I remained rooted to the spot. Néstor gestured toward a boy of about twelve who was coming towards us.

"Go find Eleuterio," he ordered.

The boy obeyed. We saw Eleuterio come out of the cabin that housed the puma. He, too, had not changed his uniform of faded orange cap, Cobreloa T-shirt, pants cut off at the knee and dusty sandals. He was a little shorter than I'd remembered, surely because of the height difference between me and Matías.

"This gentleman's here to work on the movie."

Eleuterio smiled, revealing his gold crown. He looked at me in open admiration.

"He needs a ride to the theater," added Néstor.

"No problem," said Eleuterio. "I'm actually heading out soon for El Litio."

"How soon?" I asked.

"About ten minutes."

"Perfect, thanks."

The old man switched the hand holding up his pants.

"What are you going to be doing on the movie?" he wanted to know.

"I'm the creative director."

"Forgive my ignorance, but what does a creative director do?"

"Uh…different things…" I improvised. "I'm like a… consultant about…various aspects of the production."

The old man studied me with obvious mistrust.

"I can't drive for medical reasons. That's why I came by bus," I apologized, which did nothing to diminish the old man's suspicion.

"Do you know when they're going to begin…?"

"Shooting? No, I'm not sure," I said. "But I assume it'll be soon. Almagro is sure to turn up any day now."

The more I played out this farce, the more out of place I was beginning to feel. My urge to chase after Paula was losing steam at an alarming rate. What was I doing there? I'd allowed myself to be carried along by an impulse that now seemed completely without merit. What was I going to say to her when I found her? How was I going to justify my presence there without mentioning my doublings? Was I really there to help her or was I moved by other, hidden reasons, unknown even to me? This entire thing was a monumental waste of time just five days before my flight to Paris, when I should have been focusing my energy on moving, getting my things into storage and the trip.

"Would you like to see the puma?" asked Eleuterio.

"I'd love to."

We headed for the cabin.

"Allow me to introduce Aarón," announced Eleuterio proudly.

I gazed, for the first time with my own eyes, at the sad spectacle of the imprisoned animal, who lay sleeping with its back against the rear of the cage, its paws stretched out toward the door of the cabin in a defensive posture, overwhelmed by the heat and an indescribable melancholy. Though lighter in color, the uniform shade of his pelt and the elegance of his lines made me think of Lola. I also remembered what Paula had said to Matías: that, through the movie, the puma was situated on a different level of reality from the rest of us, that we looked at him as though through a mirror.

We stood for a few minutes, silently watching him. Though he knew we were there, he didn't open his eyes. To my great embarrassment, my stomach rumbled, which seemed to have a beneficial effect on the old man.

"Don Tomás, forgive me, I haven't offered you anything to eat," he said.

"Don't worry about it."

"Come have some breakfast," he insisted, taking me by the arm again.

"Really, don't trouble yourself. I'd prefer to go straight to the theater..."

"How long will it take to drink a cup of coffee and eat a piece of toast? Ten minutes? That's how long it'll take Eleuterio to be ready to go. Right, Eleuterio?"

Eleuterio nodded, not daring to contradict his uncle.

"Then it's decided," declared Néstor.

We crossed the dirt yard together, accompanied by the dog. We climbed up onto the platform and I sat in his office, facing his desk, in the same spot Matías had occupied two days before. I set my backpack down on the wood-planked floor. The old man heated water for coffee and laid two halves of a roll on an ancient metal toaster.

"So you have no idea when the thing'll get going?" he said, turning away.

"No, I'm sorry."

"People are starting to catch on."

"Catch on to what?"

Néstor turned to face me.

"That there isn't going to be any movie," he said without hostility.

I shrugged, not knowing what to say.

"Milk? Sugar?"

"Just black, please."

Néstor set a metal cup with a rusted rim down in front of me.

"A screenwriter also came around," he said, setting butter and jam on the desk. "He stayed until yesterday and then the poor kid tore out of here like the devil was after him." He gave me a significant look before continuing. "You're all in the same boat as we are."

I said nothing.

"The photographer, the screenwriter and you: you're here because they hired you. Isn't that right?"

I nodded. Néstor served me the toast.

"Aren't you going to have any?"

"It's almost lunchtime for me," he said with a gap-toothed smile.

I began to eat and asked the old man about life in Santa Ignacia and about its history, tracing a vast plot of displacements across the north of the country. My thoughts drifted to Roberts and his unknown motives, guilt and atonement being the only ones I could guess at. In the middle of a vacation that could well have been a dress rehearsal for his honeymoon, while he was sleeping (it was easy to imagine they'd argued), his girlfriend had walked away from their campsite next to the ruined theater and plunged into the cold desert night, possibly sleepwalking. But at daybreak, she'd kept walking, from sunup to sunset, without food or water, heading straight for her own demise. Why hadn't Almagro mentioned this story when he hired Matías, but had mentioned it to Paula? It was clear to me that the tall, red-haired, elegant man I'd encountered a year before in New York was Juan Pablo Roberts. In my mind's eye, I saw him at the corner of Madison Avenue, in front of the funeral home, a man for whom the external signs of success corresponded with an internal certainty. Nothing about him gave away the fissure opened up by that suicide, a wound that, to judge by the erratic and ambivalent project he'd dragged Paula and Matías and Néstor into, he'd still not found a way to stitch up. Castor, Carstensen. Just as I'd once decided to transfer the funds from Phyllis to Inés, now I would parcel out a new round of excessive advances to all of these people, in exchange for hand-written receipts that I would destroy the first chance I got. I would ask Eleuterio or anyone else to take me to Taltal, to a bank, so I could withdraw the funds. Why not? They deserved that money more than I did. But first I had to see Paula.

Eleuterio honked the horn. I went out to the platform, said goodbye to the old man and stepped down to the dusty ground. During the short ride to the house, Eleuterio told me about the puma. I was overcome by anxiety that Paula had left, destination unknown, while I'd been enjoying the old man's hospitality. I spotted the Suzuki, still half hidden by the façade, and felt a weight lift from my chest. Eleuterio stopped the pickup, shook my hand and left, heading north. Just like the station, the house corresponded to the vision down to the last detail: the façade half propped up by metal bars and the skeleton of new beams through which you could see the theater with its wooden seats, the orchestra pit, the stage and the staircase that ascended from the foyer. Also identical, as far as I could remember, were the stacks of lumber covered in canvas tarps, the bags of cement, the shack built of corrugated metal sheeting, the sawhorses and the plastic drums. I circled the house, imagining Paula's surprised expression at seeing me appear out of nowhere, silently rehearsing the dialogue I would have with her, assuming and polishing a determined attitude in which my concern for her emotional well-being took pride of place. This confirmed what I'd suspected during the days after Mariana's death: that, just like her friends and family, I was drawn to her by a raw need for attention. These ruminations momentarily distracted me from an irrefutable fact: Paula wasn't there.

I peered into the orchestra pit and the sheet metal shack, although it wouldn't be her brand of humor to hide like that. I checked her car. It was unlocked. I found the tent (which we had bought together in a fit of adventurousness, and then never once used), her sleeping bag, her suitcase — inside which, along with her clothes, was her cellphone, her iPod and two cameras, both the digital and the film — dirty utensils and a pair of plastic bags: one filled with non-perishable food and the other with garbage. I checked the glove box and every nook and cranny, but I couldn't find the key. I climbed onto the latticework of beams and scrambled up onto the second-floor balcony to scan the horizon. She must have gone to take a look around the area, though it was odd that she hadn't taken any of her cameras. Or did she have others? I saw no sign of her in any direction. The undulating terrain obscured Santa Ignacia. To the west, a few kilometers away, I made out the ruins of a nitrate mine. At that hour, the adobe walls blended into the desert and all it was possible to distinguish was a map of vaguely geometrical shadows, as if that were all that was left of the old buildings. I dropped down from the beams. I went and sat in the car, which was parked in the shade. I set about waiting for her. I took a sip from the bottle of water. My mind drifted to the image of Paula sitting on the edge of the platform, at sunset, holding a mug of soup. Her expression one of bearing up against an incessant suffering, about which Matías hadn't a clue. I retraced my steps back to the road, holding the bottle of water. I considered the possibility of walking back to the station but, instead, obeying once again a tenuous intuitive thread that connected me to her, I headed north.

I walked for more than a half hour along the road, looking for the place Paula had left it to strike out cross-country to the east. She had, I thought, picking up my pace, a maximum of three hours' head start. Maybe less. I turned on my cellphone and checked that I still had some battery left. I kicked myself for not having asked Néstor for his number. I considered calling Alejandra, but all that would accomplish would be to set her off. I decided to call the police, but I didn't have any service. I shut off the phone to conserve the battery. The most sensible thing to do, I told myself, would be to turn around and go back to Santa Ignacia, to launch a search party with the help of the authorities. But something impelled me to continue on my own. I had the feeling that I was delving deeper into the heat, step by step, as though it were an ever-thickening substance in which I'd end up trapped like an insect in amber. Sweat soaked my baseball cap and I could feel it running down my neck and back. I took another sip from the bottle, which was still about two-thirds full. I decided to save the rest for Paula. I understood that this had been her plan from the beginning: to lose herself, to dissolve. Hence her mystifying decision to take this job which, under the circumstances, couldn't possibly rank particularly high on her list of priorities; her leaving without saying where she was going. Her decision to replicate Roberts' girlfriend's tragic, rather theatrical gesture disappointed me. It was beneath her. The duplication made it seem slightly unreal, a mere allusion to other events (Mariana's accident?). I began to feel a strange resentment towards Paula, which competed with my anxiety over her fate and the exhaustion of that forced march under the desert sun. Her action seemed almost in bad taste. Her own death mattered so little to her that she had copied another person's death, in a double abandonment of herself.

I found what I thought was the place where she had strayed from the road. I turned onto a crust of hardened, cracked earth, and immediately lost her trail. I headed straight towards the mountains in the distance. After about twenty minutes, a horizontal movement to my left, just on the edge of my field of vision, caught my eye: a small blue truck heading south down the road I'd just left, kicking up a trail of dust. I waved both arms above my head. I didn't know if they saw me. The truck kept moving at the same slow speed toward Santa Ignacia. I pressed on, using two small rises in the otherwise flat landscape and a dark, cone-shaped mound as points of reference, plotting my course between those two geographical features as I headed for the base of the mountains. The midday sun beat straight down, creating the illusion that I was surrounded by a fine mist. Despite the sweat running down my face and soaking my shirt, the alarming fluttering of my heart and a slight headache, I felt in full possession of my strength and determination. My episodes were leading me to Paula and to that moment, I thought. It was my duty to intercept her and to disrupt her plans. I had no doubt whatsoever. I was desperately thirsty, but I resisted the temptation to drink. The bottle was weighing me down, the water sloshing against the plastic with every step in a sort of irregular counterpoint that I found exasperating. I tried putting the bottle in the pocket of my jeans, but it was too uncomfortable.

A chain of ideas passed through my mind in rapid succession. I thought of Lola, weaving light-footed among the multitude of dishes on the kitchen floor. I thought of the advances I was going to hand out in Santa Ignacia that same day or the next, before leaving for Santiago, just in time for my move. I thought of my trip, imagining myself in the Sahara Desert. I told myself that, with this slow-motion pursuit, Paula and I were reproducing real events, the same ones to be narrated and deformed by the movie that would probably never be filmed. Just as Matías had sensed while being hounded by the locals, the mere proximity to that project was turning all of us into actors. I remembered that two nights before his accident, Matías had a premonitory dream in which he slept with Paula in the motel in Caldera. When he went into the bathroom, the mirror had reflected not him, but me, something I'd secretly borne witness to. And what if Paula was pregnant? Her audacity, including her lack of precaution in that regard, was because of this, this plan. It had been a goodbye. A goodbye to sex, not to Matías, who was irrelevant. I thought of the destroyed Golf. I thought of Catalina, who had lost the two loves of her life in the space of two weeks. Was I the child's father? I remembered that King Arthur had been sired by King Uther while he was disguised as another man.

I came to a secondary track that traced a wide S through the rocky terrain. I followed it for a while and then veered off to continue east. I left the two small rises behind on my right. The cone-shaped mound on my left, however, turned out to be a rather tall hill (although nothing in the desert gave any sense of scale). I continued on, skirting the flank of that dark-gray hill. The vastness of the landscape opened up before me once again. Just as had happened to Aurelio when he went looking for Osvaldo on the mountain, I felt suddenly that the subtle link that had connected me to Paula up until that moment was disrupted. I was lost in the middle of nowhere. All the mistakes I'd made up until that moment came crashing down on me: not having raised the alarm, setting out on this search alone, without any gear, without the slightest idea of Paula's possible location (for all I knew, she could be back at the house at this very moment, maybe not even having noticed my backpack on the floor of the passenger seat of her car) or her intentions. I became conscious as well of my exhaustion, my pounding heart, my worsening headache and the beginnings of nausea. I noticed that I was dry. I had stopped sweating. Then I saw, on the side of the hill I'd begun to walk away from, a line of footprints. Without stopping to think, I began to climb, taking huge strides. The steep slope was hard, but it was covered in a layer of fine black dust about a foot thick, into which my feet sank just as if it were a sand dune, making the climb incredibly difficult. The dark color of the mineral radiated and multiplied the heat. My fatigued body manifested new signs of desperation: aside from the headache — which pounded in the same spot punished the previous afternoon by my hangover — and the tachycardia, my breathing had become quick and shallow. I tried to fill my lungs and couldn't do it. I felt feverish. Suddenly, I was floating, dizzy, as though I'd tuned into the wavelength of my previous drunkenness. I paused to vomit, and felt a bit better. I forced myself to take a sip of water. A precious amount that I was depriving Paula. I kept climbing. Each step was unbearable, but I pushed on. I was flooded with an unexpected tenderness for Aurelio and I told myself that this was the true nexus that joined us, beyond the degrees of separation: the arduous ascent up that black slope, the infernal heat.

I discovered, about fifteen paces higher up, a place where the slope folded into a narrow, diagonal ledge. It seemed like a good place to rest. I curled up into the fetal position, jammed the water bottle into the sand and closed my eyes. I fell asleep or lost consciousness. When I woke up my face and hands were burning from both the fever and the punishing sun. I was having difficulty breathing. I sat up on the sand and looked down, where I glimpsed a woman circling the base of the hill. It was Paula. Off to the right, I saw the silhouettes of three men who had followed the same route and were now fanning out across the open desert. On the S-shaped track was the blue pickup I'd seen pass by that morning and a police truck and, if I wasn't mistaken, the Suzuki. I judged that Paula was much closer to me than I would have estimated if I hadn't had her body as a reference. I calculated that she was about four hundred meters away from me. She was walking east, toward the mountains, just as I had imagined her doing, except that she was looking for me. I tried to scream, but no sound came out. I drank the rest of the water. I struggled to my feet. Then she saw me and waved her arms and shouted my name, which came to me hollowed-out by the distance or the fever. I started the descent. My first step sinks into the soft terrain, which gives way beneath my weight. It doesn't hold me.

TWELVE

THE lieutenant raps his knuckles on the frame of the cage, trying to get the puma's attention. The animal opens its eyes, but ignores him. He rests his indolent gaze on the last rabbit; one could easily imagine the workings of its skeleton, pumping blood, muscles soon to be torn to pieces. The officer, who'd been squatting next to the cage, stands up and adjusts his hat. Don't go anywhere on me now, Don Néstor. Yes, Lieutenant, the old man replies with a hint of derision, leaning in the doorframe, holding his pants up with one hand. They should be here by late afternoon, adds the lieutenant, as though he hadn't heard the old man, don't even think about letting it go. He leaves the cabin. He climbs into the green pickup, waiting with its engine running, and drives off in a caravan with the van carrying the body wrapped in a plastic bag. Paula waves goodbye to them with a vague gesture. She walks through the clouds of dust over to the old man. She's holding the notebook in her hand. They both stand watching the puma. Paula slides her back down the doorframe until she's sitting on the wooden floor. On her face, a mixture of sorrow and fortitude. Her attitude suggests only a partial engagement with her surroundings, as though seeing them from an oblique angle. Aren't you going with them? Néstor wants to know. In a little bit, she says in a monotone. Then she adds, pointing to Aarón: what's going to happen to him? Supposedly some officials from the Agricultural and Livestock Service in Antofagasta are coming to get him this afternoon, the old man informs her. Paula takes a small digital camera from the pocket of her jeans and snaps a picture of the impassive animal. Are they taking him to a zoo? I'm not sure. And is it going to cause trouble for you? I'm already in trouble, declares the old man with a smile. At least they didn't arrest me, he continues, that's something. And what about Eleuterio? Why drag Eleuterio into it? It's better if it's all on me. Could you lose your job as caretaker? The old man shrugs. It doesn't make much difference at this point.

Paula stands up and walks toward the Suzuki, followed by the old man. She passes the car and continues over to the platform. She sits on the edge of the wooden porch, in the shade of the eaves. She opens the notebook. She silently turns the pages. Néstor leans against the platform, too high for him to leap onto like she had. Are you okay? asks Néstor. She nods, not taking her eyes from the notebook. What are you going to do? the old man presses. I'll go to Taltal with the police. I have no other choice. Would you like me to go with you? No, no, don't worry. Are they going to transport him to Santiago? Paula closes the notebook. She sighs. Yes, she says, if I can get all the paperwork sorted out. I suppose it's a way to distract the relatives, keep us busy. What paperwork? Obtain the death certificate, record the death in the Civil Registry, find a funeral home, get authorization from the Ministry of Health and on and on. I don't know if I'll be able to get it all done on a Sunday. Let me go with you, really, says the old man, resting a bony hand on top of Paula's, it's no trouble for me. Don't worry about it, Don Néstor.

They're quiet for a moment. The car waits, pointing in

the direction of the road leading to the highway. I'd like to stay here for a while, she says. Why don't you come back after everything's taken care of? I might do that, she lies. Your husband didn't have anything to do with the movie, did he? asks Néstor. She shakes her head. Not that I know of. Do you think it'll ever get filmed? he asks. I have no idea, Don Néstor.

Now I know that the episodes — Inés, Aurelio, Matías — did, in fact, lead back to her through a web of causal links that every once in a while I glimpse and then lose sight of, like looking at a spider's web through a very fine lens that accentuates strands and unforeseen connections while obscuring others. Sometimes, one of those threads is revealed to me, fleetingly, my attention travels along it like an electric shock. Then I let it go, I forget it. The first thing that goes out is the connective tissue between one knot or juncture and the one that follows. On a vaster timeline, events are undeniable, but their meaning shifts, they become impersonal. I bear witness to those flashes through a veil of indifference, they are connected to me in an indirect and also unexpected way, as if I had taken literally something that was, in reality, only a representation, thought something crucial when it was secondary, and vice versa.

Paula climbs down from the platform and embraces the old man. See you soon, he says. The Suzuki drives away. Néstor watches it go until it disappears around the first curve as though sinking into the desert. He walks to the end of the platform, climbs the stairs and heads, his boots dragging, towards his office, trailed by the dog. After the tumult of the past few days, the station seems emptier than before. Its stillness is a withdrawal from the outside world, which has left the station behind. The new wood of the repaired shutters and doors of the cabins gleams, in contrast with the faded sign still bearing the name of the station and the tumbled down sections of eaves. The shadows lengthen across the cover of the well, the corpse of the dog, the springs of the trampoline. The old man cooks lentils. He fries onions and garlic in a skillet and scrapes them into the bubbling water. He eats slowly in his place at the desk. I keep him company, sitting on the bench. I don't know if he senses my proximity. He washes the dishes. He takes the chair out onto the porch and sits down with a cup of coffee. It's night by the time he remembers the rabbit. The next day, two officials from the Agricultural and Livestock Service arrive. Néstor leads them to the cabin. They verify that the puma has thrown itself against the bars, opening a small gap, large enough to escape.

Another thread leads to the ruins of the nitrate mine. From this vantage point, one looks out over the skeleton of the house and, in the distance, what remains of the abandoned station. This is where Paula was when I got out of Eleuterio's truck and walked around the house and climbed up the latticework of beams — which have now been plundered, along with the rest of the construction materials and a good part of the cabins facing the old station, to go on to second and third lives as parts of the locals' houses — and scanned the horizon and went and sat in the car, before setting out on my desperate search. More than likely, distracted by her work photographing the crumbling shapes with her digital camera, she hadn't known I was there. It's also possible that she saw the truck arrive and, when she recognized me, decided to hide, instinctively taking refuge from my anxious benevolence; that she watched my movements from one of the adobe's exterior walls, praying that it wouldn't occur to me to come over here, and then she hadn't found the right moment to change her mind or the right pretext to use until it was already too late. The elements are also gnawing away at the broken wall around this compound — which makes me think of parallel lines of columns — the staircase, the stone railings, the chipped edges of the wells. All that's left of the house is the façade, which, day by day, rests a bit more of its weight on the rusty poles holding it upright. The road, now rarely traveled, is almost impossible to make out at the base of the slope that peters out into open desert. All that remains of the station is the hulk of the main depot, its eaves and zinc roof now gone. Even from here, you can see the dirt yard through the gaps in the wooden planks.

Paula climbs down from the platform and embraces the old man. I see her throwing up in a motel bathroom. In the adjoining room, the flickering glow of a television, an unmade bed. Paula rinses her mouth. She brushes her teeth. She sits on the edge of the bathtub. Her face contracts and she covers it with her hands. She sobs for a long time, with her entire body. Finally, she blows her nose on a piece of toilet paper. She lies down on her back on the tiles, diagonally across the floor. She stretches her arms out as far as they'll go in the narrow space and closes her eyes. Paula in the Suzuki, driving away, I think, from her mother's house. A flock of birds startles and takes flight as she passes by. One of them maneuvers wrongly, failing to get sufficient height, and it collides with one of the headlights. The impact is gentle, no more forceful than a pat, but everything is suddenly enveloped in a cloud of feathers that covers the windshield, then diffuses and disappears. Paula doesn't stop. Later, at a red light, she gets out of the car and circles around the hood to look at the headlight. There's no trace of the bird: no internal nick or crack in the plastic like a rock would have made, no smear of blood. The other drivers lean on their horns. Paula enters the apartment on Rosal Street for the first time. She's arranged to meet with the landlady. She uses my key. She walks through the bedroom and the living room, recognizing familiar objects in that unfamiliar place, making a mental inventory of what she'll keep. In the kitchen she finds a dozen dishes spread out across the floor. Some of them are clean; others, half full. There are scraps of food scattered across the linoleum. There's no sign of Lola. Paula, sitting in the waiting room of a clinic, decides that if it's a boy, she'll name him Tomás. Paula, now visibly pregnant, drinks a glass of juice sitting in Lola's gray armchair, on a balcony with views of the river. The three-year-old has just fallen asleep. Paula watches him from the doorway. A blonde woman with short hair who looks like Mariana hugs her from behind and delicately kisses her neck. He's the spitting image of his father, says Paula. The boy dreams (and when he wakes up, he'll forget) that he is other people. He finds himself, in quick succession, in different bodies and places: in a plaza, engulfed in a snowstorm, in a chaotic city, in a desert. He perceives that those people are in some way him or that they have made his advent possible. The old woman's stay in Tomás' apartment, for example, prevented his mother from visiting, which would have altered the course of things; Osvaldo's death precipitated his ex-girlfriend's trip to the south and also her husband's trip to the north. In the dream, the strands braid together, consolidate, and the boy reconstructs, from the inside out, fragments of the lives and deaths that aligned in order to create his own life, but he confuses or shuffles them and those intersections get projected into the past and burst into the real world. The boy swings in a park as the two women look on distractedly. The woman who looks like Mariana drives north along the highway. The sun is setting. Next to her, Paula sleeps with her mouth open and her cheek pressed against the seatbelt. In the backseat, in his car seat, Tomás watches a rugged coastal landscape pass by. He struggles to stay awake. They arrive mid-afternoon at the abandoned train station. Paula takes pictures of the boy, in her partner's arms, against the side of the ruined depot. Paula in a supermarket. Paula walking on a trail through a tropical forest in a canvas hat, carrying a backpack and two heavy bags of photographic equipment. Paula, a camera on her lap, rests her forehead against the window of an airplane that has just taken off, and gazes at the map of lights of a city below.